The Broken

Joseph H.J. Leach

Published in Australia by
Stone Table Books
Hackham SA,Australia
January 2026

ISBN 978-1-7638310-6-3

Cataloguing-in-Publication entry is available from the
National Library of Australia http://catalogue.nla.gov.au.

First published in 2019. This edition 2026

Typesetting by Ben Morton

The Broken

Joseph H.J. Leach

STONE TABLE BOOKS

Dedication

This book is dedicated to all those men and women who have been wounded in body or mind in the service of their country and community. They are all too often forgotten when their service has ended.

Acknowledgements

There are many people I need to thank, without whom this book would not have been written. First of all, the good people at Stone Table Books, especially Mark Worthing who had enough faith in the book to publish it, and my great editor Ben Morton, who understood what I was trying to say and helped me say it. I would also like to thank Sam Hiyate for his mentorship, especially in structure and plot development. His help was invaluable. As was the detailed work of Ann Hancock, my proof-reader. I would also like to thank all those who read early versions of the book and were kind enough to make helpful suggestions. You have helped to make this book what it is.

Finally, I would like to thank my family, especially my wife, Mandy, whose detailed reading and support helped to bring this book to completion, and Isabella, my daughter in law, who first directed me to the sufferings of our veterans.

"…giving thanks always for all things to God the Father in the name of our Lord Jesus Christ…" Ephesians 5:20

Table of Contents

CHAPTER ONE

Breaking

They were hard, brown hills and rose steeply on either side of the valley. A convoy of mismatched trucks of various ages raised a cloud of dust as it made its way along the track that meandered through the valley floor. At the front and the rear were Toyota four-wheel drive pick-ups. These were still painted in bright, civilian colours but now had high calibre heavy machine guns hard mounted on their trays.

The men behind these guns were constantly watching the valley sides, occasionally swinging their guns to the right or left. In most of the convoy's trucks men, some of them no more than teenagers, lounged in the most comfortable position they could manage. A few even tried to get some sleep. They were mostly dressed in the loose clothing of the local people, though many of them came from far away. All of them were carrying, often carelessly, the ubiquitous AK-47, some with belts of ammunition slung across their shoulders. They were on their way to the border and to safety.

It was getting late in the afternoon and the shadows were lengthening, but the trucks didn't slow down, even as they approached the narrowest part of the valley. Speed was of the essence. The border was not far, and they needed to be across it by nightfall.

None of them noticed the hard-eyed men watching intently from the rocky hills, nor the Predator drone high above them.

As they passed a shallow bend in the track Captain Jacob Jones, one of the men watching from the rocks, whispered a code word into his radio. A command was relayed to a control centre in California and, seconds later, both the front and the rear four-wheel drives exploded in flames. The men with the machine guns were dead before they could pull their triggers. The rest of the trucks skidded and collided in their hurry to stop, the scream of their brakes joining with the sound of the burning four-wheel drives. The men who had been resting in the trucks now scrambled to get off them and into the safety of cover. Attack helicopters appeared. One after another, the remaining trucks also exploded in flame. Fire and thunder filled the valley and consumed any who had not been fast enough.

The fleeing men ran for the shelter of the rocks. High on the slope above them Captain Jones calmly pushed one of two identical buttons that he held in his hand, and the first set of claymore mines exploded. Thousands of ball bearings were propelled at high velocity through the lower slopes of the valley, shredding flesh and bone. He waited a few seconds, until some of the survivors had struggled to their feet, then pushed the second button. He then yelled a command in Arabic into his radio and the hidden men, high on the slopes, opened fire.

As the rifles and machine guns opened up, some of the men from the trucks started to run, although what shelter they thought they were running to was not clear. Those that escaped the fire from the ambushing soldiers were cut down in a hail of heavy gun fire as the attack helicopters returned and strafed the floor of the valley. As the helicopters departed, Captain Jones nodded to the captain of the national army unit lying beside him who immediately got to his feet and yelled a command. The uniformed men about him rose from their shelter and advanced towards the valley floor, firing at anything that still moved.

As was the accepted protocol, Captain Jones only followed some time later, after the last shot had sounded. This was, after all, an operation by the national army. He was only there as an advisor. He made his way down the slope, picking a path through the rocks. Although he carried his Austeyr rifle at the ready, he didn't expect to use it. Even before he got to the floor of the valley, he was stepping over the carnage that was all that remained of the men who had been in the trucks.

He approached the national army captain who was nominally in charge of the operation. 'Area secured?' he asked in Arabic.

'The area is secured,' the man assured him. 'I have sent scouts both ahead and behind. There will be no unpleasant surprises.'

'Good,' Jacob said, giving a brief nod of his head. 'Casualties?'

'None. It was a very clean operation. If only God would grant that all such encounters would go as well.'

Jacob surveyed the shredded, broken and burning bodies that littered the valley floor. 'God', he thought, 'was surely a long way from here.'

'Are any of the prisoners wounded?' he asked.

The Captain gave an unpleasant smile. 'There are no prisoners,' he said. 'It was a very efficient ambush. One hundred percent kill rate. You are to be congratulated, Captain, on your meticulous planning. Thanks to you, these animals had neither the chance to escape nor the opportunity to surrender. Now God can deal with them.' The smile didn't reach his eyes but the admiration in his voice was genuine.

Jacob nodded and turned away from the Captain. He didn't feel like accepting congratulations. The anger he felt had not subsided. He wondered if it ever would. He looked about him. The soldiers were doing as they had been trained: documenting the dead, taking finger prints and photographs. The heat from the burning trucks was uncomfortable and the smell of cordite and blood was still heavy in the air. Some of the bodies were small; too small to be carrying those guns; too small to have done…what they did.

He turned over one of the bodies with his boot and found himself looking at the face of a boy, barely able to grow the first traces of a beard. He took a deep breath and his hands started to shake. At that age, he should have been worrying about passing exams and wondering whether he would ever get up the courage to talk to that girl who got the same bus home every night. He should not have been carrying an assault rifle. He should not have been involved in doing the things that this boy had done.

He wondered, as he looked at the young face, if the boy had really believed in what he was doing or whether he was forced into it by the simple fact of being in the wrong place at the wrong time. Did he take joy in what he had done or was it a cause of anguish and confusion? He looked at the bodies scattered around him and realised it didn't matter. He hated them and it had felt good to see them die. In fact, he hated all of them, the whole wretched country, not with any great passion but with a dull, gnawing hatred. He hated them for what they had done, but even more for what they had forced him to become. He turned and walked off to arrange transport back to base, leaving the troops to bury the dead.

No one, not Captain Jones nor any of the national army soldiers, noticed the figures in white who knelt and wept beside each of those who had died, nor the other figures who stood on the burning trucks and laughed.

* * *

The room was purely functional, part of a prefabricated building. The walls were unpainted plywood and the carpet cheap and hard-wearing. There was only one window and the light it let in was shaded by a heavy metal grating. A single, unshaded light hung from the ceiling and Captain Jacob Jones sat directly under this in a straight-backed chair. Facing him were three senior officers, sitting behind a trestle table. The one in the centre was Jacob's battalion commander. To his right was the senior operational legal officer, a thin faced, dark haired woman with a frown etched as a permanent feature of her face. To his left, somewhat to Jacob's surprise, was the senior medical officer, a large man known for his jovial nature. Each of them was reading a copy of the operation report that Jacob had prepared. Jacob sat and waited.

Eventually, his commander looked up. 'Captain Jones, as you know, this is an informal hearing to review the operation at the location known as Bandit's Run. It is a simple review and in no way implies wrong doing on your part. Do you understand the nature of this hearing?'

Jacob gave a brief nod of his head. 'Yes, Sir.'

'Good,' the Commander said, looking down at his papers. 'The first thing I need to say is that this is a very impressive kill list. We have been after some of the names on this list for a long time. The American's are very pleased.'

Jacob gave a brief nod of acknowledgement but did not reply.

'The thing is,' the Legal Officer said, 'that it is almost too impressive. There were no wounded, no prisoners, no enemy survivors at all. That's very unusual. I'm sure you can see how that might raise questions. Would you like to comment?'

'Yes, Ma'am,' Jones replied, without betraying any emotion. 'The gully was the ideal site for an ambush; we caught the enemy by surprise; and we made use of significant assets. In the words of the national army officer in charge of the operation, the kill zone was very efficient. Had any survived, I would've wondered how they'd managed it.'

'Were the enemy challenged at any point prior to your forces opening fire?' the Legal Officer asked.

'No, Ma'am,' Jacob replied. 'It was an ambush, and surprise was crucial to its success. If the enemy had been challenged prior to engagement, it would have been a very different sort of battle. We had very good intel that the convoy contained only enemy combatants, and this has been confirmed by post operation investigation. The initial drone strike was approved by operational command. After that, challenges were pretty much redundant.'

The Legal Officer leant forward. 'The crucial question is; did the enemy at any time seek to surrender? Were they still carrying their weapons as they jumped off those trucks?'

'No, Ma'am. I saw no sign of any seeking to surrender, and, yes, Ma'am, they were still carrying their rifles,' Jacob replied. 'This is confirmed by the video footage from both the attack helicopters and the drone.'

'What about in the subsequent engagement, when your troops moved in to secure the area?'

'I can't speak to that, Ma'am,' Jacob replied, his body stiff and tense. 'As per the current protocols, I held my position and left the actual combat to the national army. I only went down to the valley floor after the fire fight had finished. At that time, all the enemy combatants were dead.' He paused and then added, 'I understand the national army were pleased with the operation.' Jacob noticed that the Medical Officer was watching him intently. He tried to relax.

The Legal Officer leaned back in her seat and smiled. 'Well, from my angle, that just about covers it. If they still had their weapons, they were still combatants and legitimate targets. All clear and good.'

The Commander nodded. 'Thank you, Major. I never doubted it.' He looked down at his papers, then looked up, directly at Jacob. 'While, as you say, this was technically a national army operation, it is true, is it not, that you gathered the information, co-ordinated the strike assets; in fact, planned the whole thing. The national army were effectively acting under your direction, even if not under your direct command.'

Jacob swallowed. 'Yes, Sir,' he said. 'I think that would be a fair assessment.'

The Commander nodded and looked to those sitting either side of him. 'Any other questions?'

The Medical Officer leaned forward. 'Just a couple to finish off.' He paused, examining Jacob as if he were a patient. 'Lieutenant, some of those killed in this operation were very young, weren't they?'

'Yes, Sir.'

'How do you feel about that?'

'I don't agree with turning children into soldiers, Sir. I think it is a disgusting and immoral practice and I very much wish that it didn't happen. However, if one of them points a gun at me, I'm not going to let him shoot me.'

The Medical Officer seemed to consider this response, then asked. 'This is your third tour of duty, is it not?'

'Yes, Sir.'

'And between those tours, you have only spent a few months back home, most of it in various training courses. Is that so?'

'Yes, Sir.'

'Why?' the Medical Officer asked. 'Why come back to this place when, with your record, you could get just about any job you wanted back home?'

Jacob was silent for a long moment; the sound of orders being given to a patrol about to leave could be heard in the background. Eventually he said, 'I'm not sure how to answer that question, Sir. I'm a soldier…'

'Right!' the Commander said, giving a barking laugh. 'Doctor, you're asking a soldier why he fights. What other answer can you expect? He fights because he's a soldier. It's his job. Isn't that right, son?'

'Yes, Sir.'

'Right,' the Commander said again. 'I think that's all. This was a professional and highly successful operation and it will be so noted on your record.' He paused and took a deep breath. 'The blocked section of your record that is. The politics here are very delicate. No one must ever hear of this operation or of…what proceeded it.'

'I understand, Sir.' Jacob said. 'Thank you.'

The Commander nodded. 'That's all. You are dismissed, Captain.'

Jacob stood smartly to attention. 'Sir!' he said, then turned on his heel, almost as if he were on a parade ground, and walked from the room.

When he had left and closed the door behind him, the Commander turned to the Medical Officer. 'Doctor?'

'I'm worried about him. His personal life has pretty much fallen apart and after what he's seen... I think he needs to be sent home, to be given care.'

The Commander shook his head, 'Can't do it.'

'Look, with all due respect, Sir, I was watching him: the way he held his body. I think he's only holding it together by force of will. It won't last. It can't. In my professional opinion, he's wounded, just as surely as if he'd taken a round.' He dug out a report from among the papers on his desk and placed it in front of the Commander. 'After what he saw...' he said, pointing at the report, 'you can't expect that he can just continue as normal.'

The Commander shook his head. 'I can't do it, doctor. He's one of our best: promoted up through the ranks, special-forces trained. This last operation was a text book example of how to neutralise the enemy. It was meticulously planned and that kill zone was absolutely lethal. All the men in those trucks could do was die. If I send him home, it will look like a disciplinary action - especially after this Bandit's Run affair. I can't do it.'

The Medical Officer looked as if he wanted to press his point, but the lawyer intervened. 'If I could make a suggestion...' the other two turned to look at her. 'Surely there are still roles in country that would take him away from the battle and yet not be seen as a demotion or disciplinary appointment. He might find being placed in charge of base security, for example, a bit boring, but it would keep him close to medical supervision and support. He only has a few weeks to run on this deployment. Would it be that unusual to give him a quieter job just prior to going home?'

The Commander looked at the Medical Officer who reluctantly gave a shrug of his shoulders. 'Better than leaving him out there, he said.

'Good,' the commander said, as he organised the papers in front of him and placed them in his briefcase. 'That's settled. I'll see you both after the morning briefing tomorrow to go over the final details with the adjutant. I thank you both for your time and your input.'

As the three of them packed up, none of them saw the figure dressed in white, standing in the corner of the room. He was staring at the chair where Jacob had been sitting. He closed his eyes and raised his head slightly, as if in deep thought. Then he nodded.

Another figure appeared beside him, also unnoticed. 'Why are you here?' he asked. 'Why aren't you out weeping over some dead body. You know, the loss of what might have been and all that…'

'It's Friday,' the first one said. 'There'll be no battles today, no souls needing mourning.'

'There will be soon,' the other man said, grinning. 'Soon there will be a lot – and children too. The plans are already in place. Tomorrow they'll kidnap the driver's family. Children to mourn, that'll keep you busy.'

'The souls of the innocent fly swiftly to their Father. It is not for the children that we mourn, but for the grief of their families.'

The second man scowled. 'Again, why are *you* here?' he asked. 'Surely your main concern is a long way away.' A certain smugness crept into his manner. 'A concern, I might add, that you have neglected for so long that my victory is now certain.' When his companion didn't react, he looked suspiciously at the empty chair in the middle of the room, taking no notice of the officers who were now leaving. The commander closed and locked the door behind him. 'What's so special about this one?' he asked. 'Surely he's just one more broken soldier: no more important than any of the others.'

The first man nodded. 'You're correct, in your own twisted way. He is just as important as all the others and, like them, he is greatly loved.'

The second man gave a dismissive snort. 'Didn't help much, did it? He's a complete mess and he won't be able to keep on hiding it for long. For him, it's all over bar the shouting.'

The first man shook his head. 'No. There you're wrong. For him, it's only just beginning. Please stay away. Do not follow me.' He left the other standing there and walked swiftly out of the room. Passing unhindered through the plywood wall, he headed down the corridor after Jacob Jones.

Chapter Two

A Walk in the Mountains

Spring sunshine warmed the old stones of Salamanca Place, although a chill wind came from the mountain, still covered in winter snow. Two figures stood, unnoticed, under the ornamental trees that lined what had once been Hobart's busiest wharf. They looked very much alike. Neither old nor young, each of them was tall, thin and dressed in unremarkable, casual clothes. They had shoulder length brown hair and light blue eyes that pierced the morning sunshine. Even their faces were in many ways similar and equally unremarkable. One, however, was calm and relaxed, leaning slightly against one of the trees, his face apparently unmarked by the passage of time. The other was agitated, his face deeply lined by both calculation and anger.

Around them, the warehouses and bordellos had long ago given way to high end restaurants, fashionable coffee houses, and shops selling expensive art to those who had the money. The harbour was filled with tourist boats and the old stone buildings were now clean and honey coloured and glowing in the morning sun. Tables had been set out on the cobblestones as tourist and local alike shared a morning coffee.

The agitated one shifted uneasily. 'What are we doing here? They can't come here. I made sure of that...'

The other raised an eyebrow as he looked at his companion. 'Strangely, I don't recall inviting you. In fact, I think I indicated that you would, as always, be most unwelcome.' Getting no reaction, he continued. 'Anyway,

I am to begin here. Now, I am to make our move. You must've known that we would, sooner or later.'

The other snorted in disgust. 'You're too late. Any counter move you were going to make should have been made years ago.' He gestured towards the crowd along the street. 'You can use as many of these as you like, they won't be able to help. The place is doomed and you've lost. Accept it.'

'Maybe, but I am to select just one. Not a tool to be used, but a person: a hero. He will be our champion.'

There was a disturbance at one of the street-side coffee shops. A tall, athletic man with a military style haircut had thrown over his chair and table and was yelling at a group of fashionable, young professionals. He stormed off, turning down a narrow alleyway and climbing up towards Battery Point and the military rehabilitation centre.

Unseen, the two figures watched him leave from under the trees.

The first figure laughed dismissively. 'You can't be that desperate, surely,' he said. 'You can't seriously have chosen him.'

'Why do you say that?' the other asked casually.

'Because he's broken. You might as well have not chosen anyone at all for all the good he'll be.'

'Perhaps she can heal him. She's very good with injured things.'

'No, this is beyond her. Those wounds are too deep. They've become part of him.'

'Sometimes it is the deepest wounds that give the greatest strength. I was sent by one who saved the world through his wounds.'

'That, I'm sure you'll agree, was an exceptional case. More often, wounds such as these destroy, not just the wounded but those they love as well.'

'Yes, that too is possible …'

'It won't matter anyway. Choose whom you want. If you had wanted to stop me, you should've acted years ago. It's too late now. My plan is too far advanced for you to disrupt it.'

'We shall see.'

The coffee shop owner was busy apologising to his shocked and angry customers as his staff cleaned up the mess. The two figures were gone.

* * *

The valley was deep and the mountains rose steeply on either side, rising like green walls into a misty sky. There was a small stream and its gurgle, and the random twittering of some birds off in the scrub, were the only sounds. High above, two hawks flew an elaborate choreography in the still air. A muddy track followed the stream with wooden duckboards laid over the wettest parts. Off into some far distance it led, its ending lost in the immensity of mountain and valley. A solitary walker followed it, dwarfed by the mountains that surrounded him.

He knew that he was a small and passing creature in such a monumental landscape. 'That's good,' he thought. 'That's the way it should be.' The stream didn't care. It was simply water flowing downhill. The mountains didn't care, they simply were. They had been before he was born. They had been before even the first primeval fist was raised in anger, and they would be long after he was gone. It was a context that he needed when the people and the past pressed in on him. Walking along the small stream through the buttongrass plains and higher into the mountains, he felt nothing but the weariness of his body. This, too, was good. To feel was to feel pain: a pain that he didn't know how to cope with.

Only two days ago he had been sitting at a café, drinking coffee when the guy at the table behind him had started complaining loudly about the evils of the latest war in the Middle East, about the waste of money and the awful loss of civilian life. The accent was affected, the clothes casually expensive, his hair cut in the lopsided style that was so fashionable among young, progressive professionals.

He had known that he shouldn't listen. 'Don't take any notice,' he had told himself. 'It's nothing to do with me.' But he had felt his pulse begin to race and the anger had taken hold of him, fierce and all consuming. All of a sudden, he couldn't hear anything that the guy was actually saying. All he could hear was a voice screaming in his head, 'People died, woman and children! Innocents. It was because of you that they died. You killed them. Murderer! Murderer!.'

Jacob was on his feet, shaking with fury - his chair crashing to the pavement. Coffee spilled from his broken cup. 'Shut up!' he had yelled. 'Just shut the hell up!' He had walked away, leaving a shocked café, afraid of what he might do. The strange thing was that he actually agreed with the guy. This war, maybe all war, had been a huge waste of humanity. Lives had been taken. Lives had been broken. Nothing had been achieved.

He had had to get away. He couldn't cope: not with the crowds and the noise, not with the doctors at the hospital, not with their questions, not with the sympathetic voices and the 'understanding' looks. He didn't know which was worse, that, or the condescending callousness of the guy in the café. Here it didn't matter. Here, in this valley, he had no name, no program. Here, all he had to do was put one foot in front of the other. Here there was neither self-righteous indifference nor anyone trying to intrude into the numbness that protected his soul.

Yet he knew it was coming. He could feel it. It was the wide, empty valley and the mountains. They reminded him of the other place, the place the psyches kept wanting him to talk about. The place he was trying so hard to forget. His pulse rate increased. He was becoming more aware, more alert. He knew it was coming but he could do nothing about it. It was like watching a train wreck in slow motion: predictable and inevitable.

He noticed a spot about two thirds of the way up a hill ahead of him where there was a break in the slope. 'Good,' he thought, 'not as obvious as the top of the hill but still with a good view up the valley and room for the section to spread out and dig in. Get 'em safe from RPGs.' He stopped and took a deep breath. There was no section, no reason for surveillance, no RPGs. 'I am home. I am safe.' He kept repeating those words to himself. The doctors had told him not to be alone any more than necessary. Perhaps they had known that he would run away. Perhaps this walk was a mistake. His pulse rate remained high. He could feel the adrenaline flowing into his body. He took a deep breath and forced himself to look down and to keep on walking. 'Just put one foot in front of the other,' he told himself. 'Just put one foot in front of the other.'

When he looked up again, there was yet another ridge up ahead, its crest lined with boulders. One part of his mind told him to relax. It didn't matter, there would be no snipers. Somehow, this time he couldn't bring himself to believe it. Suddenly, he felt exposed and vulnerable. He didn't even have a weapon. He scanned the surrounding terrain. His eyes fixed on a group of boulders to his left and part way up the hill. 'Okay,' he thought, 'if things go pear shaped, that's the way we go – dead ground from the snipers on that ridge.' Again he stopped and drew in a deep breath. There were no snipers. There was nothing to go pear shaped. He concentrated on his breathing, trying to keep his mind in the present.

It didn't work. One of the hawks swooped down to take a rabbit. As the shadow passed over him, he was back. There was no stream and the mountains were brown. It was hot and the sun shone from a bright, china-blue sky. The attack helicopter came in again and the earth around him erupted into noise and dust.

'Not us, you idiots,' he yelled. 'Not us. Go kill the bad guys. John, tell 'em they've got the wrong target.' John Brunetti, communications specialist, nice kid. Used to boast of his mum's lasagne. He was on the radio and he waved to let them know they were on the wrong target. Then he caught a fifty cal. round in the chest. Blood, and guts, and muscle exploded across the dirt.

'No!' he yelled. He screamed, and he screamed, and he screamed.

He became aware that he was lying in the mud, wedged between two boulders. Above him, the misty sky had turned into a light drizzle. A small, grey lizard on the rock next to his head was watching him curiously.

He sighed and smiled at the lizard. 'I guess you're wondering why I'm lying here,' he said. The lizard cocked its head to one side. 'Well, it's a long story and I don't have the time.' He got to his knees. The lizard scurried away. Around him the valley had not changed.

He got to his feet and continued. The rain stopped as the afternoon wore on and he started to look for a place to camp. All went well until the valley started narrow. Again, he felt his heart rate increase. This walk had been a mistake. Narrow valleys with high, rocky walls held too many memories. He forced himself to breathe slowly. There would be no ambush. There was no one to ambush him. 'I'm home. I'm safe.'

Try as he might, he couldn't stop scanning the terrain around him. To the right was too steep, you'd be trapped. The left was better, go that way and you could make a fight of it.

It was getting on to late afternoon and the sun was making the shadows uncertain. If this had been in that other place, he would be sending out scouts to slowly check the area. He reminded himself that here he didn't need scouts. Still, his pulse was racing and his hands were sweating. Funny, in the other place he'd always been calm.

Somewhere on the other side of the stream, a fox called with a series of high, yapping barks. He looked around him in sudden panic. Then there was a gust of wind and he was sure he heard it, from the cliffs behind him – the sound of an RPG being launched. 'Incoming!' he yelled. To the left, the plan was to attack to the left. He ran, all the time expecting to hear the explosions around him. When he got to the cover of the boulders, he dropped on to his belly and crawled forward. Where was his rifle? How could he have been so stupid as to leave his rifle behind? 'Gun group, report!' he yelled. 'Report!' There was no answer. The only sound was the gurgling of the stream and the soft sound of the wind blowing through a patch of rugged trees near the base of the cliff.

He was lying on his stomach behind a large boulder. When he looked up he saw her, sitting on a rock and watching him with a puzzled frown. She was the most beautiful woman he had ever seen, a few years younger than himself and with hair that hung to her waist. Where it caught the late afternoon sun, it shone red gold. She was wearing a long, deep blue cloak and had been reading from a large, leather bound book.

'Are you a'right?' she asked with the soft consonants of the Scottish west. He became aware of how ridiculous he must look, lying on his stomach in the dirt. He blushed to think of how he had come to be there. He stood up and brushed himself down.

'No, not really,' he answered. 'But I'm okay for now. Sorry if I startled you.' She hadn't moved. She just sat there, looking at him with the same puzzled frown.

'What's wrong with you?' she asked.

'That's a long story…' He paused and looked at her. She still didn't move but sat regarding him with steady, grey eyes. 'And it's one I don't really want to talk about,' he said.

'Fair enough,' she replied. 'It's getting late. Where are you staying?'

He shrugged. 'I've got my swag. I thought I'd camp out.'

Her frown deepened. 'I don't think that's a good idea. There are demons chasing you and I don't think you should face them alone.' She sounded very like one of the army psyches. 'I think you should come with me. My house isn't far.' She got up, closed her book, pulled her cloak about her, and started to walk up the hill.

'No, wait,' he called. 'You can't just ask me back to your house.'

She turned. 'Why not?' she asked in a slightly puzzled voice.

'Because you don't know anything about me,' he said. 'You don't know who I am. I might be an axe murderer.'

'Are you?' she asked.

'No, of course not,' he answered. 'But you can't just take my word for it. You need to look out for your own safety. You can't just ask stray men to your house.'

A faint smile played at the corners of her mouth. 'Actually,' she said. 'I know a good deal more than you think. You won't hurt me. You couldn't, even if you wanted to. Come on stray-man, follow me.' She turned again to walk up the hill. He looked out across the valley, parts of which were already in deep shadow. Then he shrugged and turned to follow her.

Chapter Three

The Cottage

She led him over a rise and down a narrow, mossy ravine. Each step he took was careful and balanced. He was constantly scanning the walls of the ravine. All he saw was water dripping from the moss, crows coming in to roost for the night, and the girl in the blue cloak, always on the edge of disappearing into the thickening mist. A memory came to him then, a memory from deep childhood. It was of an illustration in a favourite book: a picture of Nimwe leading Merlin to his doom. He frowned as he remembered the childhood story. This whole thing felt like something from a story book and that particular story hadn't ended well.

Eventually they came to a pair of massive oak trees and walked between them. A large valley of neat well-tended fields opened up before them. Here and there, patches of mist obscured the view, like torn fragments of a curtain, but he could clearly see the village in the centre of the valley. The walking track they were on continued down through the middle of the valley and through the village. There didn't seem to be any other roads and he wondered how they could get their supplies in.

'Come on,' the girl said, interrupting his survey. 'My house is down here. You can get to know the valley later.' Still puzzled at this strange village in the middle of the wilderness, he drew his eyes away from the view and followed her down the path. About half way down the slope, a lane led off to the right. This the girl turned down. On either side, it was lined with chestnut trees that joined overhead to form a long arch, so that he felt as if he was walking through a leafy tunnel. At the end of this tunnel there was a cottage, which also looked like an illustration from a child's storybook. It had low, whitewashed walls and a straw thatched roof. There was a stone chimney at one end. On a trellis at the other end, there grew a climbing rose which, even though it was early in the season, was covered in deep red blooms. There were two mullioned windows with frames of dark wood.

He shook his head as if to clear it. This was too perfect. It couldn't be real. 'I must be dreaming,' he thought. 'I'm unconscious and dreaming. I must've hit my head and I'm really still lying on the ground, out in that valley; either that, or I've finally totally lost it and this is all a psychotic hallucination.' He looked around. If it was a hallucination, it was a very vivid and coherent one.

Off to one side there was a small, fenced orchard where red hens scratched in the dirt. A goat was tethered near the end of the lane. It chewed contentedly as the girl passed but looked at him doubtfully. The girl led him to the rear of the cottage where a small courtyard was surrounded by a tumbled down fence. Here, there was a rock wallaby with a bandaged foot lying on some straw. There was a black and white bird with a bandaged wing pecking at the weave of its wicker cage. An orphaned lamb came over and started to nibble at the girl's fingers.

She saw him watching and laughed. 'When I find the wee things injured, I bring them home and try to patch them up,' she said. 'My Da is used to it. Come on, he's over here. I'll introduce you.'

He followed her through a gate in the tumbled down fence to where an old man was digging in a vegetable garden. He was dressed in a grey smock-like garment with a broad leather belt around his waist and a dark, broad brimmed hat on his head. His hair was long and silver-grey. It hung in a loose pony tail down his back. His beard was, if anything, even longer and was tucked into his belt, presumably to keep it out of his way.

'Da!' she called. 'Da! I have a guest. I found him crawling in the other valley.' The old man looked up from his digging and regarded Jacob as if he were a stray animal his daughter had just brought home.

'Crawling? Did ye say crawling?' Steady eyes held him in their gaze, eyes the grey-blue of the evening sky. 'Why were ye crawling up that valley, young man? That's a very strange thing to do. Most people walk.'

He felt the blood rushing to his cheeks as he tried to think of an answer to that question.

The girl saved him. 'Apparently, it's a long story, Da, and it's not one he wants to tell just now. So, you be nice.' The old man's eyes, however, never left his face. Jacob could feel the gaze of those eyes boring into his soul. He held out his hand.

'How do you do sir, I'm …' He stopped. He had been about to give his now meaningless rank. 'I'm Jacob, Jacob Jones.' The old man wiped the dirt off a hand so gnarled with age and work that it resembled a collection of old tree roots more than a human appendage. He then gripped Jacob's offered hand with a surprisingly powerful grip.

'I am pleased to meet ye Jacob Jones. I'm Noah,' he said. 'I need to tell ye it wasn't yer fault – but then ye know that already, though I doubt that there's anything I can say that will make ye believe it.' Jacob felt adrenaline flood into his body and his world began to slip.

'What wasn't my fault?' he asked, keeping his voice under tight control.

'None of it,' the old man said, still holding his hand in a vice-like grip. 'The way ye stand, the way ye walk, they give ye away. I know ye're a soldier …'

'Was,' Jacob interrupted. 'I was a soldier…'

'And yer eyes are never still,' the old man continued, ignoring the interruption. 'They're always scanning, looking for the next threat. The better part of you is still off fighting a war somewhere. Listen to me, soldier. I know war and I know it wasn't yer fault. Whatever happened, it wasn't yer fault.' He finally released Jacob's hand. 'It was the fault of those who sent ye. It always is.' Jacob realised that every muscle in his body was tensed, ready for flight. The girl touched him on the arm and he flinched. He tried to consciously relax. Deep breaths.

'You mustn't mind my father,' the girl said. 'He spends so much time in the garden that he can forget his manners and be far too direct,' She turned a fierce glare at the old man. He gave a dismissive grunt and returned to his digging.

Jacob was calmer now. 'It's okay,' he said, 'and anyway, he's right about the soldier bit.'

The old man looked up from his digging. 'I'm glad to meet ye, Jacob. Ye're welcome to stay for as long as is needed. Myriam will show ye the way.'

'Um … Thank you, sir,' Jacob said.

Jacob turned to follow Myriam back to the cottage but the old man called him back, 'One more thing, Jacob,' he said holding him in the steady gaze of his soul-piercing eyes. 'This is a peaceful place and tonight when ye sleep ye'll sleep peacefully. Ye'll sleep deeply. That gift we can give ye.'

Jacob just nodded politely. It had been a long time since his sleep had been peaceful.

The old man went back to his digging and Jacob turned and followed Myriam over to the cottage.

They entered by the rear of the cottage into what was clearly the kitchen. It was dominated by a large table with bench seats that occupied the centre and a large, open fireplace that took up most of one wall. This had a series of iron hooks to carry different kettles, ovens and grills. Next to this was a door into what Jacob later learned was the pantry. A work bench ran along the back wall, just below the windows that looked out to the vegetable garden.

Myriam took off her cloak and hung it on one of the hooks next to the door. Underneath she had on a simple, white shift that hung to her ankles. She tied her hair back with a green ribbon and put on an apron that was hanging by the door. He dropped his pack next to her cloak.

'Sit down, I'll make you a cup of tea,' she said. She retrieved a large, china teapot and two delicate cups from the wooden dresser on the wall opposite the fireplace and then went over to the fire where a large, black kettle was already boiling. She used this to fill the teapot and then brought a tray with the teapot, cups and, somehow, a jug of milk.

'I'll let you pour your own so you can add the milk as you like it.' Jacob nodded and set about serving himself. By the time he had his cup poured, there was a plate of buttered scones on the table. Jacob looked at them in surprise. He didn't see how she could have gotten them ready in that time, especially as, when he took one, they were still warm. Memories came flooding back of his grandmother, who would always have hot scones and tea for visitors. Still, they took time to prepare. He looked at Myriam, puzzled.

'Where did you get the scones from?' he asked.

'Oh, I always like to have some scones for guests,' she said dismissively. This didn't really answer his question but he let it ride.

'Do you get many guests?' he asked.

'No, not many at all,' she said. 'Our valley is hidden away. Not many people manage to find it.' She smiled at him and he was struck by how readily she smiled and how beautiful her smile was. 'When you've finished there, I'll show you to your room.'

When he had had his fill of scones and tea, she led him out of the kitchen to the front of the cottage. This proved to be mostly one large room. There were richly coloured rugs on the floor, large, comfortable chairs, a massive arched fireplace, and books everywhere. There were shelves lining the walls, full of books. There were books piled on a low table. There were even books piled on the floor. All of them large, old, and bound in leather. Mullioned windows looked out at the lane lined with chestnuts, and ladders led to curtained lofts at either end of the room.

'Those are Da's and my sleeping quarters,' she said, pointing to the lofts. 'You'll sleep in here.' She showed him to a small room that was built under one of the lofts. It was not much bigger than a large walk-in closet and there was only one small window, set high in the wall, yet in this cramped space there was a large, iron framed bed with a thick multi-coloured quilt. The only other things in the room were a narrow bench along one wall, on which were a jug of water, a washing bowl, and a candle.

Jacob looked at the jug and the wash bowl. 'You have no running water?' he asked.

'No,' she answered. 'We've no electricity either. I'm afraid you'll find us very primitive.'

'No, not at all,' he answered. 'Believe me, I understand the desire to get back to a simpler way of life.' He saw her trying to hide a smile, as if he had said something unintentionally funny. 'Anyway,' he continued, 'I was planning to sleep in my swag tonight, so this is luxury. You have been very hospitable. I hope I won't disturb you too much.'

'It's no trouble at all,' she said. 'We're pleased to have the company. I'll leave you to freshen up. Dinner will be in about an hour.' She smiled at him and left. It was then that he noticed his heavy pack leaning against one wall. He looked at it in disbelief. How on earth had that gotten there?

After a quick wash, he lay on the bed to rest before dinner. As usual, he concentrated on not going to sleep. He decided to sort out the events of the day. He tried to make sense of the girl and her father. Why had he been asked so readily into their house? Were they just very hospitable? Did they ask all the walkers they met home for dinner? He toyed with the idea that they might be a cult trying to recruit him. Possible. Certainly something to keep an eye out for. Another possibility was that they were radical greenies who had gone off the grid or just a hippy commune remnant. One thing they couldn't be was simply a remote community with few basic services. In the developed world in the twenty first century, that just didn't make sense.

He thought of the old man, he of the bony hands, iron grip, and worrying gaze. His directness, candour, and understanding were unsettling. Jacob wondered if he had ever served. Whatever, his disgust at war was clear. Perhaps he was a deserter from some long-forgotten conflict, still hiding away in the hills. Hiding in the hills… He shook himself mentally. Don't let that happen. Think of other things. How did the pack get in here?

Where did those scones come from? For that matter, where did the jug of milk come from and how was the tea ready so quickly? He thought of the girl, Myriam. He thought of how her hair shone like burnished copper in the sun. He thought of how her ready smile animated her face. She had the same grey-blue eyes as her father, but hers didn't so much pierce his soul as caress it, like the clouds of a soft day, with misty rain to soften the earth. He shook himself awake. He was getting dangerously close to sleep and he mustn't let that happen.

Just then there was a light knock on his door and he got up to join Myriam and her father at dinner. Dinner was roast lamb and vegetables washed down with a mildly alcoholic apple cider. It was dark by this time and dinner was eaten by candlelight. Miriam served the dinner, her ready smile and laughter contrasting with the silence of her father. Jacob noticed the brightness of her smile, the deep red colour of her hair in the darkened room, and the way the candle light played on her pale skin.

After dinner, the three of them sat by the fire in the front room, drinking a kind of vegetable broth spiced with a herb he didn't recognise. Myriam provided the entertainment. She read a long and humorous poem about a hapless wizard and his attempts to win a farm girl 'of coal black hair and milk white skin.' Jacob watched the way fire light and candle played across her face. He heard the light inflection of her voice as she read. He felt something wake within him that he had thought forever dead.

'I have to be careful,' he thought. 'I don't want to cause these people any trouble. I must leave tomorrow at first light.' The old man didn't say much. He smiled infrequently, laughed even more rarely, and his gaze fell often on Jacob. Yet he only spoke directly to him once and that only as Jacob was leaving for bed.

'Sleep well tonight, Jacob,' he said. 'Sleep well.'

That night he lay on his bed staring at the ceiling lit faintly by the moonlight from the window. Even though he was tired from the walk and badly sleep deprived from too many troubled nights, he fought to stay awake. He was afraid of sleep, afraid of where it would take him. This night, however, his eyes closed for only a second – and sleep overtook him.

* * *

Sweat trickled down his back. It was hot and dusty and the whole place had that washed-out look, as if the sun had bleached out all the colour. He was standing by the side of the road as his men checked the traffic. It was all routine; just old cars, broken down trucks and donkey carts; farmers and traders trying to get on with their lives. Still, it all had to be checked.

It was the same bus each day, bringing the kids back from the school in the neighbouring village. That day he noticed that it was a bit earlier than usual. It slowed down as it approached the checkpoint. There was something wrong …

He felt a hand on his shoulder and turned around to find Myriam's father, with his beard still tucked into his belt. 'Not tonight, Jacob,' he said. 'Tonight, ye need to sleep.' The other place faded and his sleep was deep and dreamless, for the first time in many months.

Chapter Four

Dreams

Jacob awoke to the smell of bacon cooking. Sunlight was streaming in through the small window and it was clear that he had slept later than he had intended. He lay still for a moment, savouring the surprise. It had been a long time since he had not woken up, anxious, in the pre-dawn grey. He got up, washed himself, dressed, and went out to the kitchen. Myriam was there, standing at a steel plate that had been placed over the fire. Her hair had been loosely tied back from her face so that it hung behind her. She was cooking bacon and eggs and a kind of vegetable fritter.

She looked up as he entered. 'There you are. I trust you slept well. I have your breakfast all ready for you.' The teapot and cups were already set up on the table, as was a plate of hot, buttered toast.

'How did you know when I would be getting up?' he asked.

'Oh, I've found that people often wake when they smell the bacon cooking,' she answered brightly. The timing still seemed strangely precise to him, but he let it go. By the time he had poured himself a cup of tea, Myriam had placed a large plate of bacon and eggs, with a couple of the vegetable fritters, in front of him. It was a big meal, very different from his usual bowl of cereal and quick cup of coffee. He felt deeply embarrassed by the extent of her hospitality.

'Look, I'm very grateful for all your kindness,' he said, reaching for his wallet. 'I insist on paying you something…'

She shook her head. 'We have no need for money.' She looked at the determined set of his jaw. 'But if you insist and can swing an axe, there's a large pile of wood out there that needs to be cut before winter comes. My Da is getting on, so any help you could give would be gratefully received. When you finish up here, of course.'

'Fair enough,' he said and set to on his breakfast.

He swung the axe and split the wood cleanly. It was good work, requiring a combination of skill and strength. It required the full concentration of both body and mind. His mind left behind memory and fear to focus on this single task, and his body rejoiced in the rhythm of the axe. He was sweating from the effort and had long since placed his shirt to one side, but he realised that he was enjoying himself. The work forced him to concentrate on the moment: this piece of wood, this swing of the axe. The pile of cut wood grew steadily through the morning.

He swung the axe again, hearing the satisfying 'thunk' as the wood split. He threw it onto the split pile and reached for the next piece to split, only to find that there wasn't one. He had spent most of the morning in single-minded concentration and had worked through all the wood to be split. He swung the axe one final time to leave it embedded in the chopping block.

'Oh my goodness,' Myriam exclaimed behind him. 'You've cut it all.' He turned to find her standing there, holding a jug and a glass. 'I thought you'd be thirsty,' she said pouring him a drink, 'but I didn't think you'd have done all this.'

'Well, I just got into it and kept going I guess,' he said, taking the drink. She looked at his bare chest and noticed a scattering of scars down one side. She reached out as if to touch them but quickly pulled back.

'How did you get those?' she asked.

'IED,' he said shortly, as he reached for his shirt. She looked at him blankly. 'Improvised explosive device.' He turned away from her and began to button up his shirt. 'It was a bomb buried in a load of tomatoes and set off remotely. It was meant to kill...' His gaze went to the surrounding hills. 'It was meant to kill anyone who came to rescue...' Then he was back there. It was the normal bus. A few minutes early, bringing the local kids back from school. Only there was something wrong. He had looked at the driver and had seen that he was terrified...

She touched his arm and the other place faded. 'Come,' she said. 'Get cleaned up and we'll get you some lunch.' He looked about him, at the cottage and the pile of wood. His pulse was racing, he was holding the axe like a weapon, and the glass lay broken on the ground.

'No, no,' he mumbled. 'I'm sorry, so sorry. Got to go. You've been too good as it is.' He needed to be away, away where the only one he might hurt was himself.

'Nonsense,' she said. She pointed to the pile of chopped wood. 'You've earned at least a week's board with that.' She looked directly into his eyes and said firmly, all trace of lightness gone, 'Do not imagine that you would ever hurt me because you wouldn't. You couldn't. Now, come in for lunch.'

'Myriam, you don't know me,' he said. 'You don't know who I am, what I've done.'

'Perhaps not, but I do know you wouldn't hurt me,' she replied. 'This discussion is over and lunch is waiting.' She turned and headed back to the cottage, leaving no room for argument. Jacob watched her go, perplexed. She talked to him as if she had known him for a long time, as if they were old friends, yet he had only just met her. Her easy familiarity made him nervous. He considered the rose-covered, thatched cottage and the small village beyond it. The whole situation was like something from a fairy tale and he again briefly considered the possibility that he might be hallucinating. He had no way of telling, everything seemed real enough. He decided to go with the flow, again buried the axe in the chopping block, finished buttoning up his shirt, and followed her down to lunch.

Lunch was a rich, pumpkin soup with warm, freshly baked bread. It was simple but filling. Jacob sat in silence, trying to make sense of his situation, while Myriam served him and her father cheerfully. Eventually the weirdness of being treated like an old friend, or one of the family, when he didn't know these people, got to him and he broke his silence. He asked the question that was uppermost in his mind.

'Myriam, how come you act as if you know me when we've only just met?' he asked. 'And don't tell me I'm imagining it because I know I'm not. None of this makes any sense, not our meeting, not your invitation, none of it. What's really going on?' Myriam stopped her serving, the smile fading from her face. She looked at her father, who gave a small shake of his head. She turned back to the stove and busied herself with the kettle.

'Maybe I do know you, Jacob,' she said lightly. 'Perhaps you remind me of someone I once knew or maybe we met in our dreams.' She turned to him and smiled. 'Aye, I think that must be it. We've met in our dreams.'

'Yeah, I'm afraid I don't believe in any of that new agey dream stuff,' Jacob said. 'When we first met, you said you knew I wouldn't hurt you. What made you so sure?'

'Actually, what I said was that you couldn't hurt me,' she said, ignoring a frown from her father. 'You couldn't because I'm magic. I would be able to stop you.'

Jacob's eyes widened slightly and he drew a deep breath. He should've known. Sargent Cooper used to say 'Get with an ugly girl, son, the pretty ones are way too much work and the prettier they are the crazier they are.' According to Sergeant Cooper's theory, Myriam would have to be the craziest woman Jacob had ever met.

Myriam gave a small, almost apologetic, smile. 'I know, the prettier they are, the crazier, right? But I'm not crazy. We have met in our dreams.' she leaned a little closer and lowered her voice. 'It's magic. Let me see if I can convince you.'

Jacob felt his heart rate increase and he gripped his spoon more tightly.

'That's enough Myriam,' Noah said abruptly. 'Ye're scaring our guest.'

Jacob turned to Noah, challenging him. 'And you, Sir. Did we meet in our dreams? I certainly dreamt of you last night. What do you know of my dreams?'

'I know yer dreams, boy,' Noah growled. 'Just like thousands of other soldiers who find they can go home but they can't quite leave the battlefield. Yer dreams are my dreams. Our dreams.' Noah's jaw clenched almost imperceptibly. 'Not the time or the place perhaps, but the threat, the horror, the fear and the helplessness; these I know all too well.' He finished the drink in his hand with one swig. 'Did ye dream of me? I hope I brought some calm to ye.'

Jacob gave a reluctant smile. 'The strange thing is, you did,' he said.

'Good,' Noah said, accepting a large mug of tea from Myriam. 'My advice, young Jacob, is to take what grace ye can; however it comes to ye.'

Myriam put a mug of tea in front of him, her face sulky from her father's reprimand. Jacob relaxed a little as he sipped from the mug. His mind was racing as he tried to analyse his situation. This all was starting to make some sort of sense. Noah was an ex-soldier and a single father trying to raise and care for a seriously delusional daughter. Maybe his wife had died or maybe she had run off, unable to cope with her husband's PTSD and her daughter's illness. Whatever the case, perhaps after psychiatry had failed, he had brought her here, out in the wild, to live a simple, stress free life. Maybe he had thought that would cure her. If so, it clearly hadn't worked.

Myriam sat down across the table from him. 'In my dreams,' she whispered, glancing anxiously at her father, 'you and I played together as children. Do you remember?.'

'No, I don't,' he said kindly. Could he blame her if her mind had run away to some comforting fantasy where a stranger was actually a lifelong dream-friend? 'I really don't believe that we meet people in dreams.'

'Are you sure?' she asked. 'How many of your dreams do you remember?'

A vision came to him of a dusty road in a brown, derelict land. She watched his face tighten. 'Not those dreams, Jacob,' she said softly. 'The normal ones you had before you went to that place.'

Jacob looked at her with her long, red hair falling in gentle waves, with her pale skin and her soft eyes. He shook his head. 'I'm sure I would have remembered it, if ever I'd dreamed of you,' he said softly.

She smiled brightly, her sulkiness forgotten. 'It's very nice of you to say that, even if you don't really mean it. Still, perhaps you do remember, somewhere deep inside. Why else would you come walking out here? Why would you turn aside to stay with a strange girl? I think you knew it was time for us to meet in person, not in your conscious mind, but deep down, in the place where dreams come from.'

He gazed at her as steadily as he could. She was absolutely gorgeous. She didn't seem threatening and she looked perfectly normal. In fact, she looked not just normal but bright and intelligent. It was just that she was saying all these crazy things.

Jacob looked at her with a slightly twisted smile and sighed. 'Maybe you're right,' he said. 'Maybe we spent our whole childhood together in our dreams. But you must admit, this sounds a little crazy. I need time to think this through.'

'Fair enough,' the old man said loudly and unexpectedly from the end of the table. In their whispered conversation, they had forgotten him. Now, he looked pointedly at Myriam.

'Fair enough,' she agreed reluctantly. 'Will you at least stay with us a few days, to give me a chance to get to know you, to reconnect with someone who was, maybe, my childhood 'dream-friend'?'

He considered this for a moment, considered her bright eyes and her perfect, pale skin. He couldn't shake the feeling that there was something he still didn't understand going on. How did his pack make its way to his bedroom? Could it be mere coincidence that she had mentioned the essence of Cooper's theory just as he had thought of it? Surely it was only logical to stay until he could figure these things out. Although, if he were honest, the fact that it was a beautiful girl wanting him to stay so she could get to know him, probably played a significant role in his decision making.

'Fair enough,' he said too. He knew that was not a good way to come to a decision, but she smiled brightly at his response and it occurred to him that he could put up with a lot of weird stuff to have that smile directed at him.

'Good,' she said happily. 'This afternoon I will take you down to the village. You need to meet Father Augustus.' He nodded, even though he had no idea who Father Augustus was or why he should meet him – and he didn't really care. He just needed to figure out this girl.

* * *

Two figures walked slowly up the path beneath the chestnut trees, each dressed in modern hiking clothes. One was talking excitedly, trying to make a point.

'None of that has solved anything,' he said. 'As I pointed out to you before, those wounds are deep. They can't be cured by a good night's sleep. The old man has just papered over the problem and nothing in the village has changed. The forces I have put into play cannot be stopped, certainly not by him. This village is facing a disaster it doesn't know and can't understand.'

The other shrugged casually. 'The old man has bandaged the hurt so that the healing can begin.'

'What healing? Those wounds cut into his soul. Even if he survives them, he will be scarred forever.'

'You don't understand,' the second figure replied, forcefully this time. 'He was only hurt because he cares. You know what he saw. If he had been uncaring and unhurt, he would never have been chosen. It is the lines and scars of love that make a face beautiful.'

The first figure snorted in disgust. 'His very soul is marred and disfigured. I see no beauty in that.'

'No, you don't,' the other replied. 'That's your problem.'

They walked in silence for a while before the first figure resumed his argument. 'You know he's only staying because he's attracted to the girl.'

'He thinks she's beautiful. He's right.'

'He's thinking with his glands, not his head. Eventually, he will reject all this talk of dreams and magic, decide he's had enough, and run away. He will leave and destroy the girl – and the village. It's as plain as day. You just won't admit that you've lost.'

'Perhaps, but I think you underestimate him.'

'I don't think so. I know how shallow and selfish young men are.'

'Really? I know of this particular young man's great capacity for love and sacrifice.'

'You're a fool. What will become of the girl? The sword I have hanging over her head is sharp and double edged. It will cut, whichever way she turns. This has taken me years to prepare and you think you can undo it with a broken soldier?'

'Perhaps.'

'As I said, you're a fool. Even if he stays, that will only add to her sorrow, and doom him to an even sorrier sorry fate.' They turned to walk down the path into the village and were gone.

Chapter Five

The Village

As they walked into the village, Jacob stopped and stood still. 'It's all a dream,' he thought desperately. 'It has to be a dream. Something I've made up out of the fragments of childhood stories. I must be asleep somewhere out on the track.'

The village was, indeed, like something from a story book illustration. There weren't many buildings and they were all strung along the walking track, which widened slightly to form a sort of gravelled main street. Each building had heavy frames of dark wood with walls either of wattle and daub, or stone. Most of the high gabled roofs were thatched but some were covered with slate tiles. The windows, where they existed, were mullioned and bayed into the street.

Jacob shook his head. 'No,' he said. 'This can't be real. I'm asleep somewhere and dreaming.' He pinched his left bicep hard and felt the sharp pain of it, but the village before him didn't change.

Myriam smiled as she watched him. 'You're not dreaming, Jacob, our village may be a little different to what you're used to but it's real enough.'

The largest building in the village was a rambling affair with a thatched roof and a series of dormer windows. It appeared to be the village tavern, since it had a sign, decorated with the image of a man in a straw hat, proclaiming it to be 'The Apple Gate'. The building nearest to the entrance of the village had no front wall and was clearly the blacksmith's shop. The sound of metal ringing out against metal was clear and, even from the street, Jacob could feel the heat of the hearth. At the far end of the village, and up a slight hill, there was a church made of dark stone, with a slate roof, and a squat bell tower.

'We need to go there,' Myriam said, pointing to the church. 'That's where we'll find Father Augustus. But first I have some shopping to do…'

'No, wait!' Jacob said. 'What is this?'

'What do you mean?' Myriam asked.

'This village, what is it?' Jacob asked. 'Is it some kind of a museum? Some sort of historical re-enactment place? A tourist thing? What gives?'

'Well,' Myriam replied carefully. 'I did tell you that you might find us a bit primitive…'

'No, no. This isn't just primitive,' Jacob replied. 'This village is like something out of the early Middle Ages.'

'Late middle ages actually, according to Father Augustus.' Myriam said. 'You need to talk to him. He keeps track of these things and he'll explain everything better than I can.' She looked at him. He was standing still as if frozen. On top of all the strange talk of dreams, this was just too much. 'Can you just, what was that phrase, go with the flow for a while?' she asked. 'Just accept that this place exists, knowing that you'll find out why later?'

He looked down at her and she smiled tentatively at him, gazing at him with her misty-grey eyes. 'Okay,' he said. 'But why can't you tell me?'

She looked uncomfortable. 'I could, but it would be better coming from Father Augustus. He'll know what to tell you,' she said gently. 'Come on, I have some shopping to do.'

He considered this for a moment, looking at the village and its odd buildings, then he shrugged. 'Whatever this place was, it wasn't really all that important to him, and the girl and her father had been kind. He was prepared to cut them some slack and wait for an explanation.

Myriam led him down the street to a tile roofed house with mullioned bay windows. Inside was a draper's showroom, with bolts of cloth hanging from the walls and lying, partially unrolled, on a large table. There was a regular clacking sound coming from the rear of the building. The sound got louder as a door at the back of the room opened and a short, intense woman entered. Jacob got a brief glimpse of looms working unattended in the background.

Myriam greeted the woman cheerfully. 'Good morning, Martha,' she said. 'This is Jacob, a visitor.' The tone was cheerful and casual but Jacob couldn't escape the impression that there was some urgency in identifying him as someone from outside the village. The woman regarded him with a gaze that would pierce concrete. In the background, the noise of the looms stopped.

'Gore-Tex,' she said after a short pause. When he looked puzzled, she pointed to his jacket, frowning in disapproval. 'Gore-Tex. Expensive. Not worth it. Better off with a woollen jumper and an oilskin. I could get ye those,' she finished hopefully.

Jacob shook his head. 'I'm just visiting I'm afraid, not buying,' She frowned in disapproval.

'I am though,' Myriam said brightly. 'I have a list here of the things I need...' The talk then quickly developed into a detailed discussion of fabric and colour, and Jacob rapidly lost interest. He wandered around the shop for a bit and then stood in the doorway, watching the street. He watched for several minutes while the discussion became animated behind him, but the street was mostly empty and quiet.

It was just as some sort of deal was being reached behind him, that the peace was broken by the sound of fast moving horses. Six riders, all dressed in black, came galloping down the street from the far end of the village.

'Going way too fast,' Jacob thought to himself. 'Someone could get hurt.' The horses were heavy and the ground shook with their tread. Some chickens scattered in panic before them. A woman coming out of her door was forced to quickly retreat back into her cottage. Someone ran to grab a young child. The riders never slowed their pace. Jacob watched them grimly. He had seen this behaviour before: warlords driving their Toyota trucks, young army recruits in Humvees, people whose only concern was their own image, people who thought they could be bigger by belittling others.

'Idiots,' he muttered.

As he watched the horses approach, a small boy wandered out of the baker's shop next to him. Concentrating only on the cake he was eating, he wandered onto the street, oblivious to the horses bearing down on him.

'Watch out!' Jacob yelled. He didn't think. He ran out into the street and grabbed the boy, holding him in his arms as he rolled out of The Riders' way. It was close enough for the leg of one of the horses to brush his shoulder but the Riders neither slowed nor varied in their path. He got to his feet, still holding the boy, who was now starting to cry. The Riders wheeled their horses about at the end of the village, then rode back the way they had come. Still at the same reckless pace.

He watched as they rode past him. One of them turned, just for a moment, to look at him. What he saw in that look shocked Jacob to his core. He had expected to see the arrogance and pride, the disdain and contempt he had seen before: all the hallmarks of the young and ego obsessed. He thought that he might also see curiosity at the presence of a stranger. What he actually saw was – nothing. The rider's expression was totally devoid of any human emotion – good, bad or neutral. It was as if the rider was not a person at all. He was a blank. There was an emptiness in that look which was just plain wrong, wrong on a fundamental level. Jacob had seen callousness, depression and even madness, but he had never seen anything like that before. It was as if the rider were already dead. He watched as they rode up the street and out of the village

Jacob had to consciously shake himself free of the gut horror that look had aroused and when he did, he found the boy's near hysterical mother taking the child from him, and thanking him profusely in a garbled mixture of Scot's Gaelic and English. People were coming out of the shops and houses and, now that the Riders had gone, there was a lot of loud and angry talk. A small crowd of women surrounded the mother and crying child, while casting curious looks in Jacob's direction. The blacksmith came out of his shop and gave Jacob a long, appraising look. Jacob turned at a touch on his arm to find Myriam standing beside him, still watching where the Riders had gone. There were tears in her eyes.

When she noticed him looking at her she wiped the tears from her eyes and said, 'Come, I've finished here and there's another shop to go to before we see Father Augustus.' Jacob nodded silently and followed her, still trying to come to terms with the blankness of that look and what it might mean.

The next shop she took him to was a simple stone building with a picture of a cow and a pig painted on the door and strings of sausages hung in the window. Inside, there was one large room with a heavy wooden table in the centre. On the table, there was the partially butchered carcass of a sheep. A heavyset man in a white tunic and a blue apron stood there, sharpening a large meat cleaver. Along one wall, fresh carcasses hung on meat hooks. There was sawdust on the floor to absorb the blood.

'Myriam, good afternoon,' the man said cheerfully. 'What can I get for ye today?'

'Afternoon, Jock,' Myriam answered. 'How's Jean? I need some lamb for dinner tonight…'

Jacob stared at the partly butchered carcass on the table. Both legs had been cut off and put aside. Jacob felt his muscles begin to tense. He had to get out of there. He turned quickly to face the street, his heart suddenly racing.

It was dry and dusty but cold. The sun gave little warmth, even though the sky was clear. There was not much traffic through the checkpoint, just an old donkey cart carrying some crates of tomatoes, which was why he paid particular attention to the bus. It was just the normal bus, a few minutes early, carrying the kids back from school in the neighbouring village, but as it got closer he knew that something was wrong. He could see the driver's face and he was terrified.

'Stop it!' he yelled to his men at the checkpoint. 'Stop the bus!' There was no hesitation, not for a moment did they question him. The bus came to a skidding halt as its tyres were shot out and its engine block hit. For a moment nothing happened. Water flowed from the ruined radiator and the kids were screaming. He knew, however. There was a horrible inevitability to it.

'Cover!' he yelled, as the bus exploded in flame. The shockwave hit him and knocked him off his feet. He got up, still stunned from the shock, with his ears ringing from the sound of the blast. The remains of the bus were burning where it had stopped, but the road in front of him now looked like the back of a butcher's shop. It took him a moment to realise that it was because it was covered by blood, blood and bits of … bits of …

She touched him on the arm and he was back in the village. He was shaking and crying. Sweat rolled down his face as he stared at the empty road. Her hand rested on his arm.

'I'm sorry, Jacob,' she said. 'I didn't realise…I didn't think… I'm so sorry.' He turned to look at her. Her soft eyes were full of concern. There was sadness there too, sadness at the horror that could have this effect on him. As she looked at his face, her eyes began to fill with tears.

'It's alright,' he said, trying to smile. 'It's not your fault. You didn't know. How could you?' He took a deep breath. 'Calm down,' he thought. 'Deep breaths, in and out. It was only meat after all. Nothing to get upset about.' As he breathed, he could feel his pulse begin to slow. It was a trick that the army psychs taught him. One of the few that worked.

'Did you get what you needed?' he asked, forcing his voice to be normal.

'Aye, I did,' she said with a break in her voice. 'Now come. We'll go up and see Father Augustus.' Jacob would rather have gone to the tavern, to lose himself in a dark corner, but he knew what lay along that road. He had seen it in all too many of his fellows. So, he nodded and walked with her towards the church. Her hand had never left his arm.

The small church was a low building made of dark stone. It had a high-gabled slate roof and a square bell tower to the left of the main door. Inside it was dark, apart from the light of a few candles. The only natural light came from the multicoloured window above the main door and three narrow windows on the opposite wall above the altar. It took a moment for Jacob's eyes to adjust. The layout was unfamiliar. There were no pews and there was a wooden screen, brightly painted and decorated with carvings of saints and angels, separating the sanctuary from the rest of the church. The screen was topped by a large crucifix, painted in bright colours. Jacob turned his face away.

While the interior layout was unfamiliar, the atmosphere was not. The relative dark, the stillness, and the red sanctuary lamp burning by the side of the altar; all of these were familiar from his earliest childhood. More from habit than devotion, he made the sign of the cross and went down on one knee. It had been a long time since he had been to mass or prayed with any conviction that he would be heard.

Myriam led him towards the altar. There, just behind the screen and in front of the altar, a figure in a black cassock was stretched out, face down on the floor, arms spread wide in the form of a cross. Jacob assumed that this was Father Augustus but he was so still, showing no reaction at all to their approach, that he briefly wondered if the priest might be asleep, or even dead.

'Reverend Father,' Myriam called softly. 'Reverend Father. We're sorry to disturb your prayer but I have brought Jacob to meet you.'

The old man rose slowly to his feet. He turned to face them, and Jacob saw years of prayer and penance etched into his skin. A few grey hairs clung feebly to his head while his beard was full and reached down to his chest. He had a severe face, one used to harsh discipline, but his eyes were bright and the smile that he gave them was kind.

'The Lord be with you, Myriam, and with you also, Jacob,' he said. His voice was full and melodious. It could have been the voice of a young and powerful man. He walked out to them through the central opening in the screen, and stood looking at them for a long, silent moment. Myriam bowed her head before his gaze.

'It is good to see you both, together at last,' he said. He turned to look at Jacob. 'Although I suspect that why I would say that is something you don't yet understand.'

'No, Father, I don't,' Jacob said. 'But it's only one of many things about this place that I don't understand, and by no means the most puzzling.'

The old priest nodded, laughing. 'I'm sure,' he said. 'You must feel as if you're walking in a strangely realistic dream.' He turned to Myriam. 'My dear, I think that perchance you have not been able to finish your shopping. Why don't you go and do that now? Jacob and I need to talk…'

CHAPTER SIX

A Story

Myriam bowed to the old priest, curtsied in front of the altar, and left Jacob alone with Father Augustus. They stood for a while with the old priest looking at Jacob in silence. Jacob started to feel very uncomfortable under the priest's calm but penetrating gaze.

He was just about to speak, when the priest said, 'Let's go outside. This could well be a long talk and I need to sit down – and maybe take a glass of wine or two. This body isn't as spry as it used to be.'

Jacob smiled. 'Lead on, Father,' he said, as he followed him. Outside, to the right of the main door, there was a stone bench. Father Augustus settled on this with a sigh and Jacob sat next to him. They had a clear view of the village, the valley, and the hills beyond. In the distance, Jacob could see the dolerite cliffs of the Tasmanian highlands. Father Augustus leaned back against the wall of the church and closed his eyes for a moment. Then he handed Jacob a glass of wine. Jacob gave a grunt and stared at the glass in surprise.

'It's a good drop,' the priest said with a smile that had an edge of playfulness about it.

Jacob took the glass and sipped the wine. It was strong but passable. When he looked back, Father Augustus also had a glass. Again, there was no obvious place it could have come from.

'Try not to concern yourself too much with what you can't explain just now, son. I'll get to that.' The priest took a few sips, then he said, 'I have to tell you a story.

You may find it hard to believe but I assure you it's true. A long time ago now, there was a village in a valley high in the Scottish mountains. The inhabitants of this village were talented in ways that had long passed out of the surrounding world. They knew their talents would arouse fear and suspicion among their neighbours – so they kept them hidden. For over a thousand years, they kept them hidden and the village and the valley were peaceful and prosperous…'

'Hang on, Father,' Jacob interrupted. 'Slow down a bit. What talents? How were the villagers talented? I'm assuming they weren't just really good at music or something.'

'No indeed,' the old priest agreed. 'It was something far more troubling.' He looked at Jacob, grinning slightly. 'How do you like your wine?'

Jacob hesitated, surprised by the question.

The priest held up his hand, still grinning. 'You're still trying to figure out where it came from. I've no bottles or glasses nearby and in any case, I assure you, I'm far too old to succeed at any sleight of hand.'

Jacob frowned at his wine glass and shook his head. Then he took a large gulp of the wine. He'd seen Myriam do something similar with scones previously. None of this made any sense and he was beginning to think that the tavern would have been a better option.

Father Augustus leaned towards Jacob and whispered, 'The people in this valley can do magic.'

Jacob looked at him blankly, trying to work out if the priest were mad or joking.

'Oh, not big magic. Not the sort of magic that can tear down mountains and twist time and space. No, those who could do that passed into the west long ago. No, the people in this valley can do simple, homely sorts of magic, like having wine when it is needed without all the bother of walking to the presbytery to get it. Magic like helping a cow to calve or give more milk; or keeping an orchard free of blight; even affecting, to some small degree, where and when the rain will fall, the simple, homey things that farmers need.'

Jacob looked at the priest impassively. 'And Myriam and her family, do they have this simple, homely magic?' he asked.

'No, at least, not exactly.' The priest shifted uncomfortably. 'Did Myriam not discuss any of this with you?'

Jacob shook his head.

The priest frowned at his wine glass. 'Then I think I must respect her silence,' he said. 'But I will say this, Myriam's family have noble blood, albeit from the wrong side of the sheet, if you take my meaning. This means that more exotic talents will sometimes emerge, some rare gifts. The same is true of Noah, her father, perhaps even more so. The talk in the village is that he can see into a person's mind – even enter there. I've been told he can even intrude into another person's dreams.'

Jacob looked long and hard at the old priest to try and see if he was joking. He looked sincere and open. If he was acting, he was very good at it. Finally, he had to concede that the old man at least believed what he was saying.

'Father, you can't expect me to believe any of this,' he said. 'It's just crazy. It's like something from that old movie, only it's even more messed up.'

'The movie I know nothing about, but no, I didn't expect to convince you,' the priest replied. 'I simply offer this as an explanation. I will let the village and its people convince you. Over time, the evidence will mount and you will come to believe. This is the normal way of belief, any belief. It doesn't come through big proofs or logical argument. It comes through little things, little things that add up to a greater whole.'

Jacob leaned back against the wall of the church and sipped his wine. Sure, there were some weird things going on, but this talk of magic was just crazy. He looked at the old priest sitting next to him, his face worn and tough. This was not a man given to practical jokes, nor was he someone to be taken lightly. Jacob closed his eyes and reviewed what he had been told. He opened his eyes and smiled.

'You talk about a thousand year old Scottish village, but we're not in Scotland. We're on the other side of the world. And a thousand years ago, there was certainly no village here. Even two hundred years ago there wasn't anything that could pass as a village.'

'I didn't actually say that this village was here a thousand years ago,' the priest pointed out.

'Oh, you mean you were talking about some other Scottish village?' Jacob asked.

The priest smiled. 'Let me explain. About 500 of your years ago, the Laird of this village took a fancy to a young woman. There's nothing unusual in that. She was most attractive, and he was rich and the most talented in magic that anyone had seen for many generations. The trouble was, she was married and when she rejected him, he forced himself upon her. This the village would not stand for and it united against him. Now, he was as talented as his ancestors, maybe even more so, but he couldn't resist the combined powers of all the village folk. They stormed his great tower house and … How can I put this delicately? … ensured that he would never bother a woman again.'

Jacob was surprised and a bit shocked. 'They castrated him?'

'Sadly, yes,' the priest said. 'It was a mistake, although the village was in no mood to accept that, especially as nine months later, the woman died giving birth to the Laird's child. The Laird, however, was not a man likely to forgive. He nursed his wounds for many years while he planned his revenge. Then, one night, he called on all his power to pronounce a terrible curse. The effort nearly killed him and broke both his power and his health forever.

He determined that just as he could not have relations with a woman, the village could not have relations with the world. The village was cast adrift in time and space, never spending more than a few weeks in any one place. Families were torn apart, lovers were separated. It was like a kind of living death. Always, we would turn up in some mountainous wilderness, but it could be anywhere in the world: Tibet, South America, Canada… Anywhere and anytime; sometimes in the future, sometimes in the past, sometimes tantalizingly close to our own time and place, but never anywhere for long. Sometimes strangers come and they anchor us for a while in their own time and place but then they leave and we are off again, blown about like an autumn leaf, on winds we didn't know or understand.'

'That's a great story Father,' Jacob said drily. 'It'd make a really good TV show. Of course, I don't believe a word of it and I really can't think that you expect me to.'

The old priest smiled. 'No, I don't, but for now, will you let me just tell the rest?'

Jacob shrugged. 'Why not?'

'Good,' the priest continued, 'because you are a part of this story, an important part.'

'How so?' Jacob asked. 'Just because I blundered in here?'

'No,' Father Augustus shook his head. 'Others have done that. No, it's because …Has Myriam not mentioned anything to you?'

'No,' Jacob said, shaking his head. 'She's told me nothing.'

Father Augustus again frowned down at his wine glass, pausing, as if uncertain how to proceed. 'At first, our travels seemed truly random,' he said at last. 'Then we noticed that the village was returning with ever greater frequency to one general time and place. We didn't know why but the village kept coming back to somewhere near this time and this place: to somewhere near you. It's as if the village is now being blown in a circle and you are at its centre.'

'Why?' Jacob asked. 'That doesn't make any sense, not even in the context of this whole crazy story.'

'That puzzled me for a long time too,' the old priest said, 'but it seems to me there must be some kind of tether to the outside world, constraining our wanderings. Some relationship. The relationship between you and Myriam, perhaps?'

'But I have no relationship with Myriam!' Jacob protested. 'I only met her yesterday.'

'Are you sure?' Father Augustus asked. 'Not even in your dreams?'

Jacob leaned back against the church and closed his eyes. Not dreams again. Why was everyone in this town obsessed with his dreams. If they really knew his dreams, they would only want to forget them.

'Dreams can reach across time and space,' Father Augustus continued. 'Those limitations mean nothing in a dream. If you had met in your dreams then, strange though it might be, it would be the first outside relationship anyone in the village has had since the curse was pronounced - and that would make you our anchor.'

'But I don't remember any such relationship!' Jacob protested.

'That's often the way with dreams,' the priest said sadly. 'We forget them.'

'Not all of them,' Jacob said grimly. 'Some stick in your mind.' He took a deep swig of the wine. 'Some lodge there and you can't get rid of them.'

'You need to be wary of dreams, Jacob,' the priest said. 'The Laird will try to get at you. You are staying with Noah and there is an old, old feud between those two: a feud that the Laird will not forget or let go. His power is mostly broken but he can still reach out with the tattered fragments of his talent and touch the unguarded mind. If Noah can intrude into people's dreams, then so can the Laird and he will show much less restraint in doing so. His attacks will become more detailed and persistent as he gets to better know your mind.'

'You know that I don't believe any of this, right?' Jacob asked. 'That I'm just humouring you?'

Father Augustus smiled and made no reply. Instead, he looked down towards the village and said, 'Ah, I see Myriam has finished her shopping.' Myriam was, indeed, walking back towards the church, although she carried nothing in her hands. As she approached the church, however, the black riders again came charging down the track, from behind the church and into the village, once again at full gallop. They rode straight at Myriam, who desperately threw herself off to the side of the track to avoid being trampled. Even so, the lead horse only missed her by inches.

Jacob was instantly on his feet and running to her assistance. Father Augustus followed, much more slowly. Myriam was getting to her feet when he got to her and offered his arm for support. By this time, the Riders had reached the end of the village, wheeled round, and were now charging back at the same reckless speed. Jacob moved to place himself between the Riders and Myriam as he urged her back up the hill towards the church.

As the Riders galloped past, Myriam turned to face them and cried out, 'Josh! Josh please!' One of the Riders turned to her as they galloped past. It was only momentary, but Jacob saw the same blankness that had chilled him earlier, only this time it was on a face that bore an uncanny resemblance to Myriam's. He turned to look at her and there were tears running down her cheeks as she watched the Riders disappear.

'What the hell is going on?' Jacob demanded. 'Who are those guys? Who's Josh?'

Father Augustus came up behind them, breathing heavily. 'It's a long story,' he said. 'Myriam, are you alright?' She nodded but her tears flowed freely and she couldn't speak. 'Then come on, come up to the presbytery. As I said, it's a long story and I have some chamomile tea which will help calm the nerves.'

Father Augustus gently guided Myriam and Jacob up the hill, towards the church. The presbytery proved to be a wing attached to the back of the church. It was built of the same materials and looked a bit like an extended vestry. The priest led them into a small, plain sitting room. The only decoration was a large, wooden crucifix on one wall. The ceiling was low and made of polished wood with massive timber beams to support the weight of the slate roof. The old priest sat them down and gave them hot cups of a herbal tea. Jacob tasted his but he didn't like the taste so he didn't really drink it. Myriam continued to sip hers gratefully.

The old priest settled himself into one of the chairs and began, 'When the curse threw the village adrift, many of the young men had sweethearts they were courting in the neighbouring villages, and some of those that didn't had the desire to. So, a group of them went to demand, to force, the laird to undo what he had done. It was a mistake. The Laird has noble blood and his talent is strong. The whole village acting together could overcome him but not ten young men, angry and full of the rash confidence of youth...' There was a break in the old priest's voice and he stopped talking for a moment, looked out of the room's small window and wiped something from his eye. 'Anyway,' he continued, 'we found four of them dead the next day, laid out in the street. The other six turned up a few days later as these riders. They function well enough and they have all their memories but they just don't care about anything. They have no human emotion or feeling. It's as if there's an emptiness where their soul should be.'

'And Joshua?' Jacob asked.

Myriam was looking out the window. 'Joshua is my brother,' she whispered. 'He was courting a girl from the next village. Agnes, her name was: beautiful girl. She was the light of his life, his greatest source of happiness. They doted on each other. He couldn't bear the thought of being separated from her, the pain of that was too great. So, he and the others went to see the Laird...'

Father Augustus continued. 'We don't know what happened. We can only mourn the results. I was able to say a requiem for the dead, but these riders... They still live even though it's as if everything human in them has died.'

'Well, okay, but why do they ride like that? What's the point?' Jacob asked. 'You could have been seriously hurt.'

'They ride like that because their lord and master told them to,' she said bitterly. 'Every now and then he sends them down through the village, just to let us know who's in charge. You saved that young boy today. He probably sent them back just to make sure we know our place.' Jacob went cold inside. He'd seen that before: only not with horses, but with four wheel drives mounted with machine guns.

Myriam had finished her tea, so Father Augustus accompanied them out to the front of the church. As they were going, he turned to Jacob and said, 'Come back and talk to me again tomorrow. I'd like to hear your story.'

'Maybe Father. We'll see,' Jacob said.

'One more question, if I may,' the priest said. 'I noticed, in the church, that you would not look at the crucifix. Could I ask, why is that? Is it that it's too realistic?'

Jacob didn't look at the priest. His hands tightened into fists, his knuckles turning white with the pressure. His throat constricted and his voice was strained as he answered, 'No, Father. That's not it. In fact, your crucifix is not realistic at all. That's not what crucifixion looks like.' He then started to walk rapidly down to the village with, Myriam running to catch up.

* * *

Two men sat unnoticed on a bench outside the tavern and watched as Jacob and Myriam walked past. They were both wrapped up warmly in their woollen cloaks. One was leaning forward, intently watching the passers-by. The other was leaning back against the wall of the tavern, sipping a tankard of cider.

'The priest is too old,' the first one said. 'Once, I grant you, he was powerful, a very useful tool, but now he is old. His body is weak and failing. He'll not be of much use to you.'

'He is a man, not a thing to be used,' the other corrected in an offhand manner, 'and it's true that he is old and his body is feeble. His mind and his spirit, however, are not.'

'Still, is this the best you can do - an old man and a broken soldier?'

The other smiled as he sipped his cider. 'Yes, it is the best we can do and I am content.'

'You risk a lot on these feeble players.'

The other raised his eyebrow at this. 'A lot?' he queried. 'No. I risk everything.'

'I still think he'll leave. All of this; with the Riders and the dreams; it will be too much for him. He has problems of his own to deal with and the girl will not be enough to hold him.'

The other considered this carefully. 'You're right about his situation. He now has a choice to make and she alone is not a sufficient reason to stay. Still, I think he will stay anyway. He has a strong sense of duty and a great capacity for compassion.'

'It was his sense of duty and his compassion that got him into trouble in the other place.'

'True... but I believe he will stay.'

'Then he and the girl will be in even greater peril.'

'Yes,' the other agreed. 'That's true.' He took another sip of his cider and closed his eyes in the morning sun, while the first man continued anxiously watching Myriam and Jacob.

CHAPTER SEVEN

Conversations

They were about half way through the village when Myriam caught up with him. 'Slow down, Jacob,' she said, grabbing his arm. 'I can't keep up.'

'Sorry,' he mumbled. 'I just needed to get away.' She looked troubled but didn't say anything. She just fell into walking alongside him as he slowed down. He knew the reaction. He had seen it before in others: in good people who could see his pain but didn't know what to do about it. He knew that she would be searching for something that she could say, some words to comfort him. There were none, only platitudes or silence. She walked alongside him in silence, for that he was grateful.

Just as they got to the blacksmith's shop, she suddenly took him by the hand. 'Come,' she said. 'I've got something to show you.'

She led him off the road and onto a narrow walking track, through some forest, away from a noisy stream, and up a rocky hill so steep that they were both breathing hard by the time they got to the top.

'They call this the Pimple,' she said. 'Not a very nice name but it's one of my favourite places.' She spread her arms wide. 'From here you can see the whole world! At least, that's what I used to think when I was little.' She sat down on a rock and motioned for him to sit beside her. 'I used to dream of going out to explore one day. Even the thought of going to the next market town seemed exciting.'

Jacob looked around before sitting down. He could see the whole valley, a patchwork of neat fields and orchards. Beyond these he could see the mountains that he had set off to walk through, mountains that now seemed to belong to another world. Again, it looked like an illustration from a story book – a small village, lost in the mountains. He looked down at Myriam, who was waiting for him to sit down. She was still breathing hard from the climb and he couldn't help but notice the way her dress followed the contours of her body. The afternoon sun shone brightly in her hair as she sat there waiting for him, with a soft smile and gentle eyes.

He knew he was in trouble. Part of him wanted to run, to leave this place with its weird stories and strange happenings, to be alone in the mountains. Yet as he looked at her, he felt the power of that which he had thought he would never feel again, and he sat down beside her.

'So, when all this was supposed to have happened, did the little Myriam, the dreamer, believe the crazy tale of a village lost in time and space?' he asked.

She laughed. 'Of course,' she said, 'once it had happened...' She paused. 'I was just twelve. The sky turned strange and there was a night darker than anyone had ever known. I can remember waking in panic and calling for my Da.' She paused again, for longer this time, gazing to the west. 'When we woke in the morning, the mountains were different and we had been cast adrift.' She turned to him suddenly and smiled. 'Of course, that made the view from up here all the more interesting. You never know which mountains you will see; sometimes tall, rocky pinnacles covered in ice and snow; sometimes forested hills; and sometimes places that look achingly like the hills of home. Always different...'

'Until we met in our dreams, of course,' Jacob said, trying to control his sarcasm. This beautiful creature clearly believed what she was saying. It would be cruel to make fun of her. 'So, we met in our dreams and because it was the only outside relationship the village still had, it acted like a kind of magnet, drawing you and the village ever closer,' Jacob said.

Myriam smiled broadly at him in delight. 'You do understand!' she exclaimed.

Jacob shook his head. 'I understand how it might work well enough – in a story,' he said. 'I just don't believe, even for a moment, that it actually happened. Look, it's a great set up for a science fiction series on TV, it only needs a guy in a blue phone box to make it perfect, but it isn't real. I admit there's a lot of weird stuff going on around here but there must be some explanation that doesn't involve magic and this crazy story of a wandering village.'

Her smile turned to a frown. 'Is it just the word magic that you object to? Would it help if I said that the Laird used an alien artefact to throw the village into a rift in the space/time continuum?'

'No,' he said shortly. 'That's just as much gobbledegook as magic. It's the idea that's the problem, not the words used to name it. I know. I have a first class honours degree in physics.'

'Aye,' Myriam interrupted, 'and you abandoned your studies to go into the army. Maybe if you had kept going, you would have learned that the universe isn't the tidy predictable place you imagine.'

He looked at her, surprised and suspicious. 'How did you know about that?' he asked. 'Have you been checking up on me?'

'Now, how would I do that?' she asked. 'I have no electrical power and no way of communicating with the outside world. We met in our dreams, remember? Maybe you told me then.' Jacob looked at her with such deep suspicion that she laughed. 'Oh, don't bother your highly-educated head about it,' she said. 'Just enjoy the view.'

Jacob looked at her for a long moment, trying to think of a reply but he had nothing. So he just sat and stared at the mountains. The view was, indeed, spectacular and Myriam beside him made it more spectacular yet.

They sat in silence until he said, 'You have me at a disadvantage. You seem to know a lot about my past but I know virtually nothing sensible about yours. Tell me about the village.'

'Gladly,' she said. It was a strange talk, with normal tales of rural and domestic life interspersed with descriptions of strange visitors; from robot drones to stone-age hunters, from armoured knights to jet pack equipped special-forces, from drugged out hippies to dedicated mountaineers, all people of different times and cultures. He listened to her talk, about how the mountains were always different and how hard it was keep track of changes in language, but he mostly heard her humour and her gentleness. Sitting on that hill, watching her with the sun in her hair and listening to the lilt of her voice, he realised that the last thing he wanted to do was run away.

Eventually the flow of words stopped and as gently as he could, he asked, 'Why do you never mention your mother?'

'She died when I was born,' Myriam said, shrugging her shoulders. 'It happens. Not too often, thank God, but it happens.'

'That's tough,' Jacob said. 'And then you lost your brother to the Laird. That must be hard.'

Myriam looked away into the mountains. 'Aye,' she said in a strained voice. 'It is.'

Jacob pointed to a square tower of dark stone that was built high on a hill behind the church. 'Is that the Laird's castle?'

'Aye,' she answered in the same tight voice. 'It wasn't always as grim as it is now.' She was suddenly all business. 'Come on, we should be getting back. I need to get dinner ready.'

Dinner that night was roast lamb and Jacob was well into his meal before it occurred to him to wonder how the meat came to be in the cottage. Surely this was the lamb that Myriam had purchased earlier today. Yet she had carried nothing home with her and he was sure that no one from the village had come up to the cottage. He looked at Myriam thoughtfully, trying to come up with an explanation that didn't involve magic. Nothing even vaguely plausible occurred to him.

After dinner, the three of them sat around the fire in the front room and the conversation from the hill continued. Myriam's father added a lot more detail about the farming in the valley; about seasons, about fortune and misfortune. Most of this was normal stuff that would be familiar to any farming community, although the technology was always medieval. Sometimes, however, he would say something, casually, that involved the use of magic. Often this was to do with the weather; 'There was so much rain that we couldn't hold it back. We had to let it fall.' Or 'It was raining on the hills where it was doing no good. We had to move the clouds over.' Sometimes it was to do with the care of animals: 'The calf was simply too big. It couldn't be born the normal way. We had to get it out using our talent. Old Rory is good at that sort of thing.'

Jacob mostly just sat and listened. He couldn't help but think that if this was a hoax, a charade, or some kind of delusion, it must be one of the most detailed, consistent and meticulously planned ever. Why would anybody bother putting together such a complicated set up just for him? He had no money to speak of and no influence or power. Also, if Myriam and her father were actors, they had the talent to be in Hollywood, not out here in the wild trying to fool him.

He looked at Myriam's father, with his long white hair, still in its ponytail and turned red by the fire light, and his ridiculously long beard still tucked into his belt. Jacob realised that he had been so concentrated on Myriam that he had pushed her father into the background. It occurred to him that Myriam wasn't his only way, or even the easiest way, into this puzzle.

'Noah,' he said. 'You must know that I find all this talk of magic and wandering in space and time impossible to accept. It's just crazy. I just don't, can't, believe it. Why do you keep at it?'

'Because it's the truth,' Noah replied. 'I wish it wasn't. I honestly wish that we were a normal village, without any special talent and anchored to our own time and place. That's not the way of it, however. The village is cursed and it is doomed. Each time we move the transition takes a little longer. It wasn't noticeable at first but the effect is accelerating.' His voice lowered to a whisper. 'If it continues, soon the village will be lost in the dark forever.' Myriam was still and silent.

'Do you have a plan to solve this crisis?' Jacob asked.

'No,' Noah said. 'Father Augustus and I think that it may pass with the death of the Laird, but crooked and broken as he is, he shows no sign of dying and I have no taste for killing.'

The sorrow in the old man's voice was palpable and, despite his disbelief, Jacob was moved by it. He felt sure of one thing, whatever else was true, the old man believed what he was saying.

'Sir,' he said. 'When we first met, you made some comments about soldiers which suggested experience. Could I ask, did you ever serve?'

The old man looked long and deeply into the fire before answering. Then he sighed. 'Aye, I served. I fought with John Stewart at Bauge and it was bloody, hand-to-hand combat. Combat where you looked into the eyes of the men you killed and watched them die. There was one, little more than a boy, with a gentle face, unmarked by the world, and soft, brown eyes. As he died, he called out for his mother. It is his face, more than that of any of the others, the many others that I see in my dreams. It is his dying cry that I hear each night.' Jacob could see the old man's knuckles whiten as he gripped the mug he was holding tightly. 'Even though when I pushed my spear into his belly I felt nothing but triumph.' The old man paused and gazed with a strange intensity into the fire. Eventually, he said, 'It wasn't my fault. I only did what I had to do. Yet he haunts my dreams.' He looked across at Jacob. 'It wasn't yer fault either. None of it. The men who make wars are not the ones who have to fight them.'

Now Jacob turned to look into the fire, at least partially, to avoid looking into the pain on the old man's face. 'Nor the ones who have to live with the outcomes,' he said softly.

'Very true,' the old man said. 'Yet even if I could banish that boy from my dreams, I would not. He reminds me of who I am, of what I've done. That boy points to the dark corruption of my soul.' He continued to look silently into the fire for a long moment, then he whispered, 'There was so much blood. Such a small body and so much blood.'

'How do you live with it?' Jacob asked, his voice shaking with the strain of his emotion. He both feared and desperately needed to know the answer. 'How do you go on living when all that death won't let you go?'

'Just keep breathing,' the old man said. 'Take one breath after another, and keep loving. Love more totally and more fiercely than ever ye fought.' Jacob looked up from the fire. Father and daughter were gazing at each other and the bond between them was almost palpable.

That night, Jacob again lay in his bed, dreading the sleep that he knew must eventually come. He kept turning the whole village situation over and over in his mind. He knew he wouldn't be able to make sense of it but it gave his mind something to do as he stared into the dark. Sleep came in the early hours of the morning and he again found himself in that brown and dusty place with the bus coming down the hill, just a few minutes early. Only, nothing in that country ever ran early.

This time, however, it was different. Someone touched his arm. He turned to see Myriam standing there. He panicked. She couldn't be here! She mustn't see what was about to happen.

'No!' he yelled, grabbing her roughly by the shoulders. 'No! Go! Get away. Get away from here.' He pushed her away just as the bus exploded and she was torn apart in front of him and showered with bits... bits of children. He woke screaming into the dark and lay there, sweating in his bed, the grey light of dawn still a long way off.

Eventually he drifted back to sleep and once again he dreamed. Only now he was lying in bed in a very different place. The fluorescent lighting, the beige walls, the impossibly clean and starched sheets: he knew this place. It was the repatriation hospital in Hobart. How could he be here?

There was a man standing next to his bed writing in a small note pad. He was wearing a white coat, had a stethoscope hanging out of his breast pocket, and had a hospital name tag: Dr. Corvus. He looked up as Jacob stirred.

'Ah, I see you're awake,' he said. 'Good. Tell me, do you recognise me at all?'

Jacob looked at him closely. It was a thin, mean face with a weak chin and a patently false smile. He had never seen the man before. 'No,' he said. 'But I figure you're a doctor. How did I get to be here?'

'Some hikers found you,' Dr. Corvus said. 'You were lying on the ground and having some sort of psychotic episode: raving and delirious. They called for help and the air ambulance brought you back here. You remember none of this?'

'No,' he said. 'None of it. I remember something quite different.'

'Well, we have you back now,' the doctor said, making some notes in his pad. 'The important thing is that you don't slip back into your delusion.'

'Delusion?' he asked.

'Yes,' Dr. Corvus said. 'It's been clear from your raving that you were experiencing a reality... How can I put this? ... somewhat different from that experienced by the rest of us? Are you hungry? Would you like me to get someone to bring you breakfast?'

'Yeah, I guess so,' Jacob said, sitting up in bed.

'Good,' Dr. Corvus said. 'I'll go and arrange it.'

Jacob watched as he left the room. It was hard to come to terms with the idea that it had all been a dream. The girl, the village, the Riders ... It had all seemed so real. A great wave of tiredness swept over him and he closed his eyes. When he opened them the bright morning sun was shining through the small window of Myriam's guest room.

CHAPTER EIGHT

Further Conversations

When he finally made his way to the kitchen, he found Myriam happily baking some bread. She turned to look at him with a concerned smile.

'I heard you scream this morning,' she said. 'I listened to hear if you had some problem but you were quiet so I figured it was just a bad dream.' He said nothing but looked at her, surprised somehow to find her whole and unaffected and very, very real. 'Well?' she persisted, 'Was it a dream or were you attacked by something?'

'You didn't...' He hesitated, unsure of how to say what he needed to ask.

She looked at him curiously. 'Did I turn up in one of your dreams last night?' He gave a brief nod. She smiled, 'I wasn't there, Jacob. I think we met in our dreams in the past but I didn't share that dream. It was just a dream.' She gave him a bowl of porridge and honey and sat down across from him. 'Why do you wake screaming? What is it that has scarred you so?'

He shook his head. He couldn't speak about it, not with her. She must never know about seeing a friend torn apart by friendly fire, about a street littered with the still bleeding arms and legs of children or what he had seen in that mountain village. All of a sudden he was crying, tears flowing freely and great sobs shaking his chest. She reached to hold his hand but he pulled away and quickly got up from the table. He needed to leave. He needed to get out. He needed space to breathe. He needed to nurse this pain on his own. He avoided her anxious look as he left the kitchen.

She came out midmorning with a cold drink and found him repairing a dry-stone wall in the cottage front yard. He was struggling, lifting the heavy rocks and setting them in place.

'I came out to see if you were still here,' she said. 'I was afraid you might've gone. Would you like a drink?'

He took the drink gratefully. 'Thank you,' he said. 'Your dad said that this wall needed fixing, so I thought I'd hang around and fix it. Hot work though.' He drained the tumbler and held it out for a refill. 'Thanks again for that. I needed it,' he said as he drained the second drink.

'This wall has been fallen down for ages,' Myriam said doubtfully, 'and it really serves no purpose. I wonder why Da asked you to fix it.'

He looked at her sheepishly. 'I think he could see that I needed something to do, something hard and physical. Sorry for running out on you earlier. I just … I just needed to get away.'

She looked at him with nothing but concern. 'You didn't finish your breakfast and you've been doing all this heavy work. Why don't you give it a rest for a while and come in and have something to eat? I have some freshly baked scones inside.'

He looked at her, standing in the morning sun with her red hair flowing across her shoulders, and, even as his body relaxed, he felt a quickening of his heart. He laughed at the lightness of it. He was surprised at the strength of his feeling for her. It had only been a few days and yet he now found it hard to contemplate leaving..

'You know, I am a bit hungry,' he said. 'A couple of scones at morning tea would be very welcome.' She smiled and led him back to the kitchen.

He was enjoying a cup of milky tea and some hot, buttered scones, although he was mostly just enjoying being in Myriam's company, when her father came in, the usual dour look on his face.

'Good job on that fence. If ye keep to that pace ye'll have it finished in a couple of days. Nothing like a fencing job to keep mind and body active.' Suddenly, Jacob was confused. He had not been planning on staying anywhere that long, yet even as the idea scared him, a part of him felt an almost painful stab of joy at the thought of spending more time with Myriam.

'Thank you, Sir' he said, 'But Myriam just suggested that that wall serves no purpose. Do you really want me to fix it?'

The old man frowned slightly. 'Humph! What Myriam doesn't know is that I haven't been able to run the pigs in the south field since they broke down that wall and got into the kitchen garden. That would've been when she was about five. Haven't had the time or strength to fix it since. So, yes, I would very much like ye to fix it. I can't pay ye but ye can have free board and lodging for as long as it takes. If ye're happy to stay with us, that is.' Jacob looked at Myriam, as she poured her father a cup of tea, and realised that there was nothing he wanted more in the world.

'Thank you, Sir,' he said. 'I'll try to do a good job.' Myriam gave him her most beautiful smile and he once again thought that he would give up a lot to see that smile.

Her father, however, just scowled. 'What's with all this 'Sir' business? My name is Noah. My mother went to all the trouble of giving it to me. Ye might as well use it.' He paused for a moment, then continued in a quiet voice. 'When I came back from the war, the thing that helped me through it was the work on the farm. It was hard, physical labour. It left me exhausted at the end of the day but it kept my body strong, even when my soul was torn.'

Jacob looked fixedly at the table. 'Did it make the dreams go away?' he asked.

Noah shook his head. 'No, but it helped me to live with them – and eventually to dream some new ones. Fix the fence, Jacob, and when ye're done, if ye still scream in the night, I'll have other tasks for ye to do.' There was a long pause until Jacob looked up and found Noah starring at him with an unsettling intensity. 'Listen to me, Jacob. I've seen strong men broken by what happened to them in war. I don't want that to happen to ye. I can't make the dreams go away. I can't make ye unsee what ye've seen, or undo what ye may have done, but I can teach ye how to live with it. Part of that is forgiveness. Fix what ye can of the fence and tomorrow go up to the church and get shriven. Make your confession to Father Augustus. If ye get the forgiveness of God, then maybe ye'll be able to forgive ye'self.' Jacob started to protest but Noah insisted. 'Jacob! Go to Father Augustus and get shriven. Then we'll speak no more of it.'

Jacob resisted for a moment, thinking of the long debriefings that had left him with a pounding headache and shaking with anxiety, but he gave in to Noah's intensity and nodded his head. Perhaps, after all, he did need that. Noah gave a grunt of approval and got up from the table.

'Potatoes to dig,' he said as he left the kitchen.

Jacob went back to fixing the wall. It was hard work, lifting the stones and fitting them into place, just one stone at a time. It was like a large, difficult and very heavy jigsaw puzzle. Noah was right. While doing this he had no time or energy to think of anything else, not even when Myriam came out to talk to him. Her questions about how he was going met with very brief answers, his mind occupied with the three dimensional puzzle that was the wall. Eventually, however, he had to take a rest.

He leaned back against the portion of the wall that he had fixed. 'Tell me about Joshua,' he said.

Myriam went quiet and started to absent-mindedly play with her hair. 'He's my big brother,' she said after a while. 'When I was little, he was my hero. Da was always a bit sad, and he worked all the time, but Josh was always there to play with me. He would carry me if I got tired and tell me stories at night. It was Josh who taught me to read, just by reading me stories with his finger running along the text. I never knew my Ma. Like I said, she died when I was born. Da always took care of me, made sure I had everything I needed, but it was Josh who was my companion. As we got older, he would go with the men to trade in the neighbouring market towns.' She smiled at the memory. 'He would come back and tell me about all the strange people he met: lowlanders and English, even Frenchmen and Irish. It all seemed so exciting. Then he met Agnes and all he could talk about was Agnes. I was so jealous, someone was taking my big brother away from me. Then the families started to negotiate and I finally got to meet Agnes. She was lovely and I changed from being really mad at her to looking forward to having her as a sister. Then...'

'Then the curse happened,' Jacob said.

'Aye, then the curse happened. Josh went mad with grief and loss. He couldn't stand the thought of living without Agnes and he especially couldn't bear the idea that she might think that he had abandoned her – that he didn't love her. The thought of how much that would hurt her drove him frantic. So he went off with the others to confront the Laird...' She was silent for a long time, looking off into the distance, in the direction of the Laird's castle, and breathing deeply.

'It's okay,' Jacob said softly. 'You don't need to tell me anymore.'

She shook her head. 'I do,' she said firmly, still looking away from him. 'Ye need to know. When the four boys turned up dead the next morning, even as we all comforted their families, we were glad that Josh and the others weren't with them and we prayed that they would come back to us. Then those riders turned up, Josh among them, and we knew that the families of those who had died were the lucky ones, that there are worse things than death.' She turned to look at him then and her eyes were filled with tears.

'I see him riding that stupid horse, looking fit and well to all the world, and yet he's not there. Everything that made him who he was, everything that I loved in him has been taken from him. My brother has been taken from me and I can't even mourn him because he isn't dead. I see him and every time I think that maybe today he will turn to me and smile and say, 'Hey there, Dreamer', just like he used to. Only, he never does…'

She was sobbing now and he reached out and pulled her to him, wrapping his arms around her. She leant against him, sobbing bitterly into his shoulder. Her hair smelt of oatmeal soap and Jacob was ashamed to realise that, despite her pain, all he was thinking about was how good it felt to hold her. Eventually she pulled away from him and wiped the tears from her eyes.

She gave him a sad, apologetic smile. 'I'm sorry…'

He shook his head. 'There's no need…'

She looked at him with her sad smile and said, 'I know. I need to go and get lunch ready. Thank you for listening.'

He watched as she walked back down to the cottage. Then he bent down and picked up a particularly heavy rock to set at the base of the wall. Part of his mind returned to the task of the jigsaw puzzle that was the fence, only now he found himself thinking, 'Okay, so six farm boys. No proper training. But if they lack proper human feeling, they'll be fanatical. Still, I've dealt with that before. I'll need to plan this carefully ...'

He was so concentrated on the task at hand that he didn't notice the silent figure, dressed all in black, who got up carefully from his position behind one of the chestnut trees and made his way towards him.

'Good morning,' the man said. 'I don't think we've met.'

Jacob looked up, surprised both by the stranger's sudden appearance and his cultured English accent. 'Morning,' he said, holding out his hand. The stranger was right, they had not met and yet his face looked familiar. 'I'm Jacob.'

The other man took his hand lightly and gingerly. 'My name is ...Well, around here they call me the Crow. Not a nice name but it's what they call me. I hope they're paying you well, paying you the proper wages for all your work.' Jacob just grunted as he lifted and placed another stone.

'This is a strange place, isn't it?' the Crow continued. 'This little village, high in the mountains. It's like something out of a story, out of a child's story.' He leaned in closer to Jacob. 'Perhaps it is. How do you know any of this is real?' Jacob looked at him in surprise. 'If it all seems impossible, surely the most logical explanation is that it's not true. With all the talk of dreams, how do you know you're not still dreaming?' He smiled: a thin, false smile.

'Just something to think about.' He turned and walked away and Jacob watched him go, his mind racing.

The Crow walked quietly across the fields. When he got far enough away from the cottage, he hummed a little tune to himself. The morning had been most satisfactory.

CHAPTER NINE

Of Dreams and Dreaming

Jacob was too tired that night to stay up by the fire. The work on the fence had left him physically exhausted and he needed to get to bed. This night he welcomed sleep, something that had not happened in a long time, because he needed the rest more than he feared the dreams. The dreams did come, however. At first, they were chaotic, lacking any coherent sequence or place. He was running through a maze of streets, unable to find his way, and the enemy were after him. They were following him ever closer, pressing in on him, though he couldn't see them, couldn't hear them. Always, they were there and he couldn't find his way out. He needed to find his way home.

Then he arrived in a familiar place: a brown and dusty checkpoint on the outskirts of town. John Brunetti was there with a bowl of his mum's lasagne. 'You really should try this,' he was saying. 'It's all good, just meat and tomatoes, just meat and tomatoes. The bus was coming down the hill. 'Here, I have some for you,' John was saying, pushing a hand-cart towards him.

'No!' he yelled in terror, as it exploded, as it always did.

He jerked himself awake, wide eyed in terror. For a moment, he panicked in the dark, but then, in faint light from the window, the familiar shapes of the room began to register: his pack still leaning against the wall, the old bed, the water jug and bowl on the shelf. He lay his head back on the pillow and forced his body to relax. His mind, however, was racing, still filled with the incoherent terror of the dream. He started the breathing exercises the psychs had taught him: deep, slow breaths, in and out. Just keep going, in and out. His mind began to slow under the rhythm of his breathing and sleep claimed him once more.

He was sitting in a soft chair by the window. The top of Mt. Wellington was shrouded in low cloud. He gave a slight, tired smile. Today, the tourists wouldn't get to see a sweeping vista of Hobart and the Derwent Estuary. Today, they would get mist, atmospheric, but not what they had hoped for. Dr. Corvus came over and stood by the window, examining him critically and analytically.

'Good morning, Jacob,' he said.

'Good morning, Doctor,' Jacob replied.

'Excellent, I see that the drug has worked. You're with us again.' Dr. Corvus pulled up a chair and sat down. 'We need you to stay with us this time, Jacob. Professor Laird is getting worried.'

'Professor Laird?' Jacob asked.

'The chief consulting psychiatrist on your case.'

'No,' Jacob said, shaking his head vigorously. 'No. My doctor is Dr. Johnson. He's a specialist in PTSD.'

'Yes...' Dr. Corvus said slowly, looking down and writing something in his notebook. 'After the incident in the mountains, it was felt that ... um ... a fresh set of eyes might be beneficial in your case. You had a very serious psychotic episode. I've never seen anyone so completely lost in their delusions.'

Jacob shook his head. 'No. That's not right. I read about it when I was first diagnosed. That sort of thing isn't a part of PTSD. Flashbacks and stuff, sure, but not consistent, detailed delusions.'

Dr. Corvus didn't look up from his notebook. 'No, not normally,' he said in a flat monotone. 'We think your experiences may have sparked an existing predisposition.' He looked up. 'Tell me, any trauma in your childhood?'

Jacob looked at the thin face; the lank, black hair; and the thin-lipped, insincere smile. He had seen this man before. 'You were there,' he said. 'You were dressed in black and were telling me that nothing I saw was real.' As he remembered the cottage, the hospital started to take on a dream-like quality.

'Was I?' Dr. Corvus asked without any apparent interest. 'It doesn't surprise me.' He finally looked up from his notepad, the same false smile fixed to his face. 'You may well have a wonderful imagination, Jacob. In fact, from what we can make out of your ravings, you most surely do. Something about a magical village lost in the mountains?'

'And a girl,' Jacob thought. 'A beautiful girl.' As he thought of her, the hospital became even more dream-like: soft somehow and blurry round the edges.

'Still,' Dr. Corvus continued. 'Even if you had the imagination of Tolkien himself, you would need to take elements from the real world. Your senses are still supplying your brain with data even if your mind can no longer properly interpret them. I'm not surprised that some distorted form of me ended up in your delusion. I've been with you almost constantly for the last two days. The whole of the delusion is probably made up of similar distortions and fragments of memory. Tell me, does this magical village remind you of anything?'

'Yes,' Jacob thought to himself, 'of fairy tales and childhood.' He said nothing, however, and remained looking out the window. He didn't trust this man. He could see the base of the cliff at the top of Mt. Wellington. The cloud was lifting.

'Jacob, don't you see. You're using your imagination to construct an ideal world, a place where you can be safe. I understand. Your mind is running from the pain into fantasy but that won't make the pain go away. We can do that, but we need you to help us,' Dr. Corvus said. 'So far, the drugs have had only a limited and temporary effect. You keep slipping back into your delusion. We think it's because you're fighting us. Your mind wants to flee back to that imaginary place. We need you to want to fight to stay here, to want to hold onto reality. Can you do that? When the delusion starts to take hold, try to convince yourself that it isn't real, that it's a kind of dream.'

'No,' Jacob said slowly. 'This is the dream.'

For the first time, Dr. Corvus showed signs of irritation. 'Come on!' he said. 'How likely is that? Use your brain. The whole village set up – it's obviously crazy. Magic isn't real.' Jacob was silent, staring at the cloud that was slowly breaking up across the mountain top. Dr. Corvus was silent for a long time too. Sitting there and watching Jacob intensely.

'Jacob, Professor Laird and I are worried,' he said eventually.

'Worried about me, about my recovery?' Jacob asked.

'Yes, of course, but more than that.' Dr. Corvus leaned forward. 'Jacob, you are a strong young man and a highly-trained soldier. We are worried that you might do something that will seem justified to you in your delusion, even noble, but here, in the real world, innocent people could get hurt. That sort of thing has happened before.'

Jacob turned to look into the thin face. He really didn't like this man.

'Jacob, if you can't do this, we'll have to take precautions. We'll have to use much stronger drugs and far more invasive techniques. These will have side effects, serious side effects. Do you understand me, Jacob? Jacob...' The voice drifted off into silence as his mind drifted back to sleep and to darkness.

He began to dream again, only now the dreams were softer, quieter. It was almost as if they weren't really his dreams at all. There was no terror, no enemy pursuing. He felt secure. It was a dream of home. Only, not his home. He was sitting in a flower bed and the flowers were huge.

He crawled out of the garden bed and tried to stand, unsteadily, on his feet. He was on a garden path with a whitewashed cottage behind him – but everything looked way too big. It was as if he were in a land of giants. He tried to walk but quickly tumbled over onto the gravel path and into a more comfortable crawling position. He made his way towards the garden gate, where two giant figures were standing. He made much better progress crawling. It was then that he realised that he was seeing the world through the eyes of a toddler, not much more than one year old.

It was a strange dream. Even stranger because it was so consistent and coherent. It was almost as if it were a memory. But he had grown up in suburban Sydney and had never known any garden like this.

One of the figures at the gate came back to pick him up. It was a boy, maybe ten or eleven years old. As soon as he saw the face, a face that looked so much like Myriam's, he recognised him. It was a young Joshua, a Joshua who was full of smiles and warmth for the little person he was picking up and holding close to his shoulder. With a shock, Jacob realised that he was dreaming the world through the eyes of a very young, Myriam.

They walked back towards the gate where Noah was standing, looking much the same as Jacob knew him. A few traces of red in the hair were the only indications that he was younger. Outside the gate was a black, horse drawn coach. Driving it was a thin man, also dressed in black. Jacob recognised him as Dr. Corvus.

'Just give her to me. I'll take her to the Laird and that will be the end of it,' he said. 'He will not let this go. He will have her.'

'Then ye've a problem, Crow,' Noah said, 'for I'll not surrender her.'

'Don't be a fool, Noah. He doesn't want to harm you. The Laird only wants what is his by right,' the man in black said.

'He has no rights!' Noah yelled. 'After what he did.'

'Don't be foolish, old man,' the Crow said.

'Fly back to yer master, Crow, and tell him if he doesn't like it to not just send his carrion bird. Let him come and face me himself - if he has the stones.'

'Don't be foolish old man,' the Crow said again. 'Do not try and stand against him. You should remember who he is.'

'And he should remember who I am, as should you,' Noah growled. Around him the air seemed to grow cold and dark and Noah seemed to grow, towering over the Crow and his coach.

The Crow yelled in panic. He stood up in his seat and from his cloak he flung a black cloud of flies towards the cottage, then he wheeled the coach around and drove wildly down the lane. Thousands of black flies infested the garden. The young Myriam began to cry and struggled to get down from Josh's arms. She tried to run but fell and the world shifted. Jacob found himself sobbing on his knees, his Austeyr assault rifle on the ground in front of him. It was a dusty street in a village filled with flies and crows: flies, crows and the awful smell of rotting meat. He screamed his anger and his despair into the dirt. He woke, screaming, as the grey light of dawn filled his small bedroom.

He lay awake for a moment before trying his experiment. He closed his eyes and tried to imagine that this wasn't real. 'This isn't real,' he said to himself. 'I'm back in the hospital, back where the world makes sense.' He repeated this message, again and again, until it became a rhythmic mantra. The trouble was, he couldn't bring himself to believe it. This place felt real. He could feel the warmth of the blanket and the cold air on his face. It was the other place that had the disconnected, insubstantial feel of a dream.

He opened his eyes, still repeating his disbelief. The light was stronger now and he could see his pack leaning against the wall; the water jug, still in its place. This room, at least, didn't care whether he believed in it or not. He sighed – so much for Dr. Corvus. He got out of bed and splashed water over his face. By the time he was dressed, he could hear the sounds of Myriam, already busy in the kitchen. Today, he had a fence to build, and a priest to visit.

CHAPTER TEN

The First Confession

Myriam was cheerfully setting out the kitchen for breakfast when he came in. She stopped when she saw him and looked at him, concerned.

'I heard you scream again this morning,' she said. 'Is it getting no better?' Jacob shrugged. He needed time to process his dream before he could talk about it with her.

'Leave the boy alone,' Noah said, as he came into the kitchen, tying a belt around his waist. 'It'll be better or it won't in its own time. Don't be always at him.' Myriam frowned, clearly unhappy at being told off.

'Very well,' she said primly. She put a plate of porridge and a bowl of honey in front of him. Each hit the table a little harder than normal. Jacob looked up and smiled at Noah. It would seem that breakfast was going to be a quiet affair that morning.

He spent the morning sorting stones for the next section of the wall: large ones for the base, flat sided ones for the facing, smaller ones to fill the core and flat, slaty ones for the capping. The army had taught him to do this: always to plan and prepare. It took time but, in the long run, it made the job go faster. As he worked, he thought of the riders. He needed more information and he knew from experience that sometimes the only way to gather the necessary intelligence was to test the enemy's forces. He frowned as he placed the first of the base stones in position. That was something he was not looking forward to.

Over lunch, Myriam apologised for her surliness that morning. 'I'm sorry,' she said. 'But I'm concerned about you.' She paused and looked down at her hands. 'I don't mean to nag.'

'It's okay,' he said. 'I'm just sorry if I woke you up. I know it must be upsetting to have this stranger screaming in your house each night.'

'You're not a stranger,' Myriam objected.

'I have upset your house though,' Jacob said, 'with all my screaming and carrying on.' He paused and played with the potatoes on his plate. 'Look, the time may come,' he said at last, 'when I need to talk to you about some things in my dreams, but not now. Okay? Please, just let me choose the time.'

'Okay,' she said. Then she smiled.

After lunch, he set off to the church. Myriam offered to go with him but he declined the offer. Talking to the priest was something he would need to do alone. As he approached the dusty street, he saw the Riders coming towards him at a gallop. The villagers had either heard them coming or knew when to stay away because there was no one else about. He kept walking. If they kept to the pattern they had used the day before, they would turn just as they got to him. His instincts told him that this was a mistake, that the kind of idiot who would terrorise the village like this, would see his apparent lack of fear, or even concern, as a challenge. Still, he kept walking. He needed to test their resolve.

The Riders brought their horses to a skidding halt at the end of the village, precisely where they had turned the day before. All six of them turned to look at him as he kept walking towards them. He expected them to challenge him, to call on him to stop but there was nothing. They just looked. There was no anger, no bravado, not even any concern in their look. There was nothing, just the same chilling blankness that he had seen the day before.

He was almost abreast of them when they turned, taking no notice of him in their actions. As their horses swung around, one of them slammed against him with surprising force. This knocked him into another horse that kicked out at him, catching him in the thigh. He yelled in pain as he went down.

They looked at him for only a moment, simply registering that he was there. Then they galloped off, back down the village street, at the same careless, breakneck speed.

Jacob watched them go with a deep feeling of unease. This was different from the other place. There the actions had been similar: when it comes to terrorising simple farmers; heavy, galloping horses or pickups with thirty cals mounted on the back do the same job. The goal had been the same: to cower the villagers into subservience. In the other place, however, the young thugs had been driven by a triumphant bravado, an arrogance that had only masked a deep seated insecurity. Ultimately, they were driven by fear and that made them both dangerous and unpredictable. Here, the terror was cold and calculated. The Riders took no joy or satisfaction from their actions. They just didn't care. It was almost like terror by remote control: easier to predict, harder to act against.

The blacksmith came running out of his shop and helped him to his feet. Jacob had expected the blacksmith to be a great ox of a man. Instead, he was a surprisingly slight figure, although there was no doubting the power of his sinewy arms. 'Well, that was stupid,' the blacksmith said. 'What did ye do that for?'

'I wanted to test them,' Jacob said. 'To see how they would react if I got in their way.'

'They don't react at all,' the blacksmith said bitterly. 'That's the problem. Anyone could be in their way, even a young child or an old woman, it wouldn't matter. Ye should know, since, if I'm not much mistaken, ye're the one that grabbed young Jimmy McTavish.'

Jacob shrugged. 'I've seen similar shows of force before. Normally, the aim is intimidation, and deliberate defiance is treated very differently to a simple accident. I had to test it. I needed to know if they'd fit the pattern that I've seen before. I want to be able to predict their reactions.'

The blacksmith shook his head. 'I know nothing of where ye've been nor what ye may have seen,' he said, 'but I ken that ye'll not have seen anything like the Riders before. They're relentless, always riding at the same careless gallop. Everyday. They give us no rest.'

Jacob winced as he stretched his bruised leg

The blacksmith frowned in concern. 'Are ye well enough to walk?'

Jacob gave a small smile and nodded. 'I think so,' he said.

The blacksmith looked at him somewhat doubtfully. 'Ye're the one staying up with Noah?' Jacob nodded. 'Well ye can tell Noah from me that it can't go on. It's got to stop, no matter what. We can't keep living like this.'

'Okay,' Jacob said slowly, unsure of what all this meant.

'Ye watch out for ye'self too,' the blacksmith said. 'If ye're with Noah, the Laird will be after ye as well. He'll not let up, that one. Keep your mind guarded, especially at night. The bastard never sleeps.'

'I can look after myself,' Jacob said.

'Oh aye, and ye wanted to prove it by headbutting a horse?' the blacksmith laughed. 'And do ye think the horse is convinced?' He was still laughing as he turned away.

Jacob watched him return to his shop as he thought back over the conversation. There was clearly a lot going on in this village that he didn't understand. He took a deep breath and continued his walk up through the village, following the path the Riders had taken. His leg hurt badly and he knew he should put ice on the bruise. He just didn't think ice would be an option in this village. He almost wished he were back in the other place, in all the dust and chaos. There, at least, he knew the enemy and he understood the fight.

As he limped along the village street, he became acutely aware that he was in a state of hyper-alertness. He was constantly looking around him and his heart was racing. He was sharply aware of the dust beneath his feet, the hoof prints left by the Riders, and the increasingly cold wind blowing from the south. He could clearly hear that, when the blacksmith restarted work in his shop, the sound of his hammer blows was different from what it had been the day before, as if the blacksmith was now working on a different metal.

The weaver was standing outside her shop. She smiled and waved at him and he returned her greeting. Then he stopped. He stared at the shop with a mixture of fear and wonder. In his heightened state of awareness, it had suddenly occurred to him that the looms he had seen working at the back of her shop yesterday had been hand looms, not automatic machines. Of course, they were. This village had no electricity. Yet they had been working and there had been no one attending them. The hair on the back of his neck stood up. How could he not have noticed that earlier?

The village, and the memories it recalled of another simple, rural society, assaulted him all the way up the street. The smell from the butcher's shop sickened him and he had to resist the urge to run. He also had to resist the sweet smell of the tavern. He knew that the temporary comfort, behind its door would be all too brief, and costly in ways he didn't want to deal with. He couldn't help but remember Purvis, that great ox of a man who had saved him more times than he could count, both in training and battle. In desperation, Purvis had turned to that comfort and his life had fallen apart. Jacob briefly wondered where Judy and the kids were now before shaking his head and forcing himself to keep on walking.

A child cried suddenly in one of the houses and his hands clenched tightly into fists. Despite the cold wind, he was sweating by the time he reached the path up to the church.

The old priest was waiting for him at the church door. 'Hello, Jacob,' he said. 'I'm sorry you had to endure that.' Jacob looked at him questioningly. The priest smiled. 'One of my talents is to know who is coming to see me and to know something of their worries in advance. Come in, we can sit and talk. Here, hold this against that bruise.' The priest gave him an ice pack wrapped in cotton. Jacob took it and gratefully held it against his aching leg. He didn't bother to ask where it had come from. He was pretty sure he wouldn't like the explanation.

It was dark inside the church but it was out of the wind and something about the dark and the stillness of the place helped Jacob to calm down. Father Augustus led him up to the left of the carved screen where he had placed two stools.

'Now Jacob,' he said, 'tell me what is troubling you.' Jacob looked at the old priest sitting in the darkened church, his time worn face illuminated by the rose window above the door. How could he answer that question? How could he even make a start? He was quiet for a long time, wondering what, if anything, he could say. Father Augustus sat, patient and still, his expression never changing.

'It's been a long time, Father,' Jacob said eventually. 'A long time since I went to church or even prayed, much less gone to confession.' Another long silence followed. 'It was hard…hard to believe in God in a place where people are fighting and killing in his name.'

The priest said nothing. He just nodded and listened. Jacob had a sudden irrational desire to shock this priest, to make him see how bad the world really was.

'I've seen horrible things, Father. Some of them were just stupid accidents but most of them were done in the name of a vengeful God. I have seen nightmarish things, things that make you doubt that there was ever anything good or holy, things that make you almost hope there isn't, because if there was, it would be attacked and mutilated.' A memory came to him, a memory of a patch of blue velvet lying in a dusty street. He started to shake at the thought of it. He must not go there.

'I had a friend, John Brunetti. He was a good kid, went to church when he could. He was one of those guys who just seemed full of life, always had a joke. He had a girlfriend back home whom he was desperate to marry. He was blown apart because someone got the coordinates on a map wrong. I was close enough to be splattered by his blood and bits of his flesh.' He became aware of how loudly he was speaking. He paused and took a deep breath, then continued in a quieter voice, 'Sometimes, even now, I panic when I shower and I scrub myself raw trying to wash it off.' He looked directly at the priest. 'Why?' he challenged him. 'Why did God want Brunetti to die when he had barely had the chance to live, when he had so much to live for?'

'I don't know much about war,' the priest answered quietly, not shocked by this story but deeply sad, his sadness etched into the lines of his face. 'But I do know that God did not want your friend to die. He loved him and wanted him to live a long and happy life, to marry the girl he loved and to raise lots of happy and healthy children. God never desires war or death.'

'There are those who would disagree with you, Father,' Jacob said bitterly, 'and they have the guns. They have the power. There are those who kill, kill even little children, and claim that God commanded them to do it.' He paused, breathing heavily.

'I have trouble sleeping. Actually, I lie on my bed trying not to fall asleep. Do you know why? It's because when I dream, I'm back there. I keep reliving that place every single night...' He paused, again taking some deep breaths. His head was starting to hurt. 'I was once in charge of a checkpoint on the outskirts of this town. It was routine, boring sort of work. We just had to check all the vehicles for explosives or weapons. I saw the school bus coming in from the next village, loaded with kids. Just like it did every day. Only this day it was a bit early and I looked at the driver. He was terrified. Then I knew. I knew with a certainty that was like lead in my gut. I shouted to my men to stop the bus and they did. A few seconds later it exploded. I was knocked off my feet by the blast. When I got up the road with littered with...with burning bits of children.' Jacob stopped speaking. His head was throbbing, his breath coming in great gasps.

He looked across at Father Augustus who was still sitting quietly, tears flowing down his cheeks.

'You can't seriously believe that God wanted those children to die that way,' the priest almost whispered.

'The guys who planted those explosives thought he did,' Jacob replied. 'They would say that killing those children was God's work if it could kill even one Christian soldier.'

'Don't ask me to explain that, Jacob. I don't know how men can get things that twisted. I don't understand how they can do such...utterly evil things. I have heard of such things before, all too often, but I don't understand it. I don't think I want to.' The old priest was making no effort to stem the tears flowing across his deeply lined face, gathering in pools in the creases of his cheek.

'I'm not asking you to understand the men,' Jacob said, quietly but savagely. 'I understand them. Trust me, I understand them all too well. I want you to explain God to me. If he loved those children, then why did he allow that? Those children were killed in his name!'

Father August didn't answer straight away. He spent a long moment looking thoughtfully at the former soldier. 'Jacob,' he said eventually, 'the explanations of theology will not help your pain.'

Jacob turned to face the priest, his face taut with emotion. 'Nothing can help my pain. I don't want comforting words. I've had those aplenty. I need to know. I want to understand how you can reconcile a loving god with existence of men who can do things like this. Why would God allow those bastards to stamp his name on something so cruel and unfair?'

The old priest didn't answer for a long time. It was quiet, the wind could be faintly heard blowing around the eves of the church. Then Father Augustus breathed a deep sigh. 'Because he values our freedom,' he said, 'he will not intervene. You see, we were made to love and he values our ability to love above all else. Now, love must be given freely or it is not love at all. So, he values our freedom.' The priest wiped the tears away from his face. 'Of course, he wants us to use it to choose to love but the freedom to choose to love necessarily means the freedom to choose not to. If you are free to love then you are also free to hate. If you are free to be kind and just, then you are also free to be cruel and unfair. We are, unfortunately, in the habit of choosing…very poorly.'

'I'll tell you what choosing poorly means, Father. When I got to my feet, I ran forward. I wanted to see if any of them were alive, if any needed help. That's when the second explosion occurred.' He got to his feet suddenly, knocking over the stool. He pulled up his shirt to reveal the scars all down his side and back. 'It was designed to kill anyone who tried to help. These scars are the result of my choice to run forward. I should've stayed down. Running to try and help was the poor choice.'

'No!' the priest said in a firm voice. 'No. You did nothing wrong. Those scars are the marks of your compassion. You should wear them proudly.'

Jacob smiled grimly and let his shirt fall. 'I shouldn't be around to wear them at all. I was lucky. The second bomb was in a wagon of tomatoes and the bus blast had knocked it sideways. I only caught the edge of the blast. I don't remember anything after that until I woke up in a hospital in Germany. They said that, for me, the war was over. They were wrong.' A memory came to him then, a memory of a piece of blue velvet lying in a dusty street. No! He couldn't go there – not now, not ever.

The sunlight was fading from the window above the door. The priest still sat there, listening, and Jacob became aware that he was standing in the darkening church. He was breathing heavily, his head was throbbing and his heart racing. His hands were clenched into fists and his whole body was tense. He was ready to fight. He flinched as Father Augustus got up and put his hand on his shoulder.

'I think that's enough for today,' the priest said. 'You are, of course, welcome to stay for vespers but I think that maybe you should go back to Noah's place. Go back and have a good dinner and talk to Myriam. Go back and talk about cows and weather. Get her to sing for you or read you a story from one of those books they have. Sit by the fire and listen to her read. Learn that the war is far, far away.'

Jacob nodded and tucked his shirt in as he turned to go, but he knew the priest was wrong. The war was never far from him.

He was almost out of the church when the priest called out to him, 'Jacob, that's not the worst of it, is it?' Jacob half turned and shook his head.

'Come back tomorrow,' the priest said. 'Come in the morning, when everything is fresh.'

Jacob nodded briefly and then walked out of the church and into a world painted red by the sinking sun. Neither he nor the priest saw a dark figure slink silently from the church through the vestry door.

* * *

Two men watched from a hill as Jacob left the church. They might almost have been shepherds watching the sheep who were grazing nearby. One was angry. The other smiled as he leant on his staff.

'I suppose you think that's a triumph, a great victory,' the first man said angrily. 'It's not, I tell you.'

'No, not a great victory, but it is progress,' the other said calmly. 'I'm pleased.'

'He's now more vulnerable than ever. You have opened a raw wound, a wound that is all too easily infected, a wound that I know how to infect. He's now in greater danger than ever before and I know how to use that danger.'

'Yes, indeed,' the other agreed. 'He will soon have need of all his courage and strength, but that's why he was chosen..'

The first man stopped and looked at his companion with a puzzled frown. 'You must be afraid that he will fail,' he said. 'Their time is running out. What I have set in place will happen and soon. He is your last chance to alter the outcome and his failure will destroy the girl and doom the village. You could lose all their souls'

'Maybe, but I have faith in him,' the other replied.

'Yet can you not see the peril you have placed them in? You have done my work for me. He's broken and his brokenness will destroy her. What if she enters his dreams? She'll not survive that which broke him. It would have been kinder to leave them as they were.'

'No, not kinder. Easier perhaps, safer. Still, I think you underestimate her. She is not so easily broken.'

The first man grunted contemptuously. 'These are weak and broken creatures, all of them; the soldier, the girl, the Riders, all of them. You ask too much of them. If you truly cared for them, you'd let them be.'

'No. They are stronger than you know. They have all the strength that comes from grief and pain. The resilience that comes from brokenness and need.'

The first man spat out his disgust. 'That's a stupid, sentimental fantasy. Those things destroy. They don't give strength.' He pointed his finger at his companion. 'Reality is harsh and unforgiving. It makes no time or place for sentiment. You're foolish to put your trust in these weak and broken things.'

'Yes I am, but it is a sacred foolishness,' the other said, 'and, in the end, I think my foolishness will prove wiser than your unforgiving wisdom.'

'Talking of wisdom and foolishness,' the first said angrily. 'He has already started thinking of dealing with the Riders via some sort of military operation. He has no idea what's going on. He'll be destroyed. He doesn't have the weapons to fight this kind of battle.'

'He has courage,' the other replied, still calm. 'He has the capacity to love and he can still feel pain and loss.' Again, the first man grunted contemptuously. The other continued as if he hadn't been interrupted. 'He needs only one more thing. He needs only to remember how to pray. The priest can teach him that.'

The first man gave a mocking smile. 'He lost that ability long ago.'

'That ability is never lost, only forgotten. Like love, it is carved into the deepest part of the human soul.'

The first man again angrily pointed his finger at his companion. 'There, you are mistaken. He's broken and no amount of prayer can change that. He'll kill or be killed. It is what happens with soldiers. Either way she'll lose everything, and she can't cope alone. The village will be lost forever.' He shook his head in disgust. 'You have played this very poorly and you constantly overestimate the abilities of these creatures.'

The other sighed. 'On the contrary, I am constantly amazed at the love that they are capable of – most of all the broken and the lonely.' He turned, then, and walked away.

Chapter Eleven

The First Battle

Jacob set off for the cottage simply because he didn't know what else to do. He was anxious, jumpy and he had a splitting headache. He knew that the peaceful evening suggested by Father Augustus was an impossibility. This felt even worse than all those sessions with the psychs. He had mostly been able to bluff his way through them, tell them what he knew they wanted to hear. This was different somehow. Talking to the old priest cut a lot deeper. Once again, he felt a desperate need to run, to get away. It was only that the path down from the church was so rough that he had to tread very carefully in the fading light which stopped him from actually, physically, running. To attempt that now would only mean a stumble and fall.

All the clouds of the previous day had passed and the moon was not yet up. The sky was clear and, as the last of the sun rapidly faded, the first stars were starting to appear above the eastern horizon. This was 'stand to' time. Time for all men to be in their positions and alert. It was the time when the tricky light made it easy to attack. He couldn't help but look about him, carefully checking every shop and shadow.

Soon the sky would be fully dark and thousands of stars would blaze across it. He knew the beauty of those stars, cold and distant though they were. In long watches between the fading light of the setting sun and the first glow of dawn, it was only the stars inching their way across the sky that marked the passage of time. Those long watches had seemed to stretch on endlessly and the memory of them was always just a thought away. Long nights when nothing happened and yet nights when you always needed to be alert to each half-imagined movement in the shadows, each whisper of the wind. Long nights spent straining into the dark, always seeking the enemy who was trying to kill you, the one you couldn't see.

Jacob's eyes darted back and forth across his surroundings, checking every shadow and hint of motion. His muscles grew tense.

He started to repeat the words that were almost becoming a mantra. 'There is no enemy here. There will be no ambush, no attack. All I have to do is to walk back to the cottage.' Still, he entered the village ready for combat, his knees slightly bent, balanced on the balls of his feet, straining for any stray noise. Nothing happened. The village was mostly dark and still although there were lights in many of the houses. The only place where there seemed to be anything going on was the tavern. There was a lantern hanging outside its door and all the windows were brightly lit. Inside, there was a low hum of conversation and the sound of someone playing a fiddle.

Jacob hesitated. Those doors, and what lay behind them, were seductive. A forgetting was there and an ease to his pain. He knew the cost all too well. He had watched, close up, as Purvis' family had been destroyed. Normally, he would just keep on walking. Tonight, however, he had a splitting headache and the events of the day had left his stomach tied in knots. The thought of going back to the quiet cottage seemed like a dream from someone else's life. The promise of relief that the tavern offered, however brief, felt so real. He knew what he should do. He should run. He should go and climb the steepest hill he could find. He should run and climb until his body cried out for rest. Instead, he turned and walked through the door and into the bar.

Inside there was only one, large room, with small alcoves off the side. It had a low ceiling with massive wooden beams of dark wood. There was a bar along one wall and a huge, log fireplace along another. Jacob surveyed the room, anxiously looking for threats. There were none. There were just farmers, ranging in age from the barely adult to the ancient, all dressed in kilts with thick woollen cloaks wrapped around them. They looked at Jacob as he walked in, but only briefly. Then they returned to their conversations. The fiddler, dressed all in black, kept playing in an alcove at the back of the room. No one seemed to be paying him much attention and the hood of his cloak covered his face.

Jacob walked over to the bar, where he was greeted by a large and red faced man in a white apron. 'A beer, please,' he said.

The barman shook his head. 'No beer, I'm afraid,' he said. 'Can't get the barley for it, see. I can do ye a good, honest cider or, if you'd be wanting something a bit harder, there's a mead made from heather honey that'll hit the spot.'

Jacob smiled ruefully. He should have known that this wouldn't be a normal pub. 'Just a cider to start then,' he said.

'A pint of cider it is,' the barman said, as he filled a large metal mug from a wooden keg behind the bar. He handed Jacob the mug. 'There you go,' he said. 'That'll keep ye going now.'

Jacob pulled out his money to pay but the barman shook his head. 'We've no use for that here,' he said, nodding towards the paper notes. 'No way to exchange it for anything, see.'

Jacob looked at him nonplussed. It was obvious and he felt stupid not to have thought of it. 'I'm afraid it's all I've got,' he said.

The barman waved his hand casually. 'You're the one stay'en up at Noah's place?' he asked. Jacob nodded. 'Then yer credit's good here. Enjoy yer drink and maybe I can get you something to eat a bit later.'

Jacob nodded his thanks and took the mug of cider over to a quiet table and settled into what he hoped would be a long night of drinking. He didn't know how they measured a pint around here, but the mug seemed to hold a lot of cider and it was good cider, not too sweet and with a real kick. He took a while to finish it and when he did, he felt a pleasingly warm buzz that had succeeded in washing away his headache and soothing his anxious nerves. If one was good, then two would be better, he reasoned. He went over and got another mug from the barman and settled back down to his solitary drinking.

It was as he was sipping his second pint that he noticed that the room had gone suddenly quiet: the music had stopped and the fiddler was leaving. Everyone in the bar watched him leave in silence and after he had left, they got up in groups of two or three and nervously made their way out into the night. Eventually, there was only Jacob and the increasingly nervous barman. He was collecting the mugs from the tables, his smile long gone.

Jacob looked at the empty bar and kept sipping his cider. He was, however, now hyper-alert, his muscles tensed and every sense stretched to its limit. This wasn't, however, like it had been when he walked in. Now, there was some very real threat and, in the midst of his battle-ready state, he felt a strange calm. It had always been this way. Before battle, some men fidgeted nervously, some men joked, and some men prayed. He had always been calm and quiet, even as his body was coiled like a spring.

All men approach battle differently but all are afraid. For all his apparent calm, Jacob was no different.

'I think ye'd better go too, son,' the barman said nervously. 'It's gone quiet tonight and …' As he was speaking, there was the sound of horses in the street outside. The barman gasped and hurried back behind the bar. Jacob remained where he was, still sipping quietly on his cider.

Three of the black riders walked into the bar. They glanced briefly around the near empty room and, ignoring the barman, walked over to Jacob.

'You will come with us now,' the centre rider said. Jacob looked closely at the Riders. They were, perhaps, a little older than him and slightly shorter. They were fit and well-built and dressed in black leather that was thick enough to count as body armour.

'No, I don't think so,' Jacob said quietly.

'The Laird would like to speak with you,' the rider replied. 'You will come with us now even if we have to drag you.' There was no anger in the voice, no impatience. In fact, there was no emotion at all. It was a plain statement of fact, as if he were commenting on a bus timetable.

Jacob took another sip from his cider. 'No. I don't think so,' he repeated. The central rider nodded to his two companions who then moved around Jacob's table to grab him. Jacob's tightly coiled muscles unwound into action. He threw the remains of his cider at the rider on his left and, jumping up from his stool, overturned the table directly onto the rider in front of him. He stepped onto the overturned table, effectively, if only momentarily, trapping the central rider underneath.

The rider on his right reached out to grab him. He took the man's arm and pulled him towards him. He then elbowed him viciously in the face. The man went down, bleeding and unconscious. Jacob stepped off the overturned table as the left hand rider grabbed him from behind. He threw the man over his shoulder and, as he got to his feet, drove his knee into his stomach just below his sternum. Body armour or not, there was a loud 'Oof!' as the air left the rider's lungs and he rolled onto the floor winded.

The central rider was now on his feet and he launched at Jacob in something like a rugby tackle and drove him back into the bar. Jacob felt the hard wood of the bar smash into his back. He punched his attacker repeatedly in the ribs but it had no effect, the leather armour was too thick. In the background, the winded rider was getting to his feet.

Jacob crossed his arms over the arms of the man holding him and dropped to his knees, forcing the rider to also drop and to lose his grip. Jacob then balanced and hit his assailant with two backhanded blows to the head: first left hand, then right hand. The man fell to the floor and Jacob stepped over his unconscious body as he got to his feet and prepared to face the remaining rider.

This man was still bent over, still slightly winded, but he pulled a wooden club from his belt like a sword and swung this backhanded at Jacob, who easily stepped out of the way. The rider then swung a forearm blow. Jacob stepped inside this, blocked the blow with his left hand and punched the rider in the face with his right. It was a powerful blow. The man staggered, dropped his club, and fell unconscious to the floor.

Jacob leaned against the bar, breathing heavily. He felt spent, even though the fight had only taken seconds. He looked at his fallen attackers. They had shown no emotion at all during the fight: no anger, no fear. They had kept coming, trying to grab him, even when it was clear that they should back off. It was like fighting zombies, except for one important detail: if you hit them hard enough, they went down and they stayed down.

He turned to look at the barman, still standing behind the bar. 'Sorry about that,' he said. 'I'll pay for any damages.'

The barman shook his head. 'Ye'r credit's still good,' he said. 'Better now, I reckon.'

Jacob nodded. 'I'll just clean up,' he said. He grabbed the two nearest riders by the collar and dragged them towards the door. In the street, there was another of the black riders, holding the reins of the four horses. He made no move to either help or hinder Jacob, so Jacob just dumped the two bodies and went back to get the other one. When he had also dumped this, he turned to face the fourth rider. It was Joshua, Myriam's brother. If he was surprised or upset to find his colleagues dumped, unconscious, at his feet, he didn't show it. He looked at Jacob with the same blank, unnerving stare that he had seen before.

'You tell the Laird that I will indeed come to see him, but at a time of my own choosing,' Jacob said. 'And if he doesn't like that, he'll need to send more men.' He then stepped over the unconscious riders, into the street, and walked off towards the cottage. He felt drained and all he wanted to do was find a bed and go to sleep. Behind him, he heard horses cantering away.

The village was dark as he walked down the street, so he kept close to one side where the faint light coming from the buildings provided some illumination. As he came close to the end of the village, the blacksmith's shop provided a bright splash of light across the street. The regular sound of a hammer ringing on metal indicated that the blacksmith was still hard at work.

He felt a wave of heat from the forge as he passed the open wall of the shop. He looked inside and starred with something like shock. He had expected to see horse shoes or plough blades. Instead, there was a long sliver of metal that could only be one thing. The blacksmith had stopped his mending of ploughshares and was forging a sword.

He looked up and nodded briefly to Jacob, who returned the greeting before continuing on into the dark that surrounded the cottage. He had to wait for his eyes to adjust after the bright light of the blacksmith's forge but even so, the road to the cottage was difficult in the moonless night and it was only after many stumbles that he found his way to the tree lined path and the lights of the cottage.

Myriam was waiting for him, standing anxiously by the door. 'Jacob! I have been so worried. What happened? Where have you been?'

'Leave him alone,' Noah said from his seat by the fire. 'He's been to The Apple Gate and I don't blame him.' Myriam looked at him in surprise and Jacob nodded in confirmation.

'Well, come through to the kitchen. I've kept your dinner for you,' she said in a resigned voice. 'Unless, of course, you had a meal there?' Jacob shook his head but he didn't say anything until he was halfway to the kitchen. Then he stopped and looked at Noah.

'The Laird sent some of those riders to bring me to him for a chat,' he said. 'They were quite forceful with their invitation.'

Noah nodded. 'I thought he might do that. I take it ye didn't go. Were any of them hurt?'

'Three,' Jacob said, 'but not seriously.' He looked at Myriam's anxious face. 'Don't worry. Joshua was there but he was simply holding the horses. He wasn't hurt.'

Myriam smiled at him, clearly relieved. 'Also, the blacksmith told me to tell you the village can't go on like this. It has to stop, no matter what.'

Noah nodded. 'I was expecting it. This means they've been talking and there'll be trouble. Still, it's true. It can't go on. That's truer than they know. I need to think on this.'

'Another thing,' Jacob said. 'There was a fiddler at the tavern tonight. I'm pretty sure he went to call the Riders. I think you know him. He was dressed all in black. You call him Crow. Who is he?'

Noah gave a contemptuous snort. 'The Laird's spy. Jamie Campbell he once was but Crow is a good name for him. Always pecking around, passing information back. There was nothing so private that he wouldn't listen.' He looked across at Jacob. 'Not even a man's confession in the church.'

'Enough,' Myriam said. She grabbed Jacob by the arm and led him into the kitchen where she sat him down and presented him with a large plate of hot steak and kidney pie. As soon as he saw it, he realised that he was ravenously hungry and he quickly ate everything on the plate and drained the cup of tea that Myriam gave him.

'Thank you,' he said.

'Don't thank me,' Myriam replied somewhat testily. 'Just stay away from that place. It's okay for some but it's not good for you. Now – go to bed.'

Jacob smiled and said, 'Yes Ma'am!' He got up from the table and made his way to his bedroom. The day's events had left him bone tired. He called goodnight to Noah as he passed.

'Goodnight, Jacob,' came the reply. 'We'll talk about this in the morning.'

Chapter Twelve

The Second Confession

Jacob woke early the next morning, calm but hyperaware. For the first time in well over a year, he had slept the way he used to. As soon as his head had hit the pillow he had entered into a deep sleep. His dreams had been vivid and puzzling but they had left his sleep undisturbed. There were no screams to call him awake this morning. He recognised the pattern. This was his combat mode. The conflict in The Apple Gate the night before, which would have made most people anxious, had actually calmed him down. It was a trained response. In combat, it was the calm but aware who survived. He knew, of course, that the calm wasn't real and that there would be a price to pay for burying his fear deep inside. That morning, however, he was just grateful for a full night's sleep.

His dreams had, indeed, been vivid. One, in particular, was as clear in his head as if it were a memory. Once again, he was Myriam: older this time, maybe nine or ten. She was walking into the village when a black coach driven by the Crow pulled up, across the laneway. The Crow looked at her and smiled a thin, unconvincing smile. She felt nothing but revulsion.

'He still wants you to come to him,' the Crow said. 'His offer still stands. You will live in the castle. You will be his heir and carry his title.' He climbed down from the coach and approached her, stretching out his hand. 'Surely you would prefer that to living in an old cottage and farming… What? Sheep? Pigs?' She was backing away and starting to get nervous. 'You could be a lady with fine dresses, and servants to braid your hair.'

Quick as the strike of a snake, his hand reached out and grabbed her wrist in an iron grip. She screamed and fought him but he was strong, much stronger than he looked. He dragged her towards the coach. Then Joshua was there and the Crow was lying on the ground, blood flowing from his nose.

Joshua said only one word, 'Go!' The Crow got up from the ground and went. He stopped and turned, as if to say something but at the sight of Joshua's face, decided not to. He climbed back onto the coach and drove off.

Joshua turned to Myriam. 'Don't worry, Dreamer,' he said. 'I won't let him get you and Da would kill him if he did.' Jacob felt the waves of relief and affection flow through Myriam. This was Joshua: her big brother, her protector, her saviour. She threw her arms around him and, if the dream had continued any longer, Jacob remembered no more of it. It was a strange dream. Again, more detailed and consistent than it should be, more like a memory than a dream. He lay there for a moment, trying to make sense of it. Why would he dream that he was a younger Myriam? Nothing came to him and he could hear the current Myriam busy about the house, so he put it to one side and got up.

He washed quickly and went out to the kitchen. Myriam was there before him, cooking porridge at the stove. She did not smile as he entered but looked tired. Her eyes were red, as if she had been crying. He thought that he was probably the cause and was surprised by how much this upset him.

Stumbling over his words, he started to explain, 'Myriam, I'm sorry about last night...'

She cut him off quickly. 'There's no need. It's not as if you came back rolling drunk. You've a perfect right to go there for a drink if you want to and you certainly have a right to defend yourself. So, there's no need for an apology.' She paused. 'I also think you were right to refuse the Laird's invitation. Nothing good could come from that.' She placed a bowl of porridge and a jug of honey on the table and gestured for him to sit. He sat down but didn't start eating. There was something wrong. Her eyes were filling with tears. She turned away quickly to hide them.

'Myriam,' he asked softly, 'What's wrong?'

She didn't answer but sat across the table from him. 'Who was he?' she asked. 'The boy who was blown apart by that flying machine. Who was he?'

Jacob felt his blood turn cold, his stomach felt like lead within him. 'How?' he asked. 'How can you know about that? Did Father Augustus tell you?'

Myriam looked shocked. 'No, of course not!' she said. 'Father Augustus would never break the seal of confession. You must know that.' He did and he was ashamed that he had suggested it.

'Then how?' he asked.

'We've met in our dreams,' she said, exasperated. 'I told you. You know that. You may not want to admit it but you must know it to be true. You must've dreamt of me.' He thought over the last two nights and he nodded reluctantly. He didn't know how it could be true, how it could happen, but he knew it to be true. Somehow, they had shared something of their past in their dreams.

She shook her head. 'But this wasn't a real dreaming. It was just a fragment of memory that you somehow shared. I wasn't there. It was more like a sort of story; a sad, brutal story. Who was he?'

Jacob sighed, then said grimly, 'His name was John Brunetti. He was a good kid but it was his fault that he was killed. He was the one who radioed in the wrong coordinates. I guess that's why he stuck his head up. He felt guilty for bringing us under fire. But it was stupid. All he did was get himself killed.' He poured honey over his porridge and began to eat with a single-minded determination.

'He was just a boy,' Myriam whispered, her eyes again filling with tears.

Jacob put his spoon down. 'Yes,' he said. 'He was just a boy but he should have known better. Look, it was war and sometimes stuff like that happens. I'm sorry you got to see it. You shouldn't have. That's my burden to carry, not yours.' He looked at her anxiously. 'Myriam, I don't know how this works but please, please, do everything you can to not share my dreams or memories. There are… worse things. Things I don't want anybody else to see.' Especially not you, he added in his mind. He remembered the limbs of children littering the road and a piece of blue velvet lying in a deserted village. He stared into his porridge bowl for a moment, then said in a rush, 'I've got to go. I've a fence to fix.' He got up suddenly, nearly overturning the bench, and almost ran from the kitchen.

Noah found him a short time later. He was fitting together a line of the heavy base stones and although the day was cold and overcast, he was sweating from the heavy work.

'Ye're getting good at that,' Noah observed. 'A bit more practice and ye could make it yer trade. The valley always needs good stone workers.' Jacob only grunted in reply as he shifted a particularly heavy stone to sit flush against its neighbour.

Noah waited until Jacob straightened up to reach for the next stone. 'Ye want to talk about last night?'

Jacob paused. Then he leaned against the partially completed fence. 'After talking to the priest, I went to the tavern. Just to forget for a while, you know?' Noah nodded. 'It was my intention to get well and truly plastered. Anyway, that didn't work. Some of the Riders came to take me to the Laird.' He looked down, as if selecting his next stone. 'Didn't like their manner, so I decided not to go. They tried to insist, didn't work. That's about it.' He straightened up and looked directly at Noah. 'The time will come, soon, when I'll need to have a conversation with this Laird but it'll be when I choose and he's not going to like it.' He reached down to get the next stone, wincing slightly – the bruises from both the horse and the fight were beginning to make themselves felt.

'They'll be back and ye're hurt,' Noah said simply.

Jacob looked at him with a slight smile. 'I'm not sure how much they'll care, but three of them are certainly hurting a lot more than me right now.'

'It won't matter. Unless ye've incapacitated them, they'll be back,' Noah said. 'Ye just mounted a huge challenge to the Laird. He depends on those black riders to strike fear into the villagers. Without that, he's just a broken man in a big, stone house.'

Jacob shrugged. 'They don't bother me that much, to tell you the truth. There are only six of them and they're only farm boys on horses. As you noticed when you first met me, until very recently I was a soldier. I was trained to fight and I was good at it. I've also fought against fanatics before. The six of them working together might take me down but –'

'These are not like any other foes ye may have fought,' Noah interrupted. 'Those others ye fought against may have been fanatical but they still had human feeling. If nothing else, they knew fear and had a desire for self-preservation. These do not. They'll not stop to consider the chances of success and they'll not retreat when the situation is hopeless. They'll not worry about being hurt. In fact, they'll have no fear at all,' he straightened up and looked off to the horizon, 'and one of them is Myriam's brother, my son, Joshua.'

'I know,' Jacob said softly. 'I'll do my best to –'

Noah shook his head, his face set hard. 'Do not fight with one hand tied behind yer back. Do what ye have to do.' A light rain had begun to fall and Noah looked at the stones of the wall, now becoming wet and hard to handle. 'Leave this now. Go and see Father Augustus. I doubt that ye're finished there and this will soon become dangerous.'

Jacob straightened up and stretched. He knew he had been stalling. He dreaded going back to talk to the priest. Working these stones had been far easier. He wished then that he had lied, had told Father Augustus that he was fine, that everything was sunshine and flowers. He smiled wryly to himself. He had a feeling that Father Augustus would be a lot harder to fool than the army psyches.

'Okay,' he said. 'I'll just go and get my …' He turned around and Myriam was standing behind him, holding out his Gortex jacket. He paused for a moment, looking at her as she stood in the rain, her red hair straying from beneath the hood of her deep blue cloak. 'Thanks,' he said simply, as he put on his coat and turned to go.

He stopped before he had gone far and turned back to Noah. 'I have a question,' he said. 'Why is the blacksmith forging a sword?'

Noah shrugged. 'Ye'd need to ask him but he does make a fine sword.' Jacob nodded and then turned again, to walk back up through the village in the rain. It was mostly due to the rain that he didn't notice the stealthy, black clad figure following behind him.

The rain only got heavier as he left the shelter of the cottage's chestnut trees. Grey sheets of rain dropped, one after another, across the village and turned the main street to mud. The heat from the blacksmith's forge provided some welcome, if temporary, relief from the grey and the cold. The Apple Gate, however, was empty and dark. When he arrived at the church, Father Augustus was waiting at the front door, even though the rain now fell in torrents and sluiced off the slate roof of the church.

'Welcome Jacob,' he said. 'Come in, come in out of the rain. I would like to say come in out of the cold, but I'm afraid that the church is, if anything, even colder.' Jacob simply nodded in greeting and followed the priest into the church. He didn't feel like smiling or exchanging pleasantries.

It was dark inside the church, even though the weak sunlight struggled through the rose windows and candles were lit before the rood screen. As his eyes adjusted to the dark, Jacob could see that Father Augustus was leading him to a simple wooden bench that had been placed in front of the screen, beneath the crucifix. The church was cold, so cold that he could feel the feeble heat of the candles as he sat next to the priest. He kept his coat on, even though it dripped steadily onto the bare stone floor.

'You have something you need to talk about, Jacob?' Father Augustus asked.

Jacob looked at the priest, his face almost lost in the shadows of the church. The light from the windows was so dim that he was really only illuminated by the votive candles whose light emphasised the deep lines cut into his face by time and care.

'I don't think so, Father,' he said. 'I think we pretty much covered it yesterday. It was a bad place. It was war and I saw horrible things, things I find hard to forget. I think that pretty much covers it.'

The priest was quiet for a long time, perhaps waiting for Jacob to continue. Eventually he said, 'No, I don't think it does. You haven't told me the worst of it. You haven't told me why the crucifix causes you so much pain that you can't look at it.'

Jacob shook his head, a vision of blue velvet coming unbidden to his mind. 'No Father, I can't,' he said.

'Very well,' the priest replied softly. 'Tell me, Jacob. Are you angry with God?'

'Yes,' he answered, just as softly. 'Yes I am. Why does he let all these things happen - these things that are so horrible...so horrible that they make you doubt your very sanity? Why?' His voice had been slowly rising so that now he was yelling. 'You talk about freedom but that doesn't stop children dying in the most awful ways imaginable. He could stop it. All of it! But he doesn't! He just doesn't!'

If Father Augustus was shocked by this outburst, he gave no indication. Instead he asked, still in the same soft voice, 'Have you told him how angry you are? Have you told him about all the pain you have seen, the pain you suffer?' Jacob looked at the priest in surprise but Father Augustus continued, speaking softly in the dark church. 'Have you asked him why the innocent suffer and the evil go free? I know I have. Many times I have stood here and screamed in my anger, yelled until tears came for all the hurt and pain.'

In the flickering candle light, the old priest's face had never seemed more haggard or deeply lined.

Jacob sat, still and silent, listening to the rain pound against the roof of the church. Eventually, he asked bitterly, 'And did you get an answer?'

Father Augustus spent some moments looking up at the dull grey of the rose window. Then he said, 'Tell me, Jacob. How do you come to know what crucifixion actually looks like?'

Chapter Thirteen

Blue Velvet

A memory came to him then, a memory of a piece of blue velvet lying in a dusty street. Instinctively, his mind turned away but he forced himself to turn back and look squarely at that which haunted him.

'I was with a patrol of the national army,' he said, his voice flat, almost a monotone, as far from any emotion as possible. 'Technically, I was just a foreign advisor, but in reality I was the officer in charge. We'd heard rumours of a raid on a local Christian village, a small place on top of a hill, so we went to investigate. We knew we had trouble long before we got to the village. It was the smell, the smell of meat gone bad.

When we got there, the village street was lined on both sides with crosses. They had crucified all the males in the village, from young boys to old men, then left their bodies to rot.' He paused and took a deep breath. 'The stench was terrible. I had hardened soldiers throwing up in the street. I just started yelling; cut them down, cut them down!' He paused again and took another deep breath, this one more like a sob. 'It wasn't the right thing to do. We should have left them there for the war crimes investigators but ... It couldn't be allowed to stand. You know? It couldn't be allowed to stand...'

'I know nothing of war crimes investigations,' Father Augustus said. 'But I know you did not do wrong. To cut down those poor, abused bodies was an act of mercy, an act of love. As you say, such evil cannot be allowed to stand.'

Jacob was quiet for a while, then he continued, struggling to hold his voice together. 'I looked into each face as they cut them down. Mostly, the eyes had been pecked out by birds and there were... maggots.' He paused to gain control of his voice. 'Dark, empty sockets where eyes should have been. It was indiscriminate: old men and young boys. All staring at me with those empty sockets, all accusing me, convicting me ...'

Father Augustus looked at him, alarmed and puzzled. 'Why accusing you? You didn't do this thing. It wasn't your fault –'

'Wasn't it?' Jacob asked bitterly. 'That was a nothing village on top of a small hill. It had no strategic significance. For over a thousand years it had been there and nobody had ever bothered to attack it. Why then? What had changed?' Father Augustus shook his head, his face still puzzled. 'It was a Christian village and those others, they don't like Christians. Even so, this place wasn't worth the effort they put into it – except to send a message. It was their way of telling people like me to get out.'

Father Augustus looked at him, with furrowed brows, clearly not understanding.

'Look, I was there as part of a foreign army,' Jacob explained to the puzzled priest. 'They saw it as a Christian army, a band of crusaders, although that's so far off the beam, that it's laughable. They couldn't get at us: too dangerous. But those defenceless villagers – they could get at them and use them to send us a message.'

Jacob was quiet for a moment, looking at his hands. Father Augustus waited.

Eventually Jacob continued, still looking at his hands. 'If I hadn't been there, if I hadn't just done what my government told me to do – something that had no real relationship to the defence of my country, then maybe that village would have been happily ignored for another thousand years.'

'You were a soldier, Jacob,' the priest said quietly. 'Was it not your duty to serve your king? To obey the orders given you?'

'Even if those orders were futile and only caused more death and strife?' He looked into the priest's eyes. 'Even if they only increased the suffering of the small Christian community? A community that may have been oppressed but which was mostly just ignored or at least – was allowed to live.' He paused and took another deep breath. 'We found the body of the village priest in the burnt out remains of the church. They had nailed him to the iconostasis and burnt the church around him.'

The priest quickly made the sign of the cross. 'Miserere Domine,' he whispered.

'There was no doubt,' Jacob continued. 'This was saying 'Christians go home' in the most forceful way possible.' Jacob and Father Augustus sat in silence for a long time. The church gradually grew brighter as the sun rose higher and the rain started to let up.

Eventually the priest asked, 'What did you do?'

'We hunted them,' Jacob replied. '…the band that did this. It was wild country but we knew they'd sell the women and be heading to the border. I called in every surveillance asset I could get through every channel I knew. We caught up with them three days later and ambushed them in a steep sided valley.' He looked into the priest's eyes. 'They died, every last one of them. They deserved to die and we killed them. It wasn't justice. It wasn't war. It was vengeance, pure and simple: vengeance for those who couldn't fight back, and we took it because we could.' The only sound in the church was water dripping somewhere back in the sanctuary. Father Augustus had a leak in his roof. Jacob waited, tense and anxious.

The priest sat still and silent, listening to the water dripping onto the stone floor. Eventually he gave a deep sigh. 'Will you tell me the rest of it, Jacob?' he asked. Jacob looked at him in surprise. 'I've lived a long time, Jacob, and I know that there is a further horror pressing on your mind. Here, in this church, you are safe. Whatever happened, it happened a long way from here. Tell me, why did you hunt those men so savagely?'

'Isn't what I've told you already enough?' Jacob asked. The priest made no reply but sat quietly, waiting. Jacob looked down at his hands. He gripped them tightly together to try and stop them shaking. The rain had now completely passed and the sound of the dripping water was becoming slower and softer.

Eventually he spoke, beads of sweat forming on his forehead. 'Most of the ones who were crucified were actually shot first. They were nailed up there after they were dead, or at least dying. You know, just to send a message.' Jacob drew a long, shuddering breath. 'The head man of the village, however, was actually crucified. He must have annoyed them in some way – perhaps he defied them or organised some form of resistance. Perhaps they just wanted to use him as an example. I don't know.' Jacob drew another long, shuddering breath before forcing himself to continue. 'He was separated from the rest, right up the top of the village's main street. I could see he was different as I walked up to him. I don't know what it was, just something about the way his body was hanging there I guess.'

Jacob stopped, his eyes filling with unwanted tears. The sun was beginning to shine brightly through the windows behind the sanctuary, splashing patches of colour across the stone floor of the nave.

'Go on, Jacob,' Father Augustus said gently. 'You are safe here. In this church, no threat can reach you. Nothing can harm you.'

'There was this bit of cloth lying in the street in front of him, blue velvet it was. As I walked towards it, I kept praying and praying: "O Lord, let it just be some bit of cast off cloth. Please, let it be just something someone has dropped." I prayed so damn hard that it would just be a bit of random rubbish but I knew it wasn't. It was … it was…' It swept over him suddenly and without warning, a great wave of sadness. He broke down, crying unrestrainedly, the sound of his sobbing echoing in the quiet church.

After a while, he pulled himself together and said, 'Sorry Father, that shouldn't have happened,' he said, looking apologetically at the priest.

Father Augustus only said, 'You have nothing to apologise for. Those are not the first tears to have fallen in this church. They will not be the last.'

Jacob drew a deep breath and sat up straighter on the stool. When he continued, his voice was firm. 'They had killed the head man by actual crucifixion, nailed him to the cross while he was still alive. You'd think that would be enough but it wasn't. They'd brought out his young daughter and beheaded her in front of him, while he was helpless and in agony on the cross. It must have been a party or something when they attacked because she was wearing a pretty blue, velvet dress, trimmed with white lace – a party dress. They left her headless body in the street and carried her head off as some kind of sick souvenir. I was physically sick when I saw what was lying in the street. I threw up and almost fainted.'

Father Augustus sat in shocked silence for a moment, too appalled to talk. Then he asked quietly, 'And when you recovered, you pursued the men who had done this … thing?'

Jacob nodded. 'I was furious beyond reason. I had never felt anger like that before. I couldn't think of anything else, was hardly aware of anything else. We just had to get the men who had done this and make them suffer. That's why I was glad when we trapped them in that ravine. We rained all kinds of hell down on them from the sky and from the hills. We shot them as they ran away. I know all the talk about forgiveness and understanding, even for those who do the most horrible things, but I just couldn't. Maybe I wanted to at some level, wanted to let go of this awful anger, but I couldn't. It felt good to see them die.'

'And did the anger pass once these men were dead?' Father Augustus asked.

Jacob shook his head. 'No. No it didn't. It's always there. I don't know – maybe it's not anger anymore. Sometimes it just feels like a deep sadness, a kind of despair, but most of the time I'm just anxious and afraid.' He lifted his head and looked at the priest, his eyes still red from his tears. 'That was an obscenity. It's not just that it was a horrible crime, one that shouldn't ever have happened. It was an act that set out to make foul and dirty all that is good and pure. And please, don't tell me that God can bring good from evil. What good can come from the slaughter of an innocent, young girl? What good can come from the grotesque torture of her father?' Father Augustus was silent. Jacob continued, his voice growing louder. 'Things like that just shouldn't be possible, no one should ever think, should ever even be able to think of doing such a thing. How could a loving God make creatures who could do…that?' He paused, and then said quietly, 'How could a good god have such things done in his name?'

'He had nothing to do with it,' Father Augustus answered quietly. 'I'm afraid both your sadness and your fear are well founded, Jacob. We choose this. It is not our nature to kill. It is our choice. However comforting it might be to blame nature, it was men like you and me who did this thing and they could've decided not to. We can't blame God or nature, much as we might like to, much as we might want to deny the dark demons of our own soul.'

'I certainly don't deny them. I know those demons all too well, Father,' Jacob said bitterly.

'I know you do, Jacob,' the priest said gently. 'Jacob, I have a penance for you - look at the crucifix behind you.' Jacob reluctantly got up from his stool, slowly turned around, and forced himself to look at the cross at the top of the rood screen. It was a graphic, over the top depiction of a man who had been tortured to death. The figure's bones showed prominently, as did the bruises and the dried blood. It was the image of a man who had been starved and beaten badly before being hung up to die.

'Horrible, isn't it,' Father Augustus said. 'The artist was deliberately brutal. He wanted to make a point. He wanted to say that God doesn't stop us from causing suffering and death, he couldn't without turning us into slaves, but he did do the only thing he could: he suffered and died with us.' Jacob gazed at the figure on the cross. He knew what the priest was saying. He knew that this was an image of innocence and love violently abused. All he could feel, however, was a kind of dull resentment.

'What good did it do?' he asked. 'What good is a dead and beaten god?'

'Not all death is defeat, Jacob,' the priest said softly. 'Sometimes, if you can love even to the bitter end, death is victory. What good did it do? It changed the world. Death now doesn't have the last word, love does. Yes, the innocent suffer and die but that's not the end of their story. Easter Sunday will always follow on from Good Friday. Even in death there is hope. This I believe with all that I am.'

The word 'hope' hit him, almost like a physical blow. This time he had warning. As he looked at the battered figure on the cross, he knew he was going to have an incident. He had time to recognise the symptoms; he was sweating and his hands were starting to shake. The words formed, unbidden, in his mind: faith, hope and love, these things remain, death has no power over them. He was shaking uncontrollably and his eyes filled with tears. He could clearly see the poor, defiled body of the girl, in her pretty, party dress of blue velvet.

'Don't worry, I have her.' The words were clear, although he could not have said who uttered them. He found himself on his knees and, for the second time that morning, crying uncontrollably, his tears flowing freely and great sobs shaking his body.

Next to him, Father Augustus was saying some prayers in Latin. Jacob barely heard him until near the end. '… *Ego te absolvo a peccatis tuis in nomine Patris, et Filii, et Spiritus Sancti…* ' Jacob looked up at him with tear reddened eyes. '…whatever good you do, whatever evil you suffer, may they bring you the remission of your sins, an increase of grace, and the reward of eternal life. Amen.'

'Jacob, there is no need for you to ever think of these things again,' the priest said. When Jacob started to protest, he held up his hand in conciliatory motion. 'Oh, I don't say that you won't. I don't say that these things will not continue to haunt your dreams and blight your days. Even the risen Christ still carried the wounds of his crucifixion. I just say that you *need* not. Remember, when the fear grips you, there is no need.' The priest looked to the church door. 'Now, I believe Myriam has come to rescue you. Go, you have a long life ahead of you.'

Jacob didn't know what to do or what to say. He got up from his knees and looked across at the priest. Father Augustus' face was calm but Jacob was surprised to see tears in his eyes.

The words he was struggling to say died on his lips. Instead, he simply said, 'Thank you, Father.'

'Go now,' the priest said. 'I will pray for you. I will pray that your life will be filled with joy to match your sorrow.'

Jacob nodded and turned to walk out of the church, his eyes still red from his tears. Then he paused. He turned around and bowed deeply to the cross before leaving.

* * *

Two men sat on the stone bench outside the church and watched as Jacob walked down to meet Myriam. Both had the hoods of their cloaks pulled down to shade their faces. One watched dully as the couple met and started to walk through the village. The other smiled happily.

'This isn't over,' the first man said quietly. 'He's still broken. The dreams will still torment him. He'll still be dogged by anxiety and fear.'

'That is true,' the other agreed, 'and yet I count this as a great triumph.'

'It changes nothing.'

'There you're wrong. This changes everything.'

'Are you satisfied with how this is going? Really?' the first asked angrily 'I don't see why. Did you intend that the confrontation in the tavern should occur?'

'No. I would rather that had not happened. At least, not yet.'

'They'll come for him again,' the first man insisted with a fierce intensity, 'and next time they'll be prepared. He will have to fight her brother. No matter who wins, she loses and it will destroy her.'

'I think she is stronger than you imagine her to be.'

CHAPTER FOURTEEN

A Town Meeting

Outside the church, the rain clouds were banked high to the north east and a watery sun was shining over a world washed by rain. Myriam was coming up the path to the church. She was wearing her dark blue cloak with the hood pulled back and her red hair fanned out in wild curls behind her. She looked at him anxiously and then smiled at him in welcome.

'Have you finished?' Myriam asked. When Jacob nodded, she said, 'Good. I figured we might have a picnic now that the rain has stopped. Come on, the fence can wait. I've packed lunch for both of us.' She spoke quickly and with a kind of false cheerfulness. 'I thought you might need some time off after being grilled by Father Augustus.'

Jacob shook his head and smiled. 'It wasn't really a grilling. It was just a friendly chat – a fairly in depth friendly chat.'

Myriam studied his face: the tear stained cheeks and reddened eyes. 'Hmm,' she said, not dropping her cheerful charade. 'You're lucky then. I've seen grown men stumble out of there in tears.' She stopped, appalled at what she had just said. 'I didn't mean to… to…'

Jacob only smiled. 'In tears you say? I can believe it. He's a tough old bird. I don't think he'd ever let you off with three Hail Marys and on your way.'

She smiled and took his arm. They walked down the hill to the village through the damp freshness and the suddenly bright sunlight. This time, he didn't feel anxious or on edge. He felt tired and strangely relaxed, as if he had just done a long day's work. As they were approaching the tavern, one of the villagers, a young man, came running towards them. He was clearly distressed.

'Charlie, what's wrong?' Myriam asked, alarmed.

'It's the Riders,' the young man answered. 'They've just destroyed old Tom McCredden's kitchen garden and all the gardens in that row. They've chased the chickens half to death and damaged the orchard. There's going to be a town meeting in the tavern. I'm running to get Father Augustus. You'd better come too.' He looked slyly at Jacob. 'Both of you.' Then he ran on past them, up the hill.

'Come on, Jacob,' Myriam said. 'He's right. We need to be there.' Myriam hurried on ahead but Jacob followed more slowly. He was looking at the village, considering options, as his training came to bear. He needed a plan. The layout of the village was very open. Apart from the street, it could be easily approached from the west, across the fields, while to the east, the forest and a small river formed some minimal protection. The whole place was not easily defensible. That was a problem.

The main room of the tavern was already crowded when Jacob arrived. A series of wooden benches had been set up and the crowd sat, facing the rear of the tavern. There was a lot of loud and angry talk, each person vying to complain more bitterly than any of the others. At the far end of the room, three men; Noah, the blacksmith, and a man Jacob didn't know; sat in silence facing the crowd. Jacob spotted Myriam, made his way over, and sat on the bench next to her.

She leaned over to him and whispered, 'This is bad. It's been brewing for a while now. People are scared. What with the stays getting shorter and the in between times getting longer – and now the Riders becoming more aggressive…it's too much. I know Da will ask them to be patient but it's too much.' Just then, Father Augustus hurried into the room and made his way to the far end. He joined the other three men and sat facing the crowd.

'Okay, all settle down now,' Noah called. 'We're all here and it's time to start.' This had no effect on the crowd who were still as noisy as ever. 'We'll start with a prayer,' Noah yelled. 'Father…'

Father Augustus stood and made the sign of the cross. 'In the name of the Father, and of the Son, and of the Holy Ghost.' This quietened the crowd as they followed out of habit. 'Lord, we ask you to bless all here. May we come to know your will and what it is best to do. Amen.'

Everyone answered 'Amen' and Noah rose to talk to the now quiet crowd. 'As I heard it, Tom suffered the most. So, he has the right to speak first. Tom? Where is he?'

'The shock of it was too much,' a woman answered in a shrill voice. 'It's sent him to his bed. His garden trampled, his chickens scattered or dead, what's he going to eat? What'll he have put by when the snow comes?' There was a rise of angry murmur at this and several men stood up and shouted comments.

'Settle down, settle down,' Noah called. 'It's no use if we all talk over each other.'

A thick set man stood in the middle of the crowd. 'Don't ye be telling us to settle down,' he yelled. 'This is as much yer fault as it is that bastard's in the tower. If ye could've kept yer own wife…'

'That's enough, Angus,' the man Jacob didn't know said sharply. 'That has no place here. Do we know, was Tom's son one of them?'

'Aye, Ezekiel, we do, and he was,' a woman on the left answered. 'That was the worst of it. His own son, destroying where he once played as a child. It's too much…' She turned and the woman behind her wrapped her in her arms as she sobbed into her shoulder.

Angus hadn't sat down. 'It's like he's some dead thing,' he said. 'Something that should've died years ago but didn't. Now he's done this to his own father! Something's got to be done! Who knows what they'll do next or who'll be next?'

'Sit down, Angus,' Noah said. 'I don't think this was the start of a campaign. It was just the Laird sending us a message…'

'Aye!' Angus yelled, still not sitting down. 'And why was the message sent? Because of him!' He swung around and pointed at Jacob. 'Him, who's a guest up at Noah's place. He comes in here and stirs up trouble. He beat up three of the Riders, including old Tom's son, here in this very room and this morning, this very morning, he got in the way of their ride. Do you deny it?' he challenged. 'Do you?'

Jacob shook his head. 'No,' he said simply.

'He also grabbed young Jimmy McTavish out of the rider's path the other day,' the blacksmith said. 'Should he not have caused trouble then? Maybe, sometimes, we can get a bit too used to things not being as they should and a bit of trouble is what we need.'

'Tell that to old Tom,' Angus said. There was a murmur of agreement around the room. 'But it's too late for any of that. We're up to our necks in it now and we need to do something. Noah's a good one for sitting on his hands. We all know that. If he had claimed his inheritance, or protected his wife, or even given the Laird what he claimed he had a right to, then none of this would've happened. But he didn't do any of that and now we get to cop it. Well, take that for a bloody joke. I say we all get what implements we can and we go up and kill the Laird. Who's with me?' There was a roar of approval from many in the room. Noah dropped his head to his hands.

'And if he sends the Riders to stop you?' the blacksmith asked.

'Then we kill them too,' Angus answered. 'We kill them so that they're properly dead.' There was no roar of approval now. Only silence.

'Would you kill my son, Angus?' the blacksmith asked softly. 'Would you kill Tom's? Which do you think Tom would rather have die: his chickens or his son?'

Angus looked at the silent faces around him. 'They're kind of dead already,' he said weakly, but it was clear that he had lost the support of the crowd.

Noah raised his head from his hands. 'Sit down Angus – please!' After a moment's hesitation, Angus sat down. 'We have all been injured by the Laird, I perhaps more than anyone, but we can't kill him without killing the Riders and I have already done enough killing, more than enough killing. Those of you who have the good fortune not to have killed, be very wary of starting. It's not a good road to walk down.'

A young man in the front of the crowd timidly raised his hand. Noah nodded at him. 'But the curse is getting worse,' he said. 'Soon we may be stuck in the in between forever.' A deep silence fell on the room. 'Father, didn't you say that the curse would probably be broken on the death of the Laird? Can we not kill him to save the village? If we get stuck in the between, we'll all die.'

The old priest nodded. 'Would the curse be broken by the Laird's death? Yes, probably. I'm not certain, but probably. I've said that before. Death but not murder. No good can ever come from murder.'

'So, we simply have to wait and hope that the Laird dies of old age before the village is lost forever?' the young man asked. No one seemed to want to answer.

'Actually, if I could make a suggestion,' Jacob said. 'There are some things you could do.' Everyone in the room turned to look at him. 'I suggest you place a sentry up on the road the Riders take into the village and give him a horn or something to warn you of when the Riders are on their way. That way, you can make sure the street is clear. Also, put a horse barrier around your most critical gardens and orchards. It doesn't need to be solid, just something to spook the horses and stop them jumping over your walls. A brightly coloured strand of rope about six feet off the ground should do it.' There was a general murmur of conversations and many nodding heads as people considered this. Noah looked at Jacob across the room and gave a brief nod of approval.

'Okay, I think our visitor has given us a reasonable plan of action. Anyone have any objections to that? Anyone have anything better?' Ezekiel asked. 'No? Then that's the plan. Meeting over. You can all go home now.'

'Or you can stay,' the barman yelled from behind the bar. 'The bar's open and the kitchen's waiting.' There were few who took up his offer. Jacob watched as the crowd was getting up from the benches, their faces still angry and fearful. Nothing had been resolved. Myriam grabbed Jacob by the elbow and began to hurry him out of the tavern. As they walked past the bar, she gripped his arm even more tightly. The barman waved a friendly greeting. Myriam returned his greeting but walked just a little bit faster till they were well past the bar and out into the street. In her other hand she had a picnic basket. Jacob had given up wondering how she came to have these things.

'Come on,' she said. 'We have a picnic to get to and the rain won't hold off forever.'

Chapter Fifteen

Myriam

Jacob smiled. 'I think that the real reason you organised this picnic,' he said, 'was to stop me spending too much time in the tavern. It's not really a bad place you know.'

She looked at him sternly. 'It's a bad place for you. Jock is a good man and it's a fine spot for most to meet and talk. But it's not a good place for you. Not for my Da either.' She hesitated and stumbled slightly as she said, 'But that's not why… I just thought it might be good…'

'To enjoy the sunshine while it lasts,' Jacob finished for her. 'Yes, I think that's a very good idea. Where did you have in mind?'

'Come and I'll show you,' she said smiling. She led him through the village.

His smile hid some furious thinking. He had almost dared to believe that he might, one day, be happy again but there were things said in the meeting that troubled him greatly. He paused as they passed the blacksmith's. The blacksmith was already back at work, as if he were driven by some desperate urgency, and the hammer blows rang rapidly. He was again working on the thin band of metal that would one day soon be a sword blade. Jacob didn't know why, but each hammer blow filled him with dread. He stood transfixed as the brightness of the sunlight was beaten, momentarily, from the sky.

Myriam took his hand and the sun was shining again. She waved cheerfully to the blacksmith as she urged him forward. 'Come on,' she said. 'I want to show you another of my favourite places.' They turned to the right and off down a muddy track through farm fields and into a small forest that ran along the banks of a stream. There they entered into a green tunnel as the trees joined overhead. The clouds had passed and the forest was now dappled with bright shafts of sunlight. It was still wet from the rain and the drops of moisture glistened brightly, as if the trees were strung with lights. The path descended steeply and Jacob had to be careful to keep his footing. Several times Myriam had to grab his arm for support, laughing as she did so. Eventually they came to the bank of the stream, its clear water, fuelled by the recent rain, tumbling loudly over a stony bed. A path, even muddier than the one they had just descended, ran along the bank and along this, Myriam led Jacob upstream.

'Come on,' she said again. 'It's not far now.'

A minute or so later, they came to a place where an outcrop of rock had formed a sort of natural weir and the stream danced over the rocks in a cascade, shining brightly in the sun. Near the foot of the cascade there was a broad clearing of rock and grass and it was there that Myriam led Jacob.

She pulled a rug out of the basket she was carrying and threw it on the ground, where it spread itself out, nice and neat. Then she sat down on the rug and started to pull out food: slices of meat, bread, cakes, fruit, drinks, small pies and jars of pickles and jam. It seemed to Jacob that she pulled out more food than the small basket could possibly have held.

She smiled at him and indicated a spare spot on the rug. 'Sit down and have your lunch. I wasn't sure what you would like, so I brought a bit of everything.' Jacob sat down and there was a long moment as they looked at each other with the picnic rug between them. Jacob sat there, taking in all the details of this moment, a moment he knew he would long remember; the moment when his rational mind surrendered to his heart. She sat there with her wild, red hair framing her pale face and soft smile, with her dark blue cloak spread around her. There, with the roar of the cascade in the background, with the morning sun shining on the wet grass, and with the birds calling in the forest after the rain, he dared to believe, for the first time in a long while, that fairy tale fantasies might be true and that he might again be happy. He smiled slightly, taking a knife and slicing some bread for himself, which he then covered with ham and pickles. He watched her as she buttered some bread: her pale skin glowing from the walk and the sunlight casting bright highlights of gold in her hair. She smiled at him and once again, no matter what the truth was, he knew he would go through all sorts of trouble, just to see that smile.

'What's on your mind?' she asked.

'You', would have been the honest answer but he couldn't say that aloud, not yet at least. He looked away from her. He had to put this to one side. He needed to think clearly. There were things he needed to know. He took a deep breath. This would be a difficult conversation and he didn't know how to begin. His gaze followed over the cascade and upstream into the hills on the other side of the creek. There he saw the Laird's castle. From this angle, it stood close to a dark cliff that fell to the stream bed below: a black, stone finger on top of a rocky crag. He decided to use that as his starting point. It was as good as any.

'That's a grim place,' he said, pointing to the castle and trying to hide his nervousness about where this conversation was going to go. 'Fitting, I suppose, considering who lives there.'

Myriam followed his gaze but only looked at the castle briefly before returning her attention to the picnic.

'It wasn't always so grim,' she said softly. 'There was a time when it was the centre of the village life. All the festivals were celebrated there, the whole village gathering. There was a time when it was hung with bright banners during the day and lit with lanterns and torches during the night.'

'What happened?' Jacob asked.

Myriam sighed and began to recite what was clearly a well-remembered story. 'The father of this current Laird took a fancy to a young village girl, and she to him. Unlike his son, he was a man of honour and they were wed with all due ceremony in the village church. Their happiness was brief, however. She was a commoner and others, mostly from outside the village, considered this to be a scandal. It might seem strange to you, Jacob, but in that time and place, for one of the gentry to marry a commoner was unheard of. It was considered close to treason. Anyway, the local prince heard of it and he issued an ultimatum: either the Laird would swear that the marriage had not been consummated and have it annulled, or he would lose all land, title and privilege.' She paused and sat silently for a good minute. 'There was a problem, however,' she continued. 'The poor woman was already pregnant. The old Laird wasn't evil but he was weak. He chose to keep his land and to swear that the child was conceived before wedlock. He swore that the woman had pressured him into marriage because of this, and that he had not touched her since. Everyone knew it wasn't true but it was the legal fiction that allowed the annulment. The castle darkened that day and it has been a sad place ever since.'

'What happened to the woman?' Jacob asked.

Myriam shrugged. 'As I said, the Laird wasn't evil and he really did love her. So, he protected her and tried to look after her. He gave her a cottage and some good land on the far side of the village, far away from the castle. She gave birth to a son and the old Laird loved him dearly, although he couldn't show it too openly. When the child was grown the Laird did the best he could for him, without raising too many questions, that is. He saw to his education and arranged for him to have a position in the army, as was the custom with many of the illegitimate sons of the gentry … The son didn't much like the army, however, and, anyway, he was already in love with a girl from the village. He came home.'

'Meanwhile, the Laird had married someone more suitable?' Jacob suggested.

Myriam nodded. 'Aye. The prince selected a candidate and they were married in the prince's private chapel by his private chaplain. The whole matter was then considered closed.'

Jacob frowned. This was more complicated and twisted than he had feared. Still, he needed to know. 'That's a bit rough on the girl who was selected to marry the Old Laird,' he said. 'She walked into a situation she had nothing to do with. I can't think that it all ended happily ever after.'

Myriam nodded. 'I remember seeing her as an old lady. I felt sorry for her. She had a sad life. It was a loveless match. They had only one son, the current Laird, and most people think that that was mainly to satisfy legal expectations. Even her son brought her no joy. The current Laird was always a twisted, ill-favoured boy and he grew up bitterly resenting the first son. He was madly jealous of any love or concern that the Old Laird showed towards him.'

Jacob thought about all this, still looking at the dark castle, putting all the pieces together in sequence. 'Noah, your father, is the old Laird's son from his first marriage, isn't he?' he asked. Miriam nodded. 'So, he is actually the legitimate heir. He should be the Laird.'

'Morally, perhaps,' Miriam replied, 'but not legally. Not on paper. Come on, eat something. All this old history will just ruin our picnic.' She offered Jacob the bread and he took it to finish his sandwich, but he persisted with his questions. There was more that he guessed, more that he needed to know.

'Noah's not actually your biological father, is he? The current Laird is.' Jacob suggested.

'No,' Myriam said sharply. 'Noah is my father in all the ways that matter. The rest is just history and it makes no difference.'

'Okay. Okay, I can see that,' Jacob said, trying to placate her. 'He's the one who raised you and cared for you after your mother died: he and Joshua. Joshua, who is related to you, how?'

'He is my brother, although some would call him my half-brother,' she whispered. 'My mother was his mother, Noah's wife.' Jacob sat staring at the castle, anger rising in him, his sandwich forgotten in his hand, as he understood the implications of that statement.

'Come on,' Myriam pleaded. 'Please, just eat.' In a soft voice she added, 'I really don't want to talk about this anymore. Please, don't ask any more questions. I've got the picnic all ready. Can't we just enjoy our time together?'

Jacob took a deep breath. 'Fair enough, let's talk of something else.' He paused then, chewing thoughtfully on his sandwich. 'You had Joshua, your brother, but he was a lot older than you. Did you have other friends?' he asked. 'Would you say you had a happy childhood?'

Myriam gave a resigned sigh but then smiled. 'Happy? Aye, but lonely. There weren't many others my age in the village and even those were a bit wary of me and my family. Bad history, I suppose. I can't blame them. I always had my books and my dreams, of course, but, as you say, the only really close companion I had was Joshua. Aye, he was a lot older than me but he was my beloved brother and my great protector. He was always there when I needed him. Then, even he was taken from me.'

Jacob nodded. Having seen the young Joshua in his dream, he could understand how much it must hurt her to see the black rider who was Joshua but also not Joshua. 'What did you do for entertainment?'

'Oh, the village was never boring,' she said. 'Certainly not since being set adrift in time. You only had to wait a few weeks, at most, and some new, strange visitors would show up, some new mountains would be visible beyond the village bounds. Anyway, I always had my books. Ever since his time in the army, Da collected books whenever he could. I doubt that even the Laird has a better library, especially since we collect the ones he throws out.'

Her smile turned to a frown. 'Of course, the books were a bit of a double-edged sword. The fact that I could read and write, that I enjoyed reading more than just about anything, made me even more of an oddity. I was the child of scandal and 'not quite gentry'. People didn't know how to treat me.'

'Did you ever try to leave?' Jacob asked. 'Can you?'

'Oh aye, I think so,' she said. 'Other people have, so I suppose I could. That's one reason the village's population is shrinking. Every time we come close to our original time and place, there are some who decide to leave.'

'But not you?'

She shook her head firmly. 'No, this is my home. I'll not be driven from it. That's what the Laird wants, to destroy this town and community. Also...' She blushed and looked away to the water cascading over the rocks. 'Why all these questions?' She asked, now clearly annoyed. 'This is becoming more like an interrogation than a picnic. Please, no more questions.'

'Sorry, I just want to know you better,' Jacob replied, 'and you must admit, there's a lot about you that I wouldn't know if I hadn't asked.'

'Really? I'm so sorry,' she said sarcastically. 'How dare I not explain my family shame to you? I should have said straight away, 'How do you do? I'm Myriam, the illegitimate daughter of the Laird through his incestuous rape of his brother's wife: the man who has since raised me as his daughter.' Would that have been better?'

'No, of course not,' Jacob said, embarrassed and suddenly ashamed of himself. He had been so determined to find out if his guesses were correct, that he had not thought of Myriam and how she might feel.

'In your relentless search for answers, did it not occur to you that this might be something I didn't want to talk about?' she asked, her sarcasm turning to anger. 'That it might be something I find shameful, even painful, to recall? Maybe that should've occurred to you when I said, 'I don't want to talk about this' or when I asked you, twice, to stop with all the questions.'

'I'm sorry,' he said formally, sitting up straight, as if coming to attention. 'You had every right to your privacy and I have been most insensitive. Please accept my apology.'

'Relax, soldier,' she said, her anger fading quickly, although she was clearly still annoyed. 'I accept your apology. Now, I'm the daughter of the Laird and it's something I don't like talking about. Can we please just forget about it and enjoy this time together. We have so little time left… Here, have a pie.'

Jacob accepted the pie and ate. It was very good. Not fancy, just good. He looked at Myriam, sitting in the sun. Could he just relax and enjoy being with her? No. He enjoyed looking at her, listening to her, being with her more than anything he could think of, but he couldn't relax. There was one more thing that he desperately needed to know. When he had finished the pie, he picked up an apple and bit into it, savouring the tart sweetness of that first bite.

'People have left the village. Have any of your visitors ever stayed?' he asked casually.

Myriam looked at him warily. 'No,' she said, as he deliberately took another bite of his apple. 'When the village is getting ready to shift, they get an overpowering urge to leave; a powerful feeling that they don't belong and need to get away. It becomes urgent, irresistible, almost to the point of panic. None of them, not even those bound by military discipline, have ever managed to stay. When the time comes, you will leave. Does that tell you what you wanted to know?'

Jacob put his apple down. 'How much time do we have left?' he asked.

Myriam frowned and started packing all the picnic things back into the basket, throwing them in roughly. 'You know, I spent a lot of time preparing this picnic and now you've ruined it. I thought we could talk about silly, nothing things; about dreams and hopes. The kind of things any young couple might share. But no, you need to know. You need to ask. That analytical mind of yours — always asking questions…Some questions are better left unasked.'

'How much time?' he asked again, as gently as he could.

She stopped still for a moment and when she looked at him there were tears in her eyes. 'A week, maybe less,' she said. 'It's hard to say. You being here may act as an anchor and give us a bit longer but the stays have been getting shorter, so we can't be sure. When the time comes, you will leave and once again become just a dream.'

'What about the village?' Jacob asked.

Myriam shrugged. 'No one knows. The stays are getting shorter and the times in between are getting longer. Maybe soon there will be no stay and the village will be lost in the dark place between times.'

'Unless the Laird dies first?' Jacob suggested.

'Unless the Laird dies first,' she agreed. 'Mind you, the old coot shows no sign of obliging.' She closed the lid of the picnic basket. 'Do you know how long I have been planning this picnic? Ever since I was a girl, I planned to bring you here, to my favourite place, so we could have a picnic together. It was one of the reasons I never left the village, even when Noah said I should. I waited. I waited for you. I knew that, sooner or later, you would come. The attraction of the bond between us meant that it had to happen eventually.'

'You were waiting for me?' Jacob was stunned, momentarily too surprised to speak.

'Aye, for all the good it's done me,' she said. 'I was waiting for you.'

CHAPTER SIXTEEN

Dreamkin

There was a long moment of awkward silence as they sat and looked at each other, the only sound being the rush of water over the rocks. Eventually Jacob said softly, 'I'm very glad you were there, waiting for me, but – how come and how could you be waiting for me when you didn't even know that I existed? How can there be any bond between us? We've only just met. You don't really even know me.'

'I do know you Jacob, though perhaps you don't know me, or at least, you don't know that you know me,' she said. 'I told you before, I've dreamed with you since we were little. This is not some romantic notion. It's simple fact. It's part of my gift.' Jacob drew a deep breath and drew back. Myriam gave a small, almost apologetic, smile. 'Let me see if I can convince you, I dreamed with you when you had that bright red peddle car. You peddled around in that until your knees wouldn't fit. I dreamed with you when you got your first dog. I dreamed the joy you had, holding that small bundle of life. He was black with a brown patch over his left eye and ear – so you called him Patch.' Her voice lowered to little more than a whisper. 'I dreamed with you when he was killed by that car. He limped to the gutter and died. I dreamed with you when your mother died too – long and slow. I dreamed with you when your father ran away from the pain and buried himself in his work, leaving you to face the dark alone…' Jacob felt his blood turn cold. This was just plain creepy. Nobody could know this stuff. Not even his closest friends. Not even his dwindling supply of remaining family. Certainly not some girl he had only met a few days before. He was standing still and stiff, every muscle in his body tense.

'How!' he yelled, angry and frightened. 'How do you know all this stuff?'

'We're connected,' she answered calmly. 'I've told you this already, Jacob. It's part of my gift. In our dreams, we've been friends since we were very little. I've always been with you. I've dreamed your life just as you have lived it. I dreamed with you when you would walk home from school and that girl would always walk down the same street as you. You thought she was pretty but you never had the courage to say hello,' she stopped and smiled. 'I think she always wondered why you didn't. I'm sure she wanted you to. I dreamed with you through all those long lectures at university and through those embarrassing times when you and your university friends attempted to play some sort of Quidditch game in real life and during that even more embarrassing first date with Anne Golding.' Her smile passed and she looked at him with sorrow and pity. 'I dreamed with you when Heather broke your heart and all your world seemed to fall in ruins.'

Jacob was looking at her with a mixture of fear and horror. 'No!' he said. 'Stop. Just stop!' It wasn't possible. It had to be some sort of trick, but how could it be done? No one could know all these things. However it was done, he felt, somehow, violated.

Myriam, however, continued: 'I dreamed with you when you ran off to join the army and I dreamed with you through your training. You remember Purvis – the big guy? How did you describe him? Six foot four and two axe handles across the shoulders. Remember that night in the Wagga hotel? The guy who decided to prove he was tough by having a go at you? Purvis came over and literally picked him up and threw him out of the hotel. He bounced as he hit the street.' She paused and looked down at her hands. 'This is my gift but I think that, maybe, it's your gift too, that it was a two way sort of thing. I think that maybe I could only dream with you when you let me because when you went off to that other place, you held me away. I couldn't dream with you there..' She looked up at him with her misty sky eyes. 'I think you were trying to protect me.'

He looked at her wide eyed, his fear slowly giving way to something more like wonder. Could his childhood really have been so different from the way he remembered it? How could she have been with him all his life without him knowing it? He knew he was in the presence of something he didn't understand, and yet something that was of intimate concern to him. 'I didn't try to protect you,' he said, struggling to control his emotions. 'I don't have any gift. As far as I'm aware, I've only just met you! How could I do anything to protect you when I didn't even know you existed?'

'Are you sure?' she asked. 'I asked you this once before, how many of your childhood dreams do you remember?'

Jacob looked at her with her long, red hair falling in gentle waves, with her pale skin and her soft eyes. Just for a moment he felt something from deep inside him, not just a connection but more, a kind of unity. He shook his head. The whole thing was too weird, too creepy. It was as if he had been stalked; his privacy, the privacy of his most intimate thoughts, swept away by some unknown power.

'If this had happened, I'd know about it,' he insisted desperately. 'I'd remember it.'

She put the picnic basket down and turned to look at him. 'Of course you would, and you did!' she said firmly, like a teacher correcting a troublesome student. 'Did you not ever wonder why you turned aside from your walk to go and stay with a strange girl? Why? Does that seem like a sensible thing to do? Why did you even come on this walk in the first place? Your doctors must've told you not to. I think you knew it was time for us to meet. Not in your conscious mind, no, it's far too rational, but deep inside you, in the place where dreams come from.'

He gazed at her as steadily as he could. Why was she saying all these crazy, impossible, things? He kept trying to figure out how she could know all that stuff. Nothing even remotely plausible came to mind. No one could know those things.

'Tell me, Jacob,' she said, again with the strained patience of a weary school teacher. 'What images and thoughts have come into your mind since we have met? What comparisons have occurred to you?'

'Fairy tales,' he said. 'This has seemed like something from a fairy tale.'

She smiled suddenly and so widely that she almost laughed. 'Aye!' she said. 'Don't you see? That's the young Jacob, the Jacob I know, trying to remind this old Jacob of the times when we dreamed together as children.'

'No,' he said, shaking his head and refusing to accept what she was saying. Somehow, this was worse than the black riders, this was worse than the crazy village adrift in time. He knew why. This concerned him, concerned the deepest part of him. Yet even as he tried to deny it, he remembered those dreams he had had of Myriam. He remembered that he had felt her feelings as a young child...

'How?' he asked. 'How is this possible? How can we be connected by dreams and dreaming?'

Myriam looked thoughtful for a moment. 'I don't really know,' she said. 'We call this dream walking and those who are connected in this way, dreamkin. It's a very rare gift but it has happened to others in my family long ago. I don't know how or why we were connected nor even why the dream walking happens at all. I just know that it does and that I have dreamt of you from my very earliest memories.'

'Then why isn't this a two-way street?' Jacob asked. 'How come I didn't 'dream' you?'

'You did. I'm sure you did,' Myriam replied. 'It's just that you lived in a world where such things were not considered possible, so your conscious self forgot me, like it forgets the phantoms of normal dreams. That trained analytical mind of yours wouldn't let you remember anything that didn't fit into its understanding of the world. Still, I think that maybe some part of you did. I think those memories are still there, just buried deep down.' She bent down and picked up the picnic basket again. 'We shared our childhoods, Jacob, in the most intimate way possible …'

'No way,' Jacob said, still instinctively panicked. 'That sounds creepy.'

'I know how it sounds,' she sighed. 'But it wasn't like that. It wasn't creepy at all. It was like having … a friend, a very close friend. I wish you could remember.'

Jacob took deep breaths, relaxed the muscles in his arms, and unclenched his hands. He tried to calm down and to think it through rationally. Objectively, sharing dreams was small beer compared to a village that could turn up in any time or place. And he had had those strange dreams where he saw the world through the eyes of a young Myriam. Was that Myriam's memory or his own memory of sharing Myriam's childhood? Had contact with the physical Myriam stirred memories of forgotten dreams? He tried to think through all the crazy talk of dreams he had heard since coming to the village and he remembered something Father Augustus had said to him.

'Father Augustus warned me that the Laird might try to reach into my mind and my dreams.' Jacob paused, uncertain of how to ask his next question. 'Is it through the Laird that you have this ability, some sort of genetic inheritance?'

Myriam grimaced 'Aye,' she replied warily. 'Deamwalking is a talent that runs in the Laird's family. My mother was a commoner. All I've been told of her suggests that her talents were far simpler. The noble families in our community were those who showed the strongest and the rarest magical ability and this is still passed undiminished to their children and their children's children, regardless of …the circumstances of their birth.'

There was an awkward quiet between them.

After a while, Myriam broke the silence. 'Ever since you went to that other place, I haven't been able to dream with you. You held me away. I missed you but I've always comforted myself with the thought that you wanted to protect me from what you saw there. The thing is, that means that there's now a lot I don't know about you. For instance, where is home for you now?'

Jacob grimaced. 'Nowhere much … an army barracks or psych ward maybe. If they get sick of me, a rooming house somewhere or a swag rolled up under a bridge. My Dad married again while I was over there, then he died a few months later. Heart attack. At least it was quick. Now his widow lives in our old house.' He paused. 'I don't get on with her that well. I don't think I'd be a welcome guest.'

Silence descended again, each of them lost in private thought.

'You're right about one thing,' Jacob said eventually. 'If I could protect you, or anyone, from seeing what I saw in that bloody place, I would.'

Myriam had picked up the picnic basket and had started to walk back towards the path. She stopped, stood still, and took a deep breath. When she spoke, it was in a quiet and hesitant voice. 'Protect me from what you saw or from what you did?' she asked. The words shot through him like electricity. 'You are a murderer,' a nasty little voice said in his head; 'a murderer of children. She will find out and she will hate you for what you have done.'

'What do you mean?' he asked, trying to keep his voice calm against his rising, guilty panic.

She turned swiftly. 'I'm not going to blame you, Jacob,' she said quickly. 'I know war is awful and bad things happen. I'm not judging you and I really don't want to pry where I shouldn't. It's just that … well, you spent so long with Father Augustus, and when you left I could see that something pretty bad must've happened. I just wondered… is it something I should know about?'

He looked at her: a pretty girl with a sad history in a fairy tale-beautiful valley. All of a sudden, none of this seemed real. What was real was a piece of blue velvet lying in a street. What was real was another valley, just as deep but not as pretty. There he had rained down death and destruction. It had been the perfect ambush: fleeing from the attack helicopters, they had run into his claymore mines and machine guns. The killing zone was a lethal hell, nothing survived. He could still hear the screams, ringing out between the thunder of the ordinance. Most of them were grown men, some were little more than boys. Did they deserve to die? He didn't care. He had just killed them.

'I killed people,' he said, trying to keep calm. 'I was a soldier, it was war. I killed people. Is that what you wanted to know? I watched them die, horribly, and I saw the people they had killed – horribly.' He was losing control now and starting to yell. 'I was sent to that place and I saw things no one should ever see. I did things no one should ever be asked to do. Sure, they were young but they were carrying guns, so I killed them. Is that what you wanted to know? Is it?'

'Jacob, I …' She couldn't find the words but reached out her hand to take his. He pulled away from her and turned his back.

'No,' he said, breathing deeply and trying to gain some sort of calm. 'There is nothing you need to know. You don't need to worry about me. In a little while, the village will move on and I'll be gone.'

'Why were you off walking in the mountains, Jacob?' she asked, standing up straighter. 'Why were you out there, alone and without much in the way of food?' There was a break in her voice and he knew, without turning, that she was crying. 'I thought that you had come to find me but maybe there's another reason, maybe you came into those mountains to run away, to die. That would be bloody selfish! Whatever you've done, whatever happened to you, whatever is going to happen to you; choose to live, Jacob. We're connected and I don't want my dreams to end that way.'

He turned to look at her. There were tears in her eyes.

'I didn't choose this,' she said. 'I didn't choose to dream your life. It just happened. But it was a good thing, at least I thought it was. All those years, I thought of you as my closest friend. Now…now you're hidden from me and I don't know who you are.' She turned and started to run.

Jacob looked after her as she ran down the path. As he watched her go, the anger that had been coursing through his body flowed out of him like water. 'Fair enough, Myriam,' he whispered, 'neither do I'

He followed her back along the river track and up through the forest to the village. The musical ringing of the hammer blows from the blacksmith's had stopped and the main street was crowded with sheep as a farmer moved his flock from one field to another. He felt emotionally drained and couldn't help but think about the contrast between the peaceful appearance of the village and the dark and vengeful deeds that had been done there. Once again, he was filled with a kind of desperate, hopeless anger. It seemed that no matter where or how hard he looked, there was no escape from human cruelty and violence; not even in a fairy tale village: not even on a picnic with a beautiful girl. The afternoon was getting on and a chill entered the air as he made his way back to the cottage.

When he got back, he immediately went to work on the stone fence. He worked furiously, trying to wash away his anger and emotion in physical effort. His fingers were in great danger of being crushed as he carelessly hefted and placed the heavy stones. He kept at it, even when the light was fading. His body was sore and heavy when Myriam called him to dinner.

CHAPTER SEVENTEEN

More of Dreams and Dreaming

Dinner was a quiet affair that night. Jacob was too tired to talk much and Myriam was very reserved. Noah just looked from one to the other and ate his lamb stew in silence. He only spoke when Myriam was cleaning up the plates from the main course and had gone to get the desert.

'Ye made good progress on that wall today, Jacob,' he said. 'Did ye get to see Father Augustus?' Jacob nodded mutely. 'And Myriam was going to take ye a picnic lunch, how did that go?'

'It was good,' Jacob said, clearly not wanting to talk about it further.

'Really?' Noah asked. 'It's just that Myriam and yeself are both very quiet tonight. Did anything happen that I should know about?'

Myriam returned with bowls of bread and butter pudding. 'I took him down to the clearing by the cascade,' she said. A jug of cream appeared on the table. 'There is a very dramatic view of the castle there.'

'Ah, I see,' Noah said. 'And Jacob, being a curious and intelligent young man, asked about its recent past?'

'Actually,' Jacob said. 'I made a number of guesses which Miriam didn't deny.' He looked across at her. "In fact, she effectively confirmed them.'

Myriam nodded quietly, her eyes towards the table.

Jacob looked back at Noah. 'The whole story made me so angry that I don't understand how you can just sit here while that monster still lords it over you from the castle.'

'Ye think I should rise up and seek vengeance?' Noah asked.

Jacob nodded.

'We did. When we found out that … what had happened, the whole village rose up and took a terrible vengeance on the Laird. It did us no good and our present troubles all stem from that night.'

'You could get the villagers to band together again and oppose him,' Jacob said. 'After what I saw at that meeting today, they'd be happy to do it. If you said the word, they'd go.'

'Aye, I could rally them,' Noah took a deep breath and looked down at his hands, 'and we would defeat him, but our victory would cost the lives of the six young men he has in his thrall. That's not a price I'm prepared to pay. So – I can sit here and wallow in resentment and bitterness or I can get on with life. I choose to live.'

'He was your brother, or your half-brother at least, and he raped your wife!' Jacob said grimly.

'Aye he did,' Noah answered calmly, 'and if he hadn't, my beautiful Rebecca might still be with me. Still, God is good. He gave me Myriam whom I love as my own daughter.'

Jacob was silent for a long time before he said, 'I don't doubt it, sir. You are a good man. A better man than I will ever be.'

Noah chuckled. 'Time will tell,' he said. 'Time will tell. Eat up. Yer pudding is getting cold and you still haven't told me why ye and Myriam are so quiet tonight.'

'That'll be between us, Da,' Myriam said as she put a large mug of tea in front of Noah, 'and it'll stay between us. Don't pick the scab of a wound you can't bandage.' Noah raised his eyebrow at Jacob but Jacob made no response.

After dinner they went into the front room to sit by the fire. Before they sat down, however, Noah called for a toast and three glasses of wine appeared in their hands. Jacob almost dropped his in surprise.

'To Rebecca,' Noah called.

Jacob stood up straight, as if standing to attention, and raised his glass. 'To Rebecca,' he echoed.

'To my Ma,' Myriam said softly.

After the toast, the glasses disappeared and they settled down into the chairs around the fire. Myriam started to read from a book that sounded a bit like Mallory's 'Morte d'Arthur' and Jacob tried to stay awake and listen but the heat of the fire, the comfort of the chair, the emotional strain of the day and the physical effort of the afternoon, all proved too much. Soon, no matter how hard he tried to hold it erect, his head was falling onto his chest and he was drifting off to sleep.

He was watching the traffic on the dusty road. His pack and his weapon were heavy. It had been a long day. The donkey cart bringing a load of tomatoes in from the country was slow, the bus from the school in the next village would get there first. It was a bit early. He felt a tap on his shoulder. He turned around and Noah was standing there. How could he be here? He didn't belong in this place.

'Wake up, Jacob,' he said. 'The time for this dream has passed.'

Jacob woke with a start. He was still sitting in the chair. Myriam had stopped reading and was looking at him with an annoyed expression on her face. Clearly, he hadn't been forgiven and falling asleep while she was reading hadn't helped.

Noah was also watching him with a strange intensity. 'I think it might be time for ye to get to bed, Jacob,' he said. 'If ye get a good run at it, you might be able to finish that wall tomorrow.'

Jacob nodded and stood up. 'Right,' he said. 'Sorry Myriam, I love to hear you read but it's been a hard day. Goodnight to you both.'

He was halfway to his small room when he felt a hand on his arm. Myriam was standing there. 'Jacob,' she said. 'It's been a long time since I've been able to dream you, a long time without the sharing of our dreams…'

Jacob shook his head firmly. 'No,' he said. 'Trust me, if you can't see my dreams then that's a good thing. You really don't want to share what happens in my dreams.' He paused and looked across at Noah who was still sitting by the fire. 'I keep going back … I can't escape …'

'Don't worry,' she said quickly. 'Okay, I accept that you're trying to protect me and I really don't want to know what happened in that place. At least, not until you're able to tell me.' She hesitated and then said in a rush, 'What I was going to suggest was that you share my dreams.' Jacob looked at her confused. 'I know it might seem strange but, if you would let it happen, I think it would help you to understand.' She paused. 'Then you wouldn't need to ask so many questions,' she whispered.

'It's already happened, a little, I think,' he mumbled. He looked at her in silence for a long moment. Then he smiled. 'Dream your memories? Yes, I would like that,' he said.

'Good,' said Myriam. Then she turned and went back to the fire.

* * *

It was strange. He knew who he was and he knew that he was somehow dreaming Myriam's memories. Yet he was seeing the world through the eyes of a little girl, he was feeling her thoughts, and this was profoundly unsettling. It was a bright spring day and she was playing in what was recognisably the front garden, although it, and the cottage behind it, looked huge. The flowers seemed unnaturally bright and Jacob immediately doubted the objective accuracy of these memories.

There was a butterfly with intricate patterning on its wings. It seemed as big as a bird. The young Myriam badly wanted the butterfly to come and to land on her hand. The world seemed to dissolve into hundreds of possibilities, all happening at once: the butterfly stayed where it was; the butterfly flew away in every possible direction; the butterfly flew past Myriam; the butterfly landed on her hand. All of these things existed, all of them happened, until Myriam made her choice and the butterfly was sitting on her hand, delighting her with its beauty.

In his dream state, Jacob knew that Myriam had called the butterfly to her using magic. Even while dreaming, his mind tried to analyse what he had experienced: the use of magic as an ordinary part of life. The young Myriam saw nothing unusual in the calling of the butterfly and, sharing her feelings, Jacob didn't either. It simply was what it was. She laughed as the butterfly flew away and she chased it happily across the garden.

When she came to the gate it was closed and she was too short to reach up and open it. Again the world dissolved into multiple realities. In most of these the gate was latched and stayed latched. It some very few, distant and hard to see, the latch spontaneously came free and the gate swung open. The young Myriam tried hard to see these possibilities clearly enough to choose them, but they eluded her and the gate stayed shut. As he watched the dream memory, Jacob realised that magic was hard. It took effort and skill. Opening the gate was beyond the young Myriam's ability, although not by much.

Arms reached down, grabbed her and lifted her easily over the gate. 'Don't worry, Myri,' Joshua said. 'Don't worry. I've got you.' Her big brother carried her effortlessly down the path to where Noah was pruning one of the chestnut trees. Noah had more traces of red in his hair, but otherwise his appearance was not that different from what it was when Jacob was awake. There was no mistaking the calm confidence and power of that figure. Jacob felt Myriam's comfort and content. It was a feeling he had not known in a long time. Noah and Joshua: here were the two secure poles of Myriam's world.

Carried securely in his arms, Myriam hugged Joshua and smiled happily. To her, he seemed huge, grown up and strong, although Jacob could see that he was, in fact, a boy barely in his teens. The dream faded to darkness.

Later, Jacob again slipped into dreaming Myriam's memories. Judging by the apparent size of the house, she was now older as she lay on her bed and stared into the dark. All her earlier feelings of content and home were gone. Her mind was balanced close to the edge of panic. All around her the world shimmered with a thousand possibilities: nothing was certain or stable. She had tried, again and again, to choose, to make the world resolve itself, but had found that she couldn't. Someone else was doing this. Someone else was about to choose for her, for the whole village, and that knowledge filled her with dread.

The world stabilised, a choice had been made. She screamed as the stars outside her window spun and blurred. When the stars were fixed again, the familiar hills were gone and the valley was surrounded by tall mountains; sharp, hard and covered with ice and snow. She screamed again and ran from her bed crying with fear and shock. Noah and Joshua were already in the main room as she scrambled down the steps from her loft. Joshua was now a young man in his late teens or early twenties. He had a pleasant, open face with laughter lines already beginning to form around his eyes.

Noah looked just the same as when Jacob first met him. He was standing at the open door looking out. Joshua grabbed Myriam as she ran to him and held her close, as much to comfort himself as her.

'What is it Da? What has happened?' Joshua called, still, in that moment, sounding very much like a small boy looking to his father.

'Nothing good,' Noah replied slowly, 'We are not now where we were and judging by the stars, we are not when we were either. This is the devil's work, the devil and the Laird together I'll warrant. Who else could do such a thing? God help us all. What has he done?'

The dream skipped. It was morning and Myriam was running down the village street towards the church. All the villagers were out on the street, pointing at the strange mountains that now surrounded them. The men were angry and confused, the children were crying, their mothers trying vainly to comfort them, filled with their own fear. Myriam ignored the panicked villagers. She knew that she had to get to the church. Only there could she find any sense in a world gone crazy. As she ran, Myriam prayed hard that God would show Father Augustus the way to make the world normal again. Jacob was running up the village street with Myriam, towards the cross at the end. There was a piece of blue velvet lying at the foot of the cross.

'Please let it be just a piece of cloth,' he prayed. 'Let it be something someone has just dropped, some random piece of rubbish…' But it wasn't. It was her party dress: pretty, made of blue velvet and trimmed with white lace. He woke screaming and stared into the early morning grey, shaking uncontrollably.

He came quietly to the kitchen when he heard the sounds of breakfast being prepared. Noah had already finished eating his porridge and was drinking his tea when he arrived. Jacob said a simple 'morning' as he sat down. Miriam's eyes searched his face but she gave him no greeting as she put a plate of porridge and a large mug of milky tea in front of him. He smiled, trying to see in her the small child who couldn't reach the gate latch.

'I was out in the garden early, and ye've really made much better progress than I expected on that wall,' Noah said. 'How much do ye think ye'll get done today?'

'I think you were probably right last night,' Jacob answered, 'If all goes well, I should be able to finish.'

'Good, there's lots more for you to do,' Noah replied. He finished his tea and got up from the table. 'Finish your breakfast. We'll talk later.'

As soon as he had left the kitchen, Myriam sat opposite Jacob. She stared at him in silence for a few moments. Then she said, 'Jacob, there are things I need to know.'

He put his mug down firmly and looked at her warily. 'I told you yesterday,' he said. 'Wasn't that enough? It was a terrible place, I saw terrible things, did terrible things. Leave it at that! I don't want to go over it again. It does no good.'

'But we have begun to share our dreams again,' she said, 'and your experiences frighten me. I need to be prepared for what I might see. Tell me about the blue dress.'

Jacob shook his head. 'No,' he said. 'No way! I would never have agreed to this dream sharing thing if I had thought you would see that. I was supposed to share your dreams. That was our deal. You can't come inside my dreams. You just can't!'

Myriam leaned across the table and spoke softly and gently, as if to a child. 'Jacob, I didn't choose what happened last night. I have some control but dreams can be wild and unpredictable things.'

'Then we won't share dreams,' Jacob said stubbornly.

Myriam shook her head. 'It doesn't work that way. I'm a dreamwalker, Jacob. It's part of who I am and we have been dreamkin for many years. It's a powerful bond. While we were separated by space and time, it could be suppressed but now that we are living so close ... Jacob, I need to know about the blue dress. I need to be prepared, to know what I'm dealing with.'

Jacob stared at his porridge in silence. Eventually he said, 'She was the daughter of the head man of the village. The terrorists killed her by decapitation and left her body in the street. It was an evil, barbaric thing to do but she wasn't the only one. Things like that ... things happened...'

'And the horror of it still haunts you,' Myriam said. 'I know. I felt your revulsion. Jacob, you don't need to protect me. Aye, I experience these things through you but only as a dream. To me, this is a bitterly sad story but it's one I know from a dream. You know it as a lived reality. It won't have the same effect on me that it had on you, especially not if I know what's coming, if it's not a surprise.'

Jacob took a long drink of his tea, then cradled his mug in his hand. He considered his options. Eventually he said, 'In that case, there are some things you need to know.' He told her the story of young John Brunetti's death, of the bombing at the roadblock and all the details of the village crucifixions. He told her of the constant threat, of never knowing where your enemy might be, of the need to be always on your guard. He told it simply, quickly and without emotion, as if he were giving an operation report. 'The whole place was a bit of a hell hole and the whole operation a disaster really,' he said. 'The pressure never leaves you. You get used to the need to be constantly alert, to the idea that there is no safety, only constant threat. It becomes a part of you, a part you can't leave behind, even when it's no longer true...' He paused. 'However, it's those three incidents, in particular, that haunt me. Evil, cruel, dangerous and pointless, they seem to sum up the whole mess.'

When he had finished, Myriam's face had softened. She had tears running down her cheeks. She reached across the table and took his hands in hers. 'Poor Jacob,' she said. 'You carry all of that. I don't know how you manage.'

'Not well,' he replied. 'but I do the best I can.'

* * *

Two men sat under one of the chestnut trees and watched Jacob working on the wall. They watched his work with detached interest.

161

'Just what is your endgame in all this?' one of them asked the other. 'I don't mean just stopping me. What are you really hoping to achieve? What do you get out of it?'

'Their happiness,' the other replied.

'You think they can be happy by sharing that which makes them miserable?' the first asked sarcastically.

The other nodded. 'By sharing? Yes.'

'Again, what do you get out of it?'

'I will rejoice in their happiness just as you would have them share your misery.'

'Stupid,' the first said bitterly. 'You'll never get to rejoice on their account. The sadness of their past will always contaminate any possibility of happiness.'

The other man considered this. 'I would say flavour rather than contaminate,' he said eventually. 'It will add a richness and a depth that wouldn't be there otherwise.'

The first man grunted his dismissal: 'Romantic nonsense.'

'But I am a romantic,' the other man said smiling. 'I always have been.'

'He's angry,' the first man insisted, pointing at Jacob. 'He's angry at all the past hurt, both his own and hers. He'll fight and he'll kill and all you hope for will be lost.'

His companion shook his head and gave a sad smile. 'You understand nothing.'

'I understand that he's a soldier, a trained killer. What do you expect him to do?'

'He's a man, an image of the living God.'

'You're a fool!' the first man insisted.

The other man shrugged. 'Maybe. You've certainly made that comment before. We'll see.'

CHAPTER EIGHTEEN

The Second Battle

Select, lift, place. One stone after another. Rebuilding the wall was like doing a great jigsaw puzzle; a jigsaw puzzle that required a lot of effort and strain. In the last section of the wall, he had already placed most of the heavy basal stones and was now working with progressively lighter stones as he worked his way to the higher rows. By mid-morning, he was happy with his progress. If he was able to keep working at this rate, he would finish the wall well before evening. He very deliberately did not think about what would happen after that.

Jacob knew that this wall had, in a very real sense, saved him. It had forced his mind to concentrate on a present, here and now, problem and had exhausted his body so that he ate and slept properly even in the midst of trauma. It had given him an outlet for his emotional energy. It wasn't really the wall, of course. It was Noah, who had known, perhaps from personal experience, what he needed. Jacob didn't know what would happen when he finished. Noah had hinted at other work but he also knew that in a few days the village would be moving on and he would have to leave. He found the prospect hugely unattractive and turned his mind from it. Select, lift, place.

It was around this time that Myriam came out with some mugs of apple cider. 'Time for a break,' she said coolly. 'Da will be along soon.'

He straightened up, his back stiff from lifting. 'Thanks,' he said, as he took one of the mugs. He was thirsty and drank deeply. As he put the mug back on the tray, he heard a low rumbling sound that was getting louder.

Myriam looked anxiously in the direction of the village. 'It's just the Riders,' she said, 'doing their normal thing.' Only the sound didn't stop but kept getting louder. Soon it could be clearly distinguished as the sound of galloping horses. They obviously hadn't stopped at the end of the village and Jacob turned to face them as they swung into view and galloped between the chestnut trees at breakneck speed. All six of them were there: dressed in black and riding jet black horses: all with Scottish claymores slung across their backs.

Jacob stepped through the gate and closed it behind him, instinctively putting barriers between the Riders and Myriam. He didn't know why they had changed from their normal pattern but he knew it wasn't to make a pleasant social call.

It wasn't a situation he had ever been trained to face, nonetheless, his mind automatically started to analyse his situation. 'They're on horseback which gives them a massive advantage in power. They also outnumber me six to one. They are armed and I have no weapons to speak of.' He entered into the strange, fatalistic calm that came over him before a battle. 'The horses are their strength but maybe also a weak point. They're naturally nervous animals and I doubt these have been all that well trained. If I can panic the horses I may have a chance.' The Riders skidded to a halt in front of him. 'Attack the legs... possible but risky, those hooves can be lethal. Maybe better to dive underneath and take the risk of being trampled.' Jacob shook his head. None of this seemed very practical. If he had access to some sort of weapon it might be different.

The rider Joshua walked his horse a few steps forward and addressed Jacob, 'The Laird has told us to bring you back alive and as uninjured as possible.'

Myriam cried out, 'Joshua!' All the anguish of her loss was in her voice but he ignored her and continued to look at Jacob: flat and dead eyed. The contrast with the laughing youth who had picked up the young Myriam from behind that same gate was heartbreaking, even for Jacob who had only known the earlier Joshua in a dream.

'I don't think I want to go with you,' Jacob said slowly, still trying to work out how one man on foot could defeat six on horseback. So far, no brilliant plan had presented itself.

'What you want doesn't matter,' Joshua said, without any apparent concern or interest. 'You can't defeat the six of us, so you will come with us. The only question is how badly hurt you will be in the process' Jacob gave up any pretence at planning and decided to simply react and hope his instincts worked well.

'No!' The voice came from behind and to the left of them. It was full of authority and power. Noah came striding in from the fields. With a broad brimmed hat on his head and carrying a shepherd's crook in his hand. He looked for all the world like some wizard from a fantasy novel. Jacob again had the feeling that he had somehow stepped into a movie or a fairy tale.

'This is my land and Jacob is my guest. He is under my protection,' Noah said, as he placed himself between Jacob and the Riders. 'Here the Laird has neither right nor authority.'

'Maybe not,' Joshua said, 'but it doesn't matter. He has the power. We will do what he says.' The Riders started to fan out and walk towards Noah and Jacob.

Behind the gate, Myriam cried out, 'No Joshua! Josh, please! Please don't!' Joshua took no notice.

'Go back,' Noah said. His voice still full of command. 'Go back and tell the Laird that he would be most unwise to challenge me.' The Riders kept advancing.

Noah raised his arms, holding the shepherd's crook above his head. The Riders were advancing slowly, moving to encircle Jacob and Noah. Then the wind started to blow. It blew directly from the cottage and up the chestnut lined lane, from behind Noah and directly towards the horses. It got stronger and colder. Noah's hat flew from his head and his long white hair streamed about him in the wind. The horses started to get restive at the cold wind in their faces. Soon there was dust and sleet in the wind and the horses started to dance, becoming hard for the Riders to control, trying to turn their backs to the wind. Bits of bush and tree branch joined the debris blowing directly towards the Riders as the wind reached gale force. Eventually one of the Riders lost control. His horse, panicked by being hit by a small branch, spun around and fled back up the lane. This triggered a reaction in the other horses as they too turned and fled.

Only one rider managed to regain some control of his horse while still in the lane. Joshua pulled his horse to a halt and managed to coax it around, still dancing and panicky. He looked back at the three of them standing around the cottage gate. Just for a moment, Jacob thought he saw the blankness pass from Joshua's eyes, to be replaced by human feeling. Just for a moment, there was a trace of a smile and an expression of fondness and pride, perhaps a pride that his family could resist the power of the Laird, even if he couldn't. It was hard to be sure. He was a long way up the lane and it was only the most fleeting of glimpses before the blankness returned.

'We will wait for a time when you are not around to protect him,' Joshua called back, without any trace of feeling. He then turned his horse around and followed the others back up the lane.

'Josh!' Myriam called out desperately. 'Josh, come back!' Noah stood, still and silent, as the wind died down about him and Joshua and the other riders disappeared from view. Myriam was crying softly at the gate, her tears rolling silently down her cheeks. Jacob wondered which was worse; a continuing blank nothingness or being given a fleeting glimpse of the person he once was, only to have it taken away again.

Noah didn't move. He stood watching the place where the Riders had turned and disappeared. His face showed no expression, it was as still and as hard as if it had been carved from granite, yet there was a tense energy about him, like a predator watching its prey.

Eventually, he turned and looked at Myriam. 'He isn't safe,' he said. 'Ye know what ye need to do.' Myriam took a deep breath, then nodded and walked back to the cottage. 'Ye go too,' Noah said to Jacob.

'I haven't finished the fence,' Jacob objected.

'Forget the fence!' Noah said abruptly. 'Go with Myriam.' He then walked up the lane to collect his hat and disappeared off into the fields.

Jacob frowned. The display of magic power no longer surprised him but Noah's subsequent actions annoyed him deeply. Was the wall a real job or not? Was it just make-work, designed to keep him busy, safely occupied, while they planned what to do with him? His frown deepened. He wasn't a child to be protected and coddled and he didn't like people planning his life without telling him. He hadn't liked it in the army and he didn't like it now. Still frowning, he turned and followed Myriam into the cottage.

As he came in the front door, Myriam was putting on her cloak and Jacob noticed his pack, full and all strapped up, leaning against the wall.

'Am I going somewhere?' he asked.

'Aye, ye're leaving,' Myriam said. She grabbed his hand and started to try and drag him from the cottage. 'Come on. We don't have much time.'

She came to a stop as Jacob easily resisted her pull. 'Where are we going?' he asked quietly. 'And why now and in such a hurry? I don't like doing things without knowing the reason.'

'Please, I can't explain now,' Myriam said desperately. 'We've got to go. We don't have much time. The Laird will respond with even more force. We need to keep one step ahead of him.'

Jacob thought about it for a moment. Given some time, a weapon, and a bit of preparation, he was fairly sure he could handle the six riders but he didn't know the extent of the Laird's magical ability. Eventually he nodded and let her lead him from the cottage. He'd let it play out and see what happened.

She led him back up the lane, almost running in her haste. When they got to the main road, they turned left, away from the village, back the way he had come on his first day with Myriam. They walked along the path, towards the two oak trees that stood as guardians to the ravine entrance. There he saw his pack, already leaning against a rock at the start of the ravine.

'You're leading me out of the valley. Why?' he asked.

Myriam was still breathless from the pace of their walk. 'The valley will be moving on soon,' she said. 'If you don't go now, you could be stuck here.' She wasn't a good liar and she didn't sound convincing.

Jacob shook his head. 'I don't think so. You said that before the village moves, all the visitors are seized by an overwhelming desire to leave. I don't feel that. Quite the reverse in fact. Myriam, I'd like to stay here with you.'

Miriam looked at him with tears in her eyes. 'I'd like that too,' she said, trying to control her voice. 'I'd like that more than anything, but it just can't be. Look, I know you're a capable soldier and you might even be able to defeat the Riders but you think of this as if it's some sort of fairy story and you're just waiting for the happy ending. But this isn't like that. It just isn't. The Laird is after you and he has spies everywhere. He wants to get at Da and me through you and I think he'll try to do to you what he's done to Joshua and the others. I couldn't stand it if that happened, I just couldn't. You need to leave. You're not safe.'

Jacob shook his head firmly. 'No,' he said. 'I don't need to be safe and I don't want to leave…' He stopped and then continued in a softer voice. 'Myriam, I don't want to leave you. Yes, this all seems like some crazy dream but it's a good dream and when I came here, all I had were the nightmares and the memories of …' He shook his head to dismiss the thought. 'Here, at least I have you. If this is a dream, then it is a beautiful one. All of it…' He waved his arms wide in the direction of the village. 'The cottage, the village, Father Augustus; if it is a dream then I want to dream on. If it's all an hallucination, then I don't want reality. If I leave, I go back to being alone in a dark, empty place where, sometimes, even putting one foot in front of the other is just too hard…'

Myriam hugged him suddenly and fiercely. 'You will not be alone,' she said into his shoulder. 'We are dreamkin, remember. And you can dream me now, just as

I have always been able to dream you.' She drew back and looked him in the eye. 'I have always loved you, Jacob. I have loved you ever since I knew what it meant to love. It doesn't matter how dark or empty your world may be, I will always be with you.'

'In dreams,' Jacob said. 'Not good enough, not nearly good enough.' She looked at him anxiously, her wild red hair framing her pale face, but he didn't say anything else. Instead, he leaned forward, held her to himself, and kissed her softly on the lips. For a moment, she returned his kiss but then she pulled back.

'Please don't,' she said. 'You're only making this more difficult.'

'Myriam, I wish I could say that I have always loved you, but I can't. As far as I know, I've only known you for a few days. If we shared the dreams of or childhood, then my greatest regret is that I can't remember them. I was a lonely child and I would have loved to have you as my friend.' He paused. 'I can't say I have loved you since childhood, but what I can say is that I have loved you for as long as I've known you, from the very first time I saw you, and that, in the other world, I was sure I would never love again... I'm broken, Myriam. What happened in that other place...I can't shake it... but with you I think I could maybe hold it together. Without you...I just don't know.'

'You will always have me. Always! But you must leave! If the Laird gets hold of you, then you will be lost. If he turns you into the same sort of living-death as Josh...' She couldn't continue. He looked at her. She was overcome with tears and grief. Then he held her close and gently kissed the top of her forehead.

'Please go,' she said softly. 'Please, for my sake, just go.'

He nodded silently as he released her. Then he turned without a word, picked up his pack, and walked back down the moss covered ravine. He turned to look back at the other end but she had already gone. He turned again to look back out at the world he had always known; a world where there was no magic and where 'rose covered cottage' was a description in a real estate brochure. He could see the walking track with the poles put there by the national park rangers to help people find their way when it snowed. He sighed. If all went well, he could be back in Hobart the day after tomorrow.

* * *

Two men, each of them dressed in fashionable hiking clothes, watched from the entrance to the ravine, as Jacob walked away from them.

'Well I must say that I didn't see that coming,' one of them said. 'I thought he'd run. I never thought she'd throw him out.'

His companion gave a sad little smile. 'That's because you don't appreciate how much these, to coin your terms, 'weak and broken things' are prepared to sacrifice for those they love. You think of love only in terms of sexual attraction. You don't understand love at all.'

'Do you?'

'Yes. In fact, it's the only thing I do truly understand.'

'Are you sure?'

'Yes, I'm sure.'

CHAPTER NINETEEN

Battery Point, Hobart

The first thing he was aware of was the hard mattress. As he slowly opened his eyes, he saw the narrow bed, the white bed clothes, and beige walls. That familiar, faintly antiseptic, smell confirmed that he was back in the hospital. When the orderly, sitting by the door saw that Jacob was awake, he smiled at him and got to his feet.

'Good morning,' he said. 'Glad to see you're back with us. I'll go and get the doctor.'

Jacob looked around him. Out the window, he could see Mt. Wellington, bathed in brilliant morning sunshine. He lay back on his bed with a sigh. He was back in Hobart, back in the rehab clinic at Battery Point. A few minutes later, a man in a white coat walked in. Jacob immediately recognised him as the Laird's crow, or Dr. Corvus as he would be here.

'Hello Jacob,' he said smiling. 'Tell me, are you with us today or are you somewhere else?'

'If you are at the rehab clinic on Battery Point, then I'm with you,' Jacob answered.

'Good,' Dr. Corvus said. 'You keep slipping away from us, sometimes quite physically.' He sat down at the foot of Jacob's bed, his face becoming serious. 'I'm afraid that what we have been doing so far has not been at all effective. We need to take more drastic measures. He retrieved a very large needle from a small tray on the bedside cupboard. 'I would like your permission, your cooperation. It would make this easier but you should know, we will do it anyway.'

'No,' Jacob said. 'You can't medicate me against my will.'

'I'm afraid I can, Jacob, and I will,' Dr. Corvus replied. 'Now relax, this is for your own good. It will help you forget.' Two orderlies appeared to hold him down. Jacob struggled to get free.

'No,' he said. 'No, no, no!' There was an image of Myriam clear in his mind. He didn't want to forget. He struggled free of the orderlies and struck Dr. Corvus in the chest, sending him flying across the room. He felt a sudden pain in his arm, then it all faded to black.

When he woke, he was again lying on the hard bed, only now something was holding him down. He couldn't move. He opened his eyes to see late afternoon sun flooding the room. He was alone and he was being held down by thick leather straps. He tried to rise but it was no use. The straps had been well designed and placed. He relaxed back into the bed. He turned his head to look out the window where the face of the mountain was now covered in shadow.

He tried to sort things out. He was in Hobart and it was twice now that he had woken here. It didn't seem like a dream anymore and the straps that were holding him felt very real. Yet he didn't remember walking down from the mountains. She had, however, asked him to go, so it was possible that he had walked here. This realisation hit him like a physical blow. Even if this was a dream, this place was where he belonged. It had always been hopeless. Even if Myriam had not wanted him to leave, the curse would have meant that he would have had to leave anyway. His mind, however, kept coming back to the fact that Myriam had wanted him to leave. He would have faced any danger for her had she asked him to stay.

A nurse came into the room carrying a clipboard. 'Hi,' Jacob said. She only nodded in reply and pushed a button on the wall. A short time later, two very large male orderlies came in and stood by his bed. No one said anything to him but they all eyed him warily. It wasn't long before Dr. Corvus also came in. Jacob noticed that he took great care not to get too close to his bed.

'Jacob, where do you think you are?' he asked.

'I'm at Battery Point in Hobart, strapped to a bed,' Jacob said. 'Not something I find pleasant.'

Dr. Corvus let out a long breath and visibly relaxed. 'Good,' he said. 'It's working. The drug we gave you… Well, it was pretty much our last option to tell you the truth. But, it worked. It's kept you from lapsing back into your delusion.' He hesitated nervously. 'Now, Jacob,' he said, 'if we take off those straps, are you going to attack us?'

'That depends,' Jacob said. 'Are you going to try and stick needles in me against my will?'

Dr. Corvus shook his head. 'No need,' he said.

'Then I'm not going to attack you,' Jacob said.

'Okay then.' Dr. Corvus nodded to the two orderlies who started to loosen the straps. Both Dr. Corvus and the nurse stepped backwards.

When he was able to, Jacob sat up and rubbed his arms where the straps had been. 'How long have I been here?' he asked.

'Several days,' Dr. Corvus said. 'Although for most of that time you have been raving and quite out of your head. I can't tell you how pleased I am to have you back and rational again. Now, the long term treatment can begin. We are going to get you well again, Jacob. You do want to be well again don't you?'

He nodded. 'Yes,' he mumbled. She had asked him to leave. 'I want to be well again.'

'Good,' Dr. Corvus said. He nodded to the nurse who left the room and returned a short time later with a bottle of red liquid and a glass. Dr. Corvus took the bottle and poured a careful measure of the liquid into the glass. It was a thick, red syrup that flowed like honey. 'The label says that this has a pleasant raspberry flavour,' he said. 'Although, by the look on my patients' faces when they drink it, I'm inclined to doubt it. It will, however, stop the delusions from returning. It will calm your mind and take away your pain.' He didn't approach the bed but gave the glass to one of the orderlies. 'I'm going to ask you to drink this, Jacob. Ask, not force. The results will be more permanent if you cooperate. Please drink it.'

Jacob took the glass from the orderly. It smelled sickly sweet. He looked around the room. The walls were hard and clear, finished with a high gloss paint. 'Beige with red trim, whoever thought that was a good colour scheme?' She'd asked him to leave but that didn't really matter because people weren't magic and dreams were just random images floating up in your unconscious mind. You couldn't really meet people in dreams.

He looked down at the glass again. 'Why the hell not?' he thought. 'She asked me to leave.' He drank the liquid in one gulp. The taste was foul. Dr. Corvus smiled. It was not a pleasant smile.

* * *

It was later that day, he was standing by the window of his room. The whole of the city was now dark in the shadow of the mountain, although the tops of some of the nearby hills glowed red with the light of the setting sun. His dinner lay, getting cold, on a tray near his bed. He felt calm and quiet. So calm, in fact, that he really didn't feel

175

anything at all. The nurse came in and scolded him for not eating his dinner. She was chatty now, very different from her earlier taciturn mood.

'The doctor wants you to go out tomorrow,' she said. 'So, I'll just lay out these clothes for you.' She laid them on a chair next to the bed. They were black, all black. 'Get some sleep now,' she said. She smiled at him as she left.

'Yes, I will. Thank you,' Jacob said after her in a flat, almost toneless, voice. In the corner of his room, he thought he saw an image of a young woman with wild, red hair. She was on her knees and crying.

'O Lord, keep him safe,' she was saying. 'O Lord, please keep him safe.' He didn't take any notice. Dr. Corvus had told him to be wary of lapsing back into delusion.

CHAPTER TWENTY

Greetings and Blessings

He knew he was dreaming because he was seeing the world through the eyes of a little girl. The young Myriam was planting vegetable seedlings with Noah and a teenage Joshua. She was cross because she wanted to be somewhere else and she found the planting to be hard and dirty work. Noah looked a bit younger, his beard wasn't as long, but he was still as taciturn as ever. Joshua kept trying to cheer Myriam up, telling jokes and encouraging her. This only made her more cross and she dug fiercely in the dirt.

Dirt was lying in piles and rising as dust in the dry air. Then they found the first of the bodies. The excavator had damaged it but otherwise it was in remarkably good condition, the Australian flag showing bright blue. He realised that it was him, it was his face. He reached out to touch it but his hand hit cold canvas. He was in a body bag! They thought he was dead! He screamed and fought against the restraining cloth but it was no use. They couldn't hear him. They were going to bury him!

His struggles forced him awake. For a moment he still fought against the cloth that surrounded him until he remembered where he was. It was not a body bag. He was in his sleeping bag and swag. He lay still for a moment, shaking off the vestiges of the dream. He was alone in his camp, high in the mountains. All was as it should be. He was safe. No one was trying to kill him or bury him.

It slowly dawned on him that, in fact, something was wrong. Why was he here? Why wasn't he in hospital in

Hobart? He felt the panic begin to rise in his chest. This couldn't be real. Yet it felt real. His sleeping bag and swag were as familiar to him as old friends. He tried to reason his way back to calm. There were really only two possibilities. Either he was still in his bed in the Hobart ward and had slipped back into delusion, or this was real, in which case, it was the hospital ward in Hobart that had been some kind of weird dream. How could he know?

Trying to think this through was only making things worse. The panic kept rising. Certainly, the village and the Riders sounded like something from some mad, psychotic delusion, but why had the hospital given him an outfit of all black clothes. It wasn't something he'd normally wear. The wind blowing through the trees near his camp felt real enough. But then it would, wouldn't it. How could he decide what was real and what was not when he had no reliable data?

'You have her.' The thought came unbidden into his mind. He remembered Myriam then, remembered her walking through the mist in her deep, blue cloak, remembered her with the sunlight shining gold through the tangle of her hair ... remembered the fire warming her pale skin as she read softly from an ancient romance. The panic began to subside and he lay back and tried to relax, listening only to the wind blowing softly through the trees.

He lay still, trying to control his breathing. This wasn't a problem he could solve tonight. He remembered the deep breathing exercises the shrinks had taught him. He concentrated on feeling his breath flowing: in and out. Eventually he calmed down enough to relax once more, back into sleep and into dreams.

He knew he was dreaming because he was again experiencing the world from Myriam's point of view, not the young Myriam this time but the current one. She was lying on a large bed under the low roof of the cottage, weeping into her pillow. He wanted to reach out to her, to comfort her, to say it would be alright, but he was trapped in a dream. She stopped crying and a word formed in her mind: 'Jacob?' He remembered nothing else until he was woken by the rising sun.

The sun was just above the horizon when Jacob washed himself as best he could, dressed, boiled some water on his small, solid fuel stove, and made himself breakfast. He then went through his pack, taking out those few things he might need and stowing those things he wouldn't. He strapped on his boots, hid his pack behind the oak tree he had slept under and walked down the path towards the village.

He had made a decision. Worrying about what was real and what was not real was a waste of time. All he could do was do the best he could in the world as it presented itself to him. Here and now, in this place, there was a task he had to perform. One thing the army had taught him was that you didn't always understand the big picture, or get to choose or like the duty you were given, but if it was your job, you did it. This was his task, given to him because it needed to be done and he was the only one who could do it. He had a duty to Myriam and to the people of the village. It was time to pay the Laird a visit.

Jacob deliberately chose not to even look down the lane that led to Myriam's cottage as he walked past. It was better if she thought that he had gone back to his old life. This was something he would have to do on his own and without help. At least, without the normal sort of help. In the bright morning sun, the village seemed to him to be even more like an image from a fairy story. All the buildings could have been from a painting. Even the people, dressed in their heavy tunics and cloaks, seemed to have stepped from some story book.

There was no sound from the blacksmith's shop as he passed, although the lanterns hung about it were still burning. The lady at the weaver's shop smiled at him as she opened up. The looms had yet to start their clacking. The butcher was busy herding some sheep into yards at the back of his shop. Jacob smiled grimly. Those sheep were about to have a very bad day. The tavern keeper was cleaning up from the night before, sweeping rubbish out into the street, where some cats eagerly awaited whatever food scrapes the rubbish might contain. Jacob ignored his cheery greeting and walked straight on, his eyes fixed on the church ahead.

A small girl ran out in front of him, holding a large mug in her hands. 'Ma said ye might appreciate this,' she said breathlessly. He looked down at her in surprise. She was maybe six or seven and dressed in blue; not blue velvet but a thick woollen cloak of sky blue. It matched her bright blue eyes, and curly blond hair framed her innocent face. She smiled up at him expectantly, holding out the pewter mug. He felt his pulse begin to race as memories threatened to flood in.

'Thank you,' he said, taking the mug from her and sipping its contents. It was a hot, bitter herbal tea with a sharpness that assaulted his senses. He drank a little more and all traces of sleep left his mind. He felt more alert than he had ever been before and viewed the morning with a clarity he had never known. He drained the mug and handed it back to the girl.

'What's your name?' he asked.

'Molly,' she said, making a small curtsy.

'Well Molly, thank your Ma very much from me,' he said. 'Tell her that it was much appreciated.' She smiled and ran back to one of the houses. Jacob looked around him and realised that the whole village was watching him, either openly or from behind their curtained windows. It was as if they knew what he was about to do. He gave a slight bow to each side of the street, acknowledging their interest, before continuing on to the church. It was good to have support, no matter how hidden it was and how ineffective it would be in the end.

The front door opened as he got to the church and Father Augustus stood there, in his black cassock and white cotta, with a purple stole around his neck. 'Come in, Jacob,' he said. 'I've been waiting for you.'

It was quiet inside the church, now that rain was not beating against the roof. It was dark after the morning sun - and cold, since the day had not had time to take the chill from the stones. Father Augustus led him to the side of the church where there was a wooden bench against the wall. The priest motioned for him to sit.

'Father, I have only come for a blessing,' he protested. 'I intend to bring this to an end, no matter what you say.'

'I know boy, I know,' the old priest said. 'I don't even disagree with you. That was always the choice, either you left or you went to confront the Laird. Last night, you chose to stay. I will gladly give you God's blessing but first there are some things you should know. The Laird is a broken man, both physically and spiritually. Virtually all his magical ability is gone.'

'Not all of it, Father,' Jacob said grimly. 'I think he still has the power to invade dreams.'

'Yes, that is known,' the old priest confirmed. 'I believe I warned you about it when we first met. Still, he is no threat to you directly, physically. His one remaining weapon is his voice and his power to influence the mind. He will try to persuade you to agree to become like the

Riders. He will need to get you to agree. He will not be able to do that to you against your will.'

'He must know that there's no way I would ever agree to that,' Jacob said.

Father Augustus shook his head. 'Do not underestimate him. He is subtle and cunning. He will twist truth and lie together so that it will be hard to tell one from the other. You must be very wary of saying yes to anything he proposes; even if it's only to agree that it's a nice day.'

Jacob nodded. 'What about the Riders?' he asked.

'I very much doubt that the Laird will use them against you while there is still a chance that you could be persuaded,' the priest said. 'But once he has decided that the cause is hopeless, he will get them to attack you without mercy or pause. There are six of them and they will be armed. You need to be prepared.'

Jacob smiled grimly. 'I don't know that much about sword play but these riders are farm boys. They will probably handle their swords like clubs...' He stopped speaking as he saw the wave of sadness pass across the priest's time worn face.

'Yes, you're right. They're farm boys, or at least they once were,' the priest said softly. He stood up suddenly. 'Come,' he said firmly, 'and I will give you God's blessing.' He brought Jacob to the centre of the rood screen. There Jacob knelt beneath the crucifix and the priest placed his hands on his head.

He prayed: 'Look upon your servant, Jacob. O God, our protector, and defend him from the perils and snares of the enemy. May your gaze be upon him and keep him safe. *Benedicat vos omnipotens Deus, Pater, et Filius, et Spiritus*

Sanctus.' He traced the sign of the cross in the air above Jacob's head. '*Dominus vobiscum*, Jacob.'

'Um … Thanks Father,' he said. He knew it wasn't the right response but Father Augustus didn't seem to mind. Jacob got up and bowed awkwardly towards the altar, then turned and left the church, the priest following close behind. Now he was ready. Even in the madness of the other place he had been in the habit of seeking a blessing from the chaplain, whenever he could, before combat; even when he was angry and God had seemed cold and distant; even when he had long since ceased to pray. It just seemed right somehow. As an old soldier had once said to him, "In battle you need all the help you can get.'

He turned to shake hands with the priest before leaving, when he noticed someone running up from the village. It was the blacksmith and he was carrying a sword. Jacob and Father Augustus both waited as the blacksmith came running up to stand, panting, before them.

'Good, …' he gasped. 'I was afraid… I'd miss ye… I'm not much good… at running.' He gathered himself and paused, waiting to get his breath back. Then he held out the sword to Jacob. It was a heavy, double handed thing; finely worked in a sheath of tooled leather and with a broad shoulder strap. 'I only just finished it early this morning. I'm afraid it was a bit of a rushed job.'

Jacob looked at the sword but didn't take it. 'I'm sorry,' he said. 'Thank you for the effort and I'm sure it's a fine weapon, but I'm hoping to avoid a fight and if I can't, I'm not sure that a sword would be much help.'

The man shook his head and placed the sword in Jacob's hands. 'No, no,' he said. 'This isn't for ye. At least, it's not for ye to use. This is given to ye to give away. It's for ye to give to the one who needs it.'

'Who's that?' Jacob asked.

'Don't know,' the blacksmith said stepping back, 'but ye will, when the time comes. Anyway, I must be off. Old Rory MacAllister has a broken plough blade – again. I swear, that man must be farming rocks.' With that, he smiled at them, turned, and walked back into the town at a more sedate pace, leaving a bemused Jacob standing in front of the church. He turned and raised a quizzical eyebrow to Father Augustus.

'No need to look at me,' the old priest said, shaking his head. 'I know as little about it as you do. However, I would take notice of his words. He's a very skilled man, and not only in metal work.'

Jacob shrugged and slung the sword over his shoulder. 'Okay. Goodbye then, Father, and thank you – whatever happens' he said.

'Farewell, Jacob,' Father Augustus said. 'I'm sure God and his angels will protect you, and remember, the Laird will try to ensnare your mind. Hold on to what love you know because love is one thing he cannot understand and, though some think it soft, real love is tougher and stronger than steel.'

* * *

Jacob set off along the path he had seen the Riders take. It was a fairly broad path, rocky on the edges but worn smooth in the middle. In places, it looked as if it might once have been paved, or at least well formed, but it was rapidly becoming a horse track, worn only by the hooves of the Riders' horses. He hadn't gone far when he noticed a boy of about ten years old sitting by the side of the track. In his hands he held a large horn, made from a cow horn and bound in brass. He smiled and waved to the boy, who happily waved back. Obviously, the villagers had already put one of his suggestions into practice.

The path wound steeply up from the village and out of the valley, into hills covered by rock and heather where stunted oak trees struggled to grow in small crevasses and wind tormented pines gathered in the lee of rocks and hills.

He could see the castle tower and estimated that he was well over half way there when he heard horses riding fast towards him. It could only be the Riders, off on their morning gallop through the village, so he got off the path and waited for them to pass. As he expected, they rode past without taking any notice of him: no threats, no curiosity, not even a sideways glance. The sheer inhumanity of that blank response still chilled him. For a brief moment, he watched where they had gone. Then he shrugged off the strangeness of it and continued his walk to the castle. A little while later, he heard the horn sound. He smiled in satisfaction. At least now, the villagers would have some warning.

As he walked, from long habit he kept running through a mental check of his equipment: the heavy Gortex jacket, the long hunting knife hanging from his belt, the smaller one strapped to his ankle, the heavy sword slung across his back. He smiled as he found himself checking for ammunition he had no need of. He would certainly have felt more secure with his familiar Steyr assault rifle or even an old 9mm pistol, but those were impossible and, he hoped, unnecessary. As he had told the blacksmith, he hoped not to fight.

The Riders had still not returned from the village when he arrived at the castle. It was built of dark grey stone, with a tall keep rising above the right-hand corner of the bailey wall. The keep and the wall seemed to be in good condition although there had obviously been a number of smaller buildings around the outside of the wall that had long since fallen into ruin. All of this was abandoned and quiet with the ravens, calling and circling overhead, the only signs of life. A single figure emerged, however, as Jacob approached the open gate. It was the Crow, Dr. Corvus, the fiddler from the other night at the tavern. This time, however, he had neither fiddle nor white coat, but was dressed in a strange motley of brightly coloured cloth.

He bowed low to Jacob. 'The Laird is glad you have come,' he said. 'He is most keen to make your acquaintance. Please follow me.'

CHAPTER TWENTY-ONE

The Laird

The Crow led him across the castle courtyard and up a flight of steps to the main entrance to the keep. He entered through a low, arched doorway into a tiny, bare hall. A stone stairway spiralled off into the right hand wall. The Crow gave Jacob an insincere smile. He bowed and silently waved his hand to indicate that Jacob should climb the stairs. Jacob didn't bother to acknowledge him but simply turned and started up the stairs. Climbing the stairs turned out to be more difficult than Jacob had expected. The stairway was narrow and spiralled sharply to the left. Carrying the large, double handed sword across his back, Jacob found the climb difficult, especially as the steps were uneven and badly worn. Jacob noted, without consciously thinking about it, that this would make the upper reaches of the castle easy to defend. Attackers would find it hard to advance and even more difficult to retreat.

After several turns of the spiral, he entered directly into a large hall. This must once have been an impressive room. But now, the large fireplace was cold and filled with old ash. The tall slit windows were so grimy with dirt that even the bright sunlight struggled to penetrate the room. Furniture, rugs, and even old tapestries lay about the floor in untidy confusion. Everything was coated in a layer of dust and cobwebs and the whole room stank of decay and other, more unpleasant, things.

At the end of the room opposite Jacob there was a large table, clear of the debris that filled the rest of the room. On this there were two tarnished silver candlesticks, each with a single, burning candle. By their light, a hunched human figure could be seen sitting at the table, its head lying on its arms.

The figure lifted its head and an old man smiled at Jacob. 'Come in, come in,' he said. 'I have been most anxious to make contact with you.' His voice was weak but it flowed like warm honey.

Jacob walked forward, finding his way through the debris on the floor but always keeping his eyes on the seated figure. Age had not been kind to him. His skin was withered, yellow, and marked and his hair that was as long as Noah's, but thin and a dirty grey rather than silver. His eyes were sunken and dark. He didn't sit up straight, even as Jacob approached, but sat hunched over the table.

'I don't know how you perceive me now, Jacob, but I can assure you that I am not what you think me to be.' The Laird spoke softly but calmly. There was a friendliness and gentle welcome in the sweet, honeyed voice. 'You doubtless see me as some kind of threat, some sort of potential, if not actual, enemy. Yet I am not. I am the very opposite. I am a doctor, trying to bring you back to health, back to your normal, rational self.'

'I'm already rational,' Jacob said.

'I know you are, Jacob. I know you are and you have had some beautifully lucid moments. That's what gives us hope. Regardless of how you see me now, regardless of whatever mythical monster you believe me to be, I'm a doctor and I'm trying to cure you of your delusion. That is my sole concern.'

'What delusion?' Jacob asked cautiously. 'You don't look like a doctor to me and this certainly doesn't look like a hospital.'

'No, I daresay that to you it doesn't, but what you see isn't real. You're suffering from a psychotic delusion.

In your condition, you should never have gone off by yourself – and into the mountains too. That was almost guaranteed to bring on an episode. You were found unconscious by the side of the path by some walkers and then medevaced to Hobart. Since then you have been raving, whenever we let you wake that is: saying wild, crazy things; reliving your very worst memories. Jacob, you're very ill. Please let me help you.'

'I don't believe you,' Jacob said. 'I was warned not to trust anything you say.'

'I have no doubt that you were,' the Laird said in his soft, almost hypnotic voice. 'That was just your mind seeking to hold on to this cosy little fantasy you've built for yourself. Deep down you know that this can't be real, that it has to come to an end. But you wanted to hold on for as long as possible. So you set traps and barriers to stop reality from reasserting itself. All those who tried to help you were seen as the enemy.' He paused and took a deep breath. 'You hurt some of the nurses quite seriously the other day and poor old Dr. Corvus still carries his bruises.'

'I don't believe you,' Jacob said, shaking his head.

'Then let me see if I can convince you,' the Laird replied. 'You have been through a time when there was no safety anywhere, when you had to be constantly on alert. At the same time, your home and family in Australia ceased to exist in any real way. You had no security anywhere; no place that was safe and familiar. So, what does your mind do? It makes up just such a place.'

Jacob gave a mocking smile. 'Yeah, I've read all those books on pop psychology too.'

The Laird smiled and spread his hands wide, as if presenting something to Jacob. 'Home and comfort, the human soul craves it. The wounded human soul most of all. The village you apparently imagine yourself to be living in is just such a comforting fantasy. It's an ideal place made up of fragments of memory and old fairy stories. Ask yourself, could such a place really exist in the world as we know it. Of course not. This isn't real. It's a place you've constructed in your mind, precisely in order to run away from reality, a reality where you have only found threat and hurt. Can't you see? It's a dream, a place where magic is real, a place pulled from a simpler time, before all the traumas of the modern world.'

Jacob shook his head. 'The Riders? Your twisted history with Myriam's family? None of that sounds very comforting to me.'

The Laird brought his hands together and the smile disappeared. 'That's precisely the point. It doesn't work, does it? You can't live in dreams and you can't run away into them for long. It doesn't heal the trauma or the pain. They follow you, even into your idyllic delusion. In your mind there is no safety, not even in your dreams. So the Riders appear. They are a threat, implacable and ruthless. They can't be understood, just as you couldn't understand much of the violence you experienced. The Riders personify that violence and cruelty and they repel you, just as the violence and cruelty did.'

'There is more to the village than an idyllic setting and a weird threat,' Jacob said. 'If I made all this up, I must have a very vivid imagination.'

'You do, Jacob. You do. But there is a clear pattern to your imagining. Take for example the figure of Noah: an old man, an old soldier; one who is able to understand your problems. He is clearly a father figure replacing the father who was absent to you when you needed him and who couldn't understand you. Maybe, he didn't even try. Surely you can see that Noah is an idealised symbol of what we all want from our fathers, but so rarely get. He is strong yet gentle, firm but understanding. He is a textbook Jungian father archetype. You have even given him magical powers to protect you. Don't we all wish our fathers had those?'

'You must've read a whole stack of pop psychology books,' Jacob said sarcastically, 'but I've been treated by some of the best psyches the army could provide and I know that all this talk is nonsense. Delusions aren't this complete and they certainly aren't this coherent or consistent. Talk about Jungian archetypes all you like - I will trust what my senses tell me.'

'Will you?' the Laird asked with a slight mocking tone. 'Yet how do you know what your senses do, in fact, tell you, or indeed, if they tell you anything at all? It is your mind that perceives the world, not your senses.' He paused, nodding absently. 'Yet you are correct' he continued. 'Your delusions are unusual in their complexity, in their coherence and consistency. This is a tribute to both the power of your imagination and to the depth of the trauma you have suffered. Yet you must admit, there is a certain pattern to them.

Take Myriam for example. You have been unlucky in love and now, with this sickness, you are afraid your chance in that area is gone forever. Who would want a crazy ex-soldier? Yet here she is, a beautiful girl who already knows and loves you. Surely you can see that that is pure wish fulfilment. Even more, you grew up a lonely and isolated child and now you discover that you actually had this close friend and companion for all of your life. Come on now, isn't that very convenient? How can that possibly be real?

The same is true of Father Augustus. Surely you can see that he is the priest from central casting. He would not be out of place in an old movie. Telling you to face the evil, to name it and move on. What rubbish! Typical superego stuff.

Although I do think that, on the whole, he is a healthy element. He is your mind trying to figure out how to heal itself, providing itself with a safe way to pick at the wound to see how bad it is. I can tell you that, Jacob. It's bad, very bad. Bad enough to drive you into a psychotic state, bad enough that you will not be able to heal yourself. You need my help. In fact, you need pharmaceutical help. We need to readjust the chemistry of your brain.'

A crystal goblet appeared on the table. It was finely etched with the coils of a dragon rising from the base to the cup. It contained a thick, golden liquid that shone warmly in the candlelight.

'I would like you to drink this,' the Laird said. 'It is an antipsychotic that will deaden some of the activity in your brain and allow information from those senses you are so fond of to penetrate. It's become clear that cognitive, talking therapy alone won't break through this delusion. Drugs are the only thing that seem to work and we need to get you back to a shared understanding of reality. Then we can talk. Drink it, please.'

Jacob looked at the goblet suspiciously. This meeting with the Laird had not gone at all as he had expected. He didn't believe the story of delusion that he was being told, and yet there was a part of him that remembered the hospital ward ... that insisted that it must be true, that it was the village that was impossible and that the madness was all too real. He looked about him, at the dim, cobwebbed room. He was sure he had never seen such a place before – yet there had been places like this in the stories he was told as a kid. He looked again at the goblet but made no movement towards it.

'If it is so important that I take this drug, why not just inject me?' he asked. 'Why all this charade about getting me to drink it?' Images of Dr. Corvus and a large needle came forcibly to his mind. 'Don't say you wouldn't do it because I've known people forcibly injected with antipsychotics before.'

'We may need to,' the Laird replied. 'And if we do, we certainly will but I would only do that as a last resort. It would be much better if you would choose to drink, if you would choose to be well. Your recovery will be faster and more complete if you cooperate in your therapy. I would much rather work with you than against you. Again, I'm not the bogey man in a ruined castle, squatting in the squalid remains of a great hall, that your mind has invented me to be. I'm your doctor and it may not be possible to fully cure you against your will.'

Jacob reached out and took the goblet from the table. He looked at it closely as the Laird leaned forward in anticipation. The liquid inside was thick, like a sticky liquor, and it glowed a soft golden light in the dim room, as if it fluoresced in the candlelight. The aroma was sweet, a little too sweet to be pleasant. It made it hard to think clearly and Jacob desperately needed to think clearly. He went over all that the Laird had said in his mind, considered it as he would an intelligence report from an informant. There was a plausibility to the story and yet it was the details that were important. He had to decide – of his own free will.

'How do you know all this?' he asked. 'How could you know that nature of the place where I believe myself to be, the names and characters, of the people in my delusion?'

'I told you,' the Laird said. 'You've been raving and we've been able to piece it all together from your ravings.'

The vapours from the liquid were fogging his mind but everything the Laird said seemed to make sense, more sense than a magical village and a beautiful girl. Jacob raised the cup to his lips.

'Drink,' the Laird said eagerly. 'Drink the whole of the goblet and you will be on the road to recovery.'

Goblet? He paused and lowered the goblet as he slowly shook his head. Now he had the data he needed.

'No, I don't think so,' he said. 'It would be weird that I could have a delusion that is as consistent and coherent as this one, but even then, my ravings most certainly wouldn't be able to convey that consistency. I don't believe you could put together such a complete picture from the ravings of a delusional psychotic. There's this also, you mentioned a bogey man in a ruined castle, in the squalor of a great hall. Have I been raving as we've been talking? Yet this is the only time I've been here. How could you possibly know how I perceive you? You asked me to drain the goblet. Why would you use that word? Unless, of course, you could actually see it.' He held up the goblet. 'No, I will not be drinking this.'

He opened his hand and let the goblet fall to the floor. The crystal smashed on the stone and the golden liquid ran slowly across the floor, its sweet smell rapidly turning rancid.

* * *

Two figures watched, unnoticed, from a corner of the great hall. One waved his hand and time froze; the Laird and Jacob both paused in the act of watching the golden liquid flow across the floor.

'Now we come to it,' he said. 'He's come to the castle, armed, to confront the Laird and his riders. Your hopes have come to nothing.'

'How so?'

The first man gave a condescending smile at his companion's slowness. 'I've explained this before. There are only two possible outcomes; either the Laird still manages, somehow, to enchant him and he joins the Riders, or he resists the Laird and fights, in which case either he or Joshua will be killed. No matter which way it turns out, there's only misery. The girl's heart will be broken yet again, and the village will be lost. Whatever happens, I win.'

His companion shook his head. 'I think your analysis is too limited. There are factors you're not taking into account.'

'Such as?'

'Such as his capacity for love and sacrifice.'

The first man gave an exasperated grunt. 'You keep going on about that but it's irrelevant nonsense. Look, it's over and you're holding on to false hope. You've lost and this has been really poorly played. I told you at the beginning, you needed stronger players.'

His companion shrugged. 'I am still content with those I've been given.'

'They are broken. How many times do I have to point this out?'

'I am content with their brokenness.'

The first man was silent for a while. Then he tried another tack. 'Anyway, you cheated. You suggested the girl to him. He didn't really show strength of mind or love, you know. He only reacted out of fear, fear that he might be alone.'

'I'm not sure that you can recognise love, nor strength of mind for that matter.'

'I can recognise that he's now in an impossible position, something you seem unable to do. He's a soldier under threat and he's armed. He'll kill. A soldier is trained to take the life of those who threaten him. Now it is come to it. It's kill or be killed'

'Even if it does come to that choice, you forget – a soldier must also be prepared to die.'

'My point exactly. If he gives his life, what good is that? That's just as bad as him killing. The village is left in the same situation and girl has another reason to grieve. Kill or be killed, she loses any chance at happiness and the village runs out of time.'

'He may yet choose another option.'

'There is no other option.'

'There's always another option.' The men disappeared back into the darkness of the corner and time started to flow again.

CHAPTER TWENTY-TWO

Jacob and Joshua

The Laird looked at the shattered goblet in shocked silence, watching the golden liquid ooze into the cracks between the flagstones. He slowly rose to his feet. Then his face contorted with sudden rage.

'You fool!' he yelled. 'Do you have any idea how expensive that goblet was or how long it took to prepare that potion?' Jacob could hear heavy footsteps filing into the hall behind him. The Riders had returned from the village. 'That potion would have taken away all your pain,' the Laird raged. 'I was trying to do you a great favour. You would have been able to sleep at night. No dreams would have troubled you. You would have been able to watch that little girl die a hundred times over and it would not have bothered you.'

Jacob looked at him dispassionately. 'Is that what you promised the Riders?' he asked. 'That you would take away their pain? That the awful grief of never being able to marry the girls they loved would be gone?' The Laird looked at him warily. 'You took away a lot more than just their pain though, didn't you? Did you warn them of all the consequences: that you would also take away their joy, their hope, their love?'

The Laird looked at him with contempt. 'They were overly emotional boys,' he said. 'I did them a favour. They all rather loudly and rudely demanded that I remove the curse from the village, a curse they had brought upon themselves.' The Laird waved his arms wide. 'They very dramatically proclaimed that they didn't want to live if they couldn't marry the ones they had chosen. They even threatened me with violence. Well, I soon fixed that. Do you blame me?'

'Yes, I blame you,' Jacob said. 'What you did to them was a crime. It was certainly no favour.'

'I took away all the pain they were complaining about,' the Laird said with a thin smile, 'and I have been a generous lord and master ever since …'

'You're an inhuman monster,' Jacob said in a flat, matter of fact voice. He could hear the footsteps of the Riders coming closer behind him. 'Do you know why I wouldn't drink your potion? It was precisely because it would take away my pain. My pain is a part of me. My pain comes from my life, from my concern for others. Pain and suffering are part of what it is to be human. I would rather suffer a thousand times what I suffer now than see that young girl die once and not care.'

The Laird seemed to be struggling. He was looking at the dusty surface of the table and had a look of intense concentration on his face. The Riders stopped, standing close behind Jacob. He didn't turn around but kept his eyes on the Laird. Seven crystal goblets appeared on the table, all filled with the same golden liquid.

The Laird now looked directly at Jacob. 'I give you another chance before we use force,' he said. 'I know you are trying to enmesh me in your delusion but I am not what you think I am. I am not some evil cripple in a castle. I am your doctor and I am offering you an antipsychotic, something to bring you to yourself, to take away your pain…'

'How can I be myself without my pain?' Jacob asked. 'I've seen your riders. Sure, they're still walking around, but that's simply biological function. It's not life. They don't really live. No thanks. I choose to live. I choose to be myself.'

'Jacob,' the Laird said urgently. 'These riders are a figment of your delusion. Please Jacob, I'm a doctor. I don't want to take away your humanity or your personality. Please drink. It would be so much better if you would choose to be well but make no mistake, I will use force if I have to.'

Jacob drew the sword that hung across his back. Behind him, he heard the sound of six claymores being drawn from their sheaths. The Laird stepped quickly back, out of range, but Jacob didn't attack him. Instead, he swung the sword and sent all the crystal goblets crashing to the floor. The Laird cried out and stood staring at where the goblets had been. He looked shocked and, for the first time, afraid.

'You see, I just don't buy that whole psychosis story,' Jacob said, 'You're not a doctor and what was in those goblets was not a cure. It was a vile poison.'

'No, you are sick,' the Laird yelled. 'I am your doctor!'

'No,' Jacob replied. 'What you are is a broken old man trapped in the web of your own evil. You ask me to choose to be well? Look to yourself, look around you. What has all your scheming got you? You live hunched over, in darkness and filth. In the village they call you Laird, but as far as I can see you are nothing, nothing at all.'

The Laird's face contorted with rage. 'You think so?' He stood as straight as his broken body would allow and yelled at Jacob. 'You think that because they ripped my manhood from me that I have no power? You are very much mistaken. I am your worst nightmare!'

The old and crippled figure of the Laird trying to be intimidating in the dim filth of the castle was vaguely comical and Jacob could not stop the trace of a smile crossing his face. 'No, you're not,' he said. 'Trust me, I have nightmares that would curdle what little blood you have left.'

This infuriated the Laird even further. 'You think this is funny?' he spat. 'You would dare to laugh at me? I still have power, fool. O yes, even after all they have done to me, I still have power. Look behind you, soldier. I have six blades who will kill at my word. I wasn't lying when I said I would resort to force if I had to.'

Jacob turned to face the Riders. The six of them stood there with their swords drawn: as emotionless and uncaring as ever. If they had been listening to the conversation, they showed no sign of it.

'How many of them do you think you can kill before they kill you?' the Laird continued, his voice becoming sly. 'You're a trained soldier and they're not. So, I'm sure you will be able to get some of them but you're not superhuman. You won't be able to get all of them and how do you think the village people will love you when I tell them that you have killed their sons?' The Laird's voice became softer and, behind Jacob's back, a vicious smile crossed his face. 'Think of the poor girl. Think of how anguished she will be to learn that her lover killed her brother.' He sighed in mock sadness. 'You, get ready to fight,' he said sharply, pointing at the rider who had been Joshua. 'The rest of you fall back and take no action until one of these two is dead – then kill the one who remains alive.' Again, he gave a sigh of mock sadness. 'Poor Myriam will be so heartbroken. Who knows what she might do?'

The Laird broke into a wild, mad laugh but Jacob was concentrating on Joshua. Just for a moment, at the mention of Myriam's name, he had seen a flicker of something in the dead eyes of the rider; perhaps recognition, perhaps something else. 'What,' Jacob wondered, 'would the others do if neither of us dies? How long would they simply stand by and watch? Why were there seven goblets on the table? Does he need the potion to keep them in check? Perhaps the effect will wear off. What happens then?'

The Laird's laughter had died down and there was a moment's silence, when everything was still. Then the Laird yelled at Joshua, 'Well, attack him you fool! Kill him!'

Joshua the rider swung his sword like an axe with a downward slash at Jacob's head. Jacob easily stepped out of the way and the sword dug deep into the table behind him. Jacob waited while the Joshua pulled his blade free from the table, his sword resting in his hands.

The Laird's eyes narrowed in calculation. 'It's no good,' he said. 'You won't be able to avoid fighting him forever. Sooner or later, either you will kill him or he will kill you.'

Jacob, meanwhile, had circled out and away from the table. If he was to succeed, he would need the freedom to move. Joshua advanced on him, this time swinging a low hack at his legs. Jacob easily blocked the blow with his own sword and stepped back. This pattern continued for several minutes. Joshua kept advancing and raining blow after blow at Jacob, who parried with his sword when he had to and stepped out of the way when he could. Rubbish covered the floor and he had to be careful that he didn't trip. A slip could be fatal.

All of the blows were artless, slow and telegraphed well ahead. They were, however, delivered with a great deal of power and focus and Jacob was very much aware that he was fighting for his life. Still, he never retaliated, even when a counter attack would have been simple. Time and again, he reminded himself that this was Myriam's brother, and stayed his hand.

He didn't know that much about sword play but he knew more than Joshua. He knew that control was more important than power, that the point was more deadly than the edge, and that the rider's blade couldn't hurt him as long as his blade was between him and it. Still, he didn't attack. He just kept retreating, moving ever closer to the door.

The other riders followed, surrounding the two combatants and waiting to kill the one who survived the fight. The Laird followed too, some distance behind, laughing and calling out, 'You can't escape, you know. Eventually, you'll be forced to kill him.'

Soon the blows became more erratic and began to lose their power. Joshua might be driven by some mindless madness but his body still got tired and the wild flurry of attacks couldn't continue for long. This meant, however, that while his blows were becoming less lethal, they were also less predictable and Jacob was under no illusion about what even a relatively small injury would mean. The Riders behind him cleared away as they approached the back wall. Jacob began to edge towards the door. Still, Joshua kept up his attack, although now there were longer pauses between the blows.

As he got to the stairs and started to back down, his situation became even more difficult. The large, double-handed sword he was wielding was difficult to use in the enclosed space of the stairway and the steps were angled deliberately to aid the defender on the higher steps. Jacob was also walking backwards down worn and uneven stairs. With the advantage his place on the stairs gave him, Joshua started to break through Jacob's guard and the fight suddenly became a lot more dangerous. After being bruised badly about his arms and taking a serious cut to his leg, Jacob decided to cut his losses and run. He turned and bolted down the stairs as fast as he could. Joshua followed hard on his heels.

Jacob didn't stop running until he had gone through the antechamber and down the steps onto the relatively flat courtyard. There he turned and swung his sword just in time to parry a head high cut from the closely following rider. They faced each other in the courtyard, each of them tired and Jacob bleeding. The five other riders came down the steps and passively took up positions around them, ready to kill the victor.

The Laird stood at the top of the steps and yelled, 'What are you waiting for, kill him! Kill him now!' It was not clear which of them he was talking to but Joshua renewed his attack with a weary and clumsy strike at Jacob's legs. Jacob took the opportunity to parry heavily, close to the claymore's guard. The sword went flying from the rider's hand. He raised the point of his sword to the rider's throat.

'No! Jacob, please don't!' The anguished cry came from the main castle gate. The portcullis was down and Myriam was standing alone on the other side straining to get through. How she came to be there, Jacob didn't know, nor why, but she stood there with the morning sun shining off her red hair and his heart cried out to her. Joshua also turned to look at Myriam and Jacob again saw that momentary flicker of recognition, as if some powerful emotion was trying to force its way through the effects of the potion.

'What are all you idiots waiting for?' the Laird yelled. He pointed at Joshua. 'Someone give him a sword.'

Jacob looked at Myriam and he looked at the helpless rider. The words of the blacksmith and Father Augustus came back to him. 'Good idea,' he said. He knelt on one knee, bowed his head, reversed the sword and presented it to the rider. 'This sword was never mine to use,' he said. 'It was only ever mine to give away to the one who needed it. That's you.'

Chapter Twenty-three

Revolution

There was silence in the courtyard for a long moment. All was still as Joshua held the sword and stared, as if transfixed, at its blade. Jacob waited, still on one knee and with his head bowed. He was shaking with the effort to control his desire to run. Images flashed through his mind, vivid in their reality; images of decapitated and mutilated bodies; memories of all the cruel obscenity of war. Great beads of sweat formed on his forehead and fell to the paving stones. Yet he stayed there, unmoving.

Eventually, the Laird broke the silence. 'What are you waiting for?' he yelled. 'Kill him now, while you have the chance. Cut off his head!'

'No!' Myriam cried from the gate. 'No! Joshua, I love him. Just like you loved Agnes, I love him. Please! Please! Don't do this!'

Jacob looked up, more than half expecting to see the blade swinging down to claim his head. Yet Joshua still stood there, staring at the blade. The blade began to glow red, as if it were still in the blacksmith's forge. Names began to form along its length, outlined in red fire; Rebecca, Noah, Myriam, Agnes. Joshua closed his eyes and when he opened them, all trace of the blankness had gone. His eyes filled with great tears and where these fell onto the sword, and ran down the blade, the names blazed ever brighter, brilliant even in the sunlight.

Joshua fell to his knees. 'Oh God forgive me,' he said. 'What have I done? What have I become?'

Jacob reached out, put his arm around his shoulder and held him, as he had cradled soldiers before. 'You have come home,' he said. 'Welcome back.' Joshua sobbed into his shoulder. At the gate, Myriam held her hands to her face, tears of joy flowing down her cheeks.

'You five,' the Laird called out. 'Forget what I said before. Kill them both. Kill them now.'

Jacob dived to grab the sword that Joshua had dropped earlier. Joshua, however, simply stood up and held the blacksmith's sword high. The sunlight caught the blade and names flashed across it in red fire. The five riders stood unmoving, transfixed by the sight of the blade.

'Kill them! Kill them!' the Laird yelled, now both angry and afraid. 'Why are you just standing there?' Jacob left the fallen sword where it was and stood beside Joshua as he saw the blankness fade and tears fill the eyes of the Riders. One by one, they dropped their swords letting them clatter to the stone pavement. The first to do so, Jacob noticed, bore a striking resemblance to the blacksmith: the same black hair; the same tough, sinewy build.

No one moved. Jacob was so caught up in what was happening around Joshua and the sword that it took him a long time to notice the commotion at the gate. A large crowd had now gathered, pressing forward, crying in anger, but the portcullis was still down and it held them out. Four huge men pushed their way through the crowd, dressed in kilts and stripped to the waist. They gripped the portcullis and began to lift and, incredibly, the heavy gate began to rise.

Joshua lowered the sword. 'Go!' he said. 'They need help. We have to let them in.' The five riders ran off across the courtyard to the winch and swiftly began to raise the portcullis. Jacob saw the Crow hurry out of the keep. He grabbed the Laird and pulled him back through the door. The door of the keep slammed shut just as the portcullis was raised high enough for the people to get in. The crowd streamed into the courtyard and the five riders found themselves surrounded by family. They were hugged and held tightly. They were covered with kisses and welcomed back with tears and incredulous laughter.

Myriam ran screaming across the courtyard and flung herself at Joshua, holding him close in a vice-like grip. She didn't say anything but just sobbed into his shoulder.

For his part, Joshua returned her hug. 'Myri, Myri,' he said. 'I'm so sorry. I'm so very sorry.'

Myriam made no reply, she just gripped him tighter. Eventually, she let go of Joshua and turned to face Jacob. He was surprised to see that she was angry.

'You were meant to be safe,' she said. 'Do you know how much it cost me to send you away? Do you know what a miserable night I had? Only to wake up this morning and find that the whole village knows you've gone to the one place you mustn't go, the one place I had tried so hard to keep you away from and you had gone alone! You could've been hurt. You could've been killed. You could've been… turned into…' She gave a cry and threw herself at him, wrapping him in a hug so tight it threatened to stop his breathing.

He managed, with considerable difficulty, to disengage himself. 'Was it true?' he asked. 'What you said by the gate, did you mean it?'

'Of course,' she said indignantly. 'You know I love you. I always have.'

'And I, Myriam of the cottage in the valley, love you.' He gathered her in his arms and kissed her. It was only some time later that they became aware of the noise that surrounded them: wild clapping and cheering. They looked about them to find themselves the centre of attention with the whole village applauding them. Myriam turned bright red but Joshua grabbed both their hands in his and raised them high above his head – to the further cheers of the crowd.

It was some time later that the crowd fell silent as Noah and Father Augustus arrived. Noah stopped and was still for a long moment, looking at his son who was smiling apologetically, almost on the edge of tears, and shifting nervously from foot to foot at the bottom of the castle steps. Then Noah ran, with a speed surprising in one his age, and grabbed Joshua in a hug that lifted him off his feet – no mean feat since Joshua was taller than he was.

It only lasted a moment. Then he turned around, still with his arm around Joshua's shoulder and with tears flowing freely down his cheeks. 'Father,' he said to Father Augustus, 'We need a prayer. We need to give thanks for these sons of ours who were dead and now live again.'

Smiling, Father Augustus turned to the crowd and cried, 'Oremus!' The crowd bowed their heads. 'O God, whose mercies are beyond number, we give you thanks for graciously granting the petitions of those who called to you and returning to us our sons who had been lost. May you always preserve them from harm and keep us all in your service. *Benedicat vos omnipotens Deus Pater, et Filius, et Spiritus Sanctus.*'

He traced a cross in the air and the crowd yelled 'Amen!' and broke again into wild cheering. Food and tables began to appear and the publican turned up with a wagon loaded with barrels. Soon someone started to play the bagpipes and the party was in full swing. As this was happening, Noah nodded to the four men who had initially tried to lift the portcullis. One of them went over and stood, silently guarding the door to the keep.

The party went on all through the afternoon and well into the night. In all that time, the four men rotated the duty but the keep door was never left untended. Late in the night, Jacob found himself staring at the current guard. He was bald headed and truly huge, a massive lump of muscle. He had wrapped a woollen cloak about himself in the chill night but he stood as still as a statue. Jacob, who knew how hard and boring guard duty was, was mightily impressed.

Myriam came up beside him. 'His name is Niall,' she said. 'The others are Cormack, Liam, and Douglas. They used to compete in the highland games, mostly in the stone carrying and throwing. Personally, I think they used to cheat. I think they used their magical ability to make themselves stronger.'

Jacob looked at the massive form of the guard: broad, deep chested, made of solid muscle and well over six feet tall. He could well believe that this guy had more than a normal training regime. 'I'm guessing they have no love for the Laird,' he said.

'Oh, they love the Laird,' Myriam said smiling. 'They love the Laird the way a cat loves a mouse. Trust me, while they're there, the Laird will be wishing that door was a good deal thicker.'

Jacob nodded. Looking at the size of Niall the guard, he thought that in the Laird's place, he would feel the same.

'Let's forget about the Laird. I don't want his tired, old ghost haunting this night,' she said, suddenly grabbing his hand and laughing. 'Come with me, there's something I'd like to show you.' She led him up the battlements to a place near the keep wall. There the whole valley lay below them, silvered in the light of the full moon.

'Da told me about this spot,' she said. 'From here you can see the whole of my world.' She threw her arms wide. 'I love this place. This is my home and now it's free of the terror that darkened it, thanks to you.' She turned to face him. 'Thank you. Thank you for what you have done for my people.'

'I didn't do it for them,' Jacob said. 'I'm not that altruistic. I did it for you. I love you. I'm a sorry excuse of a broken-down soldier, but I love you. Maybe you're right and I have always loved you. It certainly feels that way. There is nothing I would like more than to spend my life with you in this valley. If I could be with you and make this my home, I would be the happiest man on Earth.'

'You can, Jacob. You must!' she said. 'Curse or no curse, we'll find a way!'

Then she was in his arms and they kissed long and deep, with an eager and hungry passion.

CHAPTER TWENTY-FOUR

The Judgement

It was in the early hours of the morning, when the frosty sky was clear and bright and the new day was just beginning to touch the east, that the last of the party goers drifted away and Noah called Jacob to a meeting in the warmth of the stables huddled against the southern wall of the courtyard. The blacksmith was also there, as was Joshua, the man called Ezekiel and Father Augustus.

'We need to decide what to do with the Laird and his fiddler crow,' Noah said. 'He can't stay locked up in that tower forever.'

'Why not?' the blacksmith asked. 'Believe me, I could forge a bolt that would seal that door forever.'

'I don't doubt it,' Noah said. 'But I don't want the village to be always living in the shadow of his evil. We need him to be gone.'

Joshua drew the sword that Jacob had given him, the names Myriam and Noah still ran like fire across the blade. 'He murdered four of my friends. It is, in fact, only to my shame that I am still alive. They died because they were smarter, nobler and stronger than me. I say we put him on trial, find him guilty, and execute him for his crimes. This blade is keen enough to do the deed.'

Father Augustus shook his head. 'Alas,' he said, 'much as I would like to see justice done, I fear that is one course we cannot take. The line between human justice and vengeance is thin at the best of times and there is not a man woman or child in this village who has not been personally and grievously hurt by this man. I don't believe we can render justice in his case…'

'And to kill him for vengeance would make us little better than him,' Ezekiel said.

'Also,' Noah said. 'The trial would open up old wounds that might be best left to heal. There is too much of this which is the result of our own foolishness and anger for me to have any desire to kill.'

'Amen,' said Father Augustus softly.

'Banish him,' Jacob said quietly.

'I wish we could,' Noah replied. 'But it wouldn't work. Unless we did it at the precise moment the village began to move, he would simply find his way back, and there's no way of knowing when the village will move. It's more or less random.'

'We could send someone back with him,' Ezekiel suggested. 'One of the big men perhaps. They could watch over him.'

'They all have families,' Father Augustus pointed out.

'And they would be banished to my time along with him,' Jacob said, almost in a whisper. His mind raced ahead and he saw the answer. His chest tightened, he felt lightheaded, and the food and drink of the party now felt like lead in his stomach. He thought that maybe he was going to be sick.

'Perhaps one of the Riders?' Ezekiel suggested. 'They have suffered so much at his hands that they would be glad to have a hand in his punishment.'

The blacksmith shook his head firmly. 'No. They have just been returned to their families. It would be cruel to take them away again, and so soon.' Jacob tried to imagine any of the Riders living in twenty first century

Australia. He shook his head. It wouldn't work. He didn't want to look at what his mind was telling him.

'The trouble is that for the most part, those who were eager to leave the village, or those who have no responsibilities here, have already left,' Father Augustus said. 'Still, there must be someone.'

'Someone who can read and write in English?' Jacob asked. His throat was tight and he found it hard to form the words. 'Because, believe me, they will not survive in my world if they can't.' Jacob wiped his eyes with the back of his hand and hung his head. For a moment he paused with his eyes closed, praying that someone would come up with another way. They didn't, and he surrendered to the inevitable. This night had been a beautiful, glorious dream but dreams end in the hard light of day.

'Let me take him back to my world, to my time,' he said, the words feeling like poison in his throat. ' I will guard him in the outside valley until the village moves. Then there will be no way back and he will be trapped in my time. There he will be nothing and nobody. He will be stripped of everything he owns, of everything he has stolen, of every honour or title he claims to himself. I don't know that my world will be kind to him. Justice will be done.'

'And yet he will still be alive,' Father Augustus said. 'He will still have some chance at redemption.'

'That would mean that ye also, would be banished from the village,' Noah said softly, his face stricken. 'All that ye have here would be lost to ye and ye would be lost to the village. A hard thing. Ye would do this?'

Jacob took a deep breath. 'It turns out you can't beat the curse,' he said. 'For a happy moment, I thought that maybe we could. With Myriam here, there's no way I would ever want to leave, curse or no curse. But it doesn't matter, does it? We all know that I can't stay when the village moves. If there's no desire to leave, then the curse finds another way, up comes a duty to leave. The result is the same.' Again, he wiped his eyes with the back of his hand. 'Anything else was a dream. A beautiful dream but a dream nonetheless. This way, at least my going does some good.'

'Father, what would that do to the curse?' Ezekiel asked.

Father Augustus shook his head slowly. 'I don't really know. The curse was a dark and terrible thing that I don't fully understand. Still, I think that, perhaps, it will be good. The Laird is at the centre of the curse. With him out of the valley, I think the shifts may slow. We may settle down. Maybe we can't get home but at least we could find a place to live out our lives in the normal way. It's possible... but, as I say, I don't really know.'

Noah was quiet for a long time. Then he said, 'The proposed sentence of this meeting is that the Laird be banished from the village and placed under Jacob's guard. How say ye?'

'Does he take his Crow with him?' the blacksmith asked.

'Oh Aye, I think so,' Joshua said. 'I definitely think so.' The others sat quietly for a moment. Noah looked at each of them in turn, trying to gauge their feeling.

Eventually he said, 'Are we agreed then? He leaves and he leaves today.' The others all nodded and Jacob felt numb. That meant that he would also be leaving today: leaving Myriam. He had known that the time would come when the village would move on in its strange journey and that he almost certainly would not go with it, but it was a shock to be faced with such an imminent departure. He remembered the warm feeling of Myriam in his arms and he felt very empty. He knew it had to be done but it was going to be the hardest thing he would ever do.

'Good,' Noah continued. 'Now all we have to do is pull him out of his little hidey hole.'

'That won't be easy,' Joshua said. 'He will have set defensive traps throughout the tower. You need to be especially careful of the entrance. Even if you can get past the door, there's a murder hole in the roof of the entrance chamber and he has a vat of some foul liquid ready to pour on any who come that way.'

'Leave that to me,' Noah said. 'I have some experience in such matters. For now, get some rest. We'll breakfast at dawn and, I give my word, by midday the Laird will be gone.'

* * *

Two men stood warming themselves by a fire set up in the castle courtyard. One was shaking his head in disbelief.

'Well, I must admit, I am surprised,' he said. 'In the kill or be killed situation, he chooses to die. I did not expect that.'

'He didn't chose to die,' his companion said. 'He chose to love. This was not some act of despair nor was it an accidental tumble down the stairs. It was a choice, a deliberate act of trust and love and that's a very powerful thing. Even you should know that.'

The first man shrugged. 'The end result is much the same.'

'There you are, once again mistaken.'

'Yes, but only because you cheated,' the first man cried. 'A magic sword? Really? Don't you think that idea is a bit old and tired? I'm surprised you didn't have him pulling it out of a stone. You really need to learn to think outside such obvious clichés.'

His companion smiled, 'Cheat? You've accused me of that before. I'm not sure I share your understanding of the rules. As for the sword,' he spread his hands in a gesture of helplessness, 'I had nothing to do with it.'

'I don't believe you,' the first man said accusingly. 'The names of those they loved outlined in red fire? It sounds a lot like you. If you had nothing to do with it, how is it that the sword wasn't simply a bit of sharpened steel?'

His companion shook his head and with a sad little smile said: 'Do you understand so little? How could a sword, formed with every hammer stroke by a father's love, not have properties absent from normal steel — properties that call forth the remembrance of love and faithfulness.'

'Nonsense. Love and faithfulness, to the extent that they exist at all, are abstract concepts and steel is material. It can't hold such things. It can't think. It doesn't have the capacity. It's just matter. Stuff. It has no soul.'

'You have, I fear, a very limited view of reality. Love is the least abstract thing in the universe and simple 'stuff' has the capacity to carry the divine.'

The two of them stood warming themselves in silence for a while. Then the first man spoke again.

'Still, this victory of yours feels very much like a defeat. You say you wanted their happiness and yet they have sacrificed that for the good of the village. Their life together ends tomorrow. What has been gained?'

'Much. The Riders are now free and the village can return to its normal life.'

'Yet the two of them,' the first man insisted. 'Your two major players in this situation, they'll be lost to each other. They'll be miserable and their misery will colour all that has happened. Where is love in all of this?'

'You have a very limited understanding of love if you think love is ended by sacrifice. Yes, he is prepared to walk away from her, just as she was willing to send him away. In their love, there is no limit to what they would sacrifice for the good of the other. And yet, all things are possible to those who love.'

The first man looked at his companion warily. 'No, they aren't,' he said slowly. 'He will leave and she will stay. It would be cruel to send her out into his world. They both know that. I doubt she'll even come to say goodbye. Even if she did, all they get is a teary goodbye. There is no happy ending.'

'We shall see.'

Chapter Twenty-five

Departure

Jacob lay in the warm hay of the stable and rested but without sleep. His heart was racing, even as he forced his body to rest. The physical memory of the warmth of Myriam's body against his was a torment to him now. Today, he would leave her forever.

To meet only in dreams was not enough, yet he could think of no way out. When the village made its next jump, he would have had to leave anyway and this way, taking the Laird with him, his departure would at least do some good. Only by walking away from Myriam could he save her. He went over it again and again in his mind but he could see no other solution.

Myriam, meanwhile, was back at the cottage, preparing a celebratory breakfast for her returned brother. They hadn't told her of their plans for the Laird, the others simply hadn't thought to do so. Jacob, on the other hand, wanted to spare her the dread that he was feeling for as long as possible.

Every minute seemed to stretch into hours as the pre-dawn light gradually became brighter, and he was glad when Noah finally came over to him and said, 'Come on, soldier. Time to earn yer rations.'

The three of them, Noah, Joshua and Jacob, met the four strongmen at the door of the keep. In the morning chill they were wrapped warmly in woollen cloaks. Noah went over and laid both hands on the door. Then he smiled.

'Aye, it is possible,' he said. He turned to the four strongmen. 'I will use my power and this door will fall outwards. When it does, you must grab it, lift it, and hold it inside the entrance chamber as a kind of false ceiling. Do ye understand?' The four nodded. 'Good, once we are on the stairway ye need to get out. Cover yer heads and be careful not to let anything that is poured onto the door touch yer skin. If it does, wash it with water, lots of water, straight away. No messing about, okay?'

Again they nodded. The one called Niall said, 'What do we do with the door and the chamber after you've gone?'

'Leave it a while and then flush it out with as much water as ye can find,' Noah answered. 'But be careful. Be very careful.' He then turned and again placed both his hands on the door. He closed his eyes. His expression was calm and very still. It was as if he was staring, through his closed eyes, at the door or at what was behind it.

Jacob listened carefully but for a long time nothing seemed to be happening. They were just standing there in the cold morning air. A few curious villagers began to arrive to clean up the remnants of the previous night's party. There was a loud thud behind the door and Jacob jumped.

'That'll be the wooden latch falling down,' Joshua said, smiling. A little while later there was loud metal clang. 'And that'll be the metal bolt.' Still, Noah did not move, even though by this time the door could presumably have been opened. Then there were two smaller metallic pings and the door started to fall outwards. The four strongmen rushed forward to catch it. 'The last two sounds were the pins falling from the hinges,' Joshua explained. 'Let's go in.'

The four strongmen hoisted the door above their heads and angled it back through the doorway, the others following close behind. In the entrance chamber, they lifted it high and rammed it against the stone ceiling. Almost immediately there was a gurgling sound and a foul, acrid smell filled the chamber. Noah, Joshua and Jacob rushed in under the door to the stairs.

As soon as he gained the bottom steps, Noah turned to the strongmen and yelled, 'Go! Get out now – and be careful.' The four strongmen backed out and only let the door drop when the last of them was through the doorway. A clear, smoking fluid ran down the door and onto the chamber floor. Its vapour stung at the eyes and noses of the three standing in the stairway.

'Hydrochloric acid,' Jacob muttered. 'Charming.'

They turned to climb the stairs, Noah leading and Jacob bringing up the rear. They hadn't been climbing long before a deafening din filled the stairway and Jacob was forced to cover his ears. Hundreds of spiked, metal balls, about the size of tennis balls, came cascading down the stairs towards them. Noah held up his hands and all sound stopped as the balls froze in mid-air.

'I thought he might try something like that,' Noah said grimly. 'Crude, but potentially very effective. Come on, I won't be able to hold these forever.' With the balls frozen as they were, they were able to push through them as though through a thorn bush. It wasn't long before they had made their way past the last of them and the stairway was again filled with noise as Noah let the balls fall once more.

At the entrance to the hall, the Crow stood in the doorway, still dressed in his strange motley and holding a Scottish claymore. Being higher, he had the advantage but when he saw Jacob holding one of the rider's claymores and Joshua with his great, double handed sword, he simply dropped his own sword and ran deeper into the hall.

Through the doorway, the hall was just as filthy but darker and even colder than Jacob remembered. It was barely possible to make out the Laird sitting in his chair behind the table, with the Crow standing at his side, whispering something into his ear.

The three of them began to walk down the hall, Noah in the middle and the others flanking him, swords at the ready. They were only half way down the hall when two monstrous creatures rose from the dust and grime of the floor. They were the stuff of nightmares; dark and twisted, with mouths frozen in the act of a scream, and empty eyes that stared into horror and despair. Noah gave an impatient wave of his hand and the horrors collapsed back into dust.

Noah looked at the Laird. 'Ye seek to scare us with children's hobgoblins,' he said contemptuously. 'I expected more of ye.'

The Laird laughed, a broken, withered sound. 'Perhaps you will appreciate these more,' he said.

A young, teenage boy appeared in the middle of the hall. He was, maybe, thirteen or fourteen, dressed as a medieval pikeman, and he had a gaping wound in his stomach, blood and entrails spilling through his hands.

'Ma!' he cried in pain and fear. 'Mamma!' He stumbled and would have fallen if Noah had not gathered him in his arms and held him close, his eyes fixed on the Laird.

'Every night I meet him in my dreams,' Noah said. 'How do ye suppose that this is any different?' He kissed the boy gently on the forehead, picked him up in his arms, and carried him as he walked forward.

The boy was still screaming as he was being carried, 'Ma, it hurts! It hurts! I'm afraid. I don't want to die!'

Jacob was still looking at Noah when he heard his own voice behind him yelling, 'Not us, you idiots. Shoot the bad guys!' He looked around to see Brunetti being blown apart, blood and flesh fountaining over the floor. Just as in his dreams, Brunetti was still yelling and screaming. Even though his body was blown apart, his head was still screaming. Jacob turned and tried to walk towards the table only now the body was in front of him, still screaming. He shut his eyes but it didn't help, he couldn't shut out the sound of the screaming. When he opened his eyes the hall seemed to be changing, becoming brighter and smaller, beige with a red border.

He shook his head. No, that wasn't real.

Across the hall, he heard a woman's voice. 'I didn't wait for ye, Joshua. I wanted to, but I didn't know why ye'd left me. I waited for a long time but ye didn't come. Ye promised, Joshua. We promised each other.' Joshua was facing a beautiful young woman with a soft, round face and long, honey blond hair. She was dressed in a simple country frock, with a tartan shawl over her shoulders and bare feet.

Jacob forced himself to look closely at Brunetti's severed head. It was still screaming only now the pitch was higher, as if it were the head of a young, frightened girl. He knelt on one knee, and gently closed the screaming mouth and the starring, fear filled eyes. His heart was racing and he was sweating heavily, but he managed to hold himself together. Around him, the hall threatened to dissolve into the hospital ward, but he wouldn't let it.

He looked at the poor, battered head lying on the floor. 'It'll be okay, Johnny,' he said softly. 'It'll be okay. Give my regards to your mother.'

The screaming had stopped but the severed head was still very real: a horrible, pitiful, unnatural thing. Jacob put down his claymore, picked the head up gently and cradled it in his left arm, as he picked up the claymore again and turned to walk forward.

Across the room, Joshua pushed roughly past the phantom. 'I didn't expect ye to wait,' he said brusquely.

'I married another,' she said as he past her. 'Joshua, I married William Campbell.'

He stopped briefly but didn't turn to look at her. 'Then I hope ye were happy, Agnes, and I pray that ye had lots of bonnie children.' The strain in his voice was evident and it was clear that he was on the verge of tears but he kept walking forward.

'I wasn't, Joshua,' the phantom yelled. 'I wasn't happy. The man was a brute. He beat me and assaulted me and every night I cried out for ye but ye wouldn't come. Why did ye leave me, Joshua? Why?' Joshua stumbled, hesitated, and almost turned but he kept walking forward, fixing his eyes on the Laird.

'Enough!' Noah yelled. 'This is pointless.' He laid the still screaming body of the young man on the table in front of the Laird. He gently closed the staring eyes and the wide-open mouth. The screaming stopped. 'What did ye imagine?' he said to the Laird. 'That faced with these things we would collapse and be unable to continue? Fool! We have all faced these, and worse, a thousand times in our dreams.'

Jacob placed Brunetti's head on the table. 'Sad to say,' he said, 'this doesn't shock me as much as it should. I have seen far too many heads without bodies. This one isn't even real.' Both the body and the head faded back to dust.

The Laird paused and took a deep breath. Then his voice changed. 'Jacob, please come back. I know you have incorporated me into your delusion but I am not what you see me to be. I am your doctor and you still have a chance to be cured. The figures you see around you, they are not real. They are projections of your delusion. Don't give in to them. Fight them and you can be free.'

'I don't think so,' Jacob said, swinging the claymore casually around his body. 'That won't work anymore. I choose not to believe it.' He brought the claymore to guard in front of him. It was a nicely balanced weapon and he smiled briefly. The Laird glanced at him with a momentary look of pure terror but he quickly turned back to Noah who was standing in front of him and watching him impassively.

'It's over,' Noah said. 'It's time for ye to go.'

'Go! I'm not the one who should go. It's you, the three of you. It's my rights and my body that were violated. I was the victim of the villagers' violence once before. I know what they want to do to me. I know that they hate me, and I will not be bullied by a mob. I will not! You're trespassing in my house! Get out! Go!' He leaned forward to stare directly at Noah. 'Go back to your pigs and dirt, old man,' the Laird said quietly. 'You don't belong here. You never did.'

'Nor do you,' Jacob said quietly as he stood beside Noah. 'Actually, you belong in a prison.'

The Laird turned to look at Joshua, who had joined his father. There were marks where the tears had run down his cheeks but the Laird saw only the anger in his eyes, how his knuckles were white with the firmness of his grip on the sword, and he quickly turned away. Standing behind the Laird, the Crow said nothing but looked wildly at each of them in turn.

'Creature of the dark: ye are a traitor, murderer, rapist and abuser of the power God gave ye,' Noah said to the Laird. 'Ye have been tried and sentenced. By rights, ye should be executed or left to rot in some dungeon; but I'm afraid that the first of those is too brutal and the second too dangerous. So, ye are to be banished – to leave this village and never return.'

'No, I won't go,' the Laird said.

'Yes you will,' Jacob said. 'I'll make sure of it. I'll escort you into my world and time and I'll make sure you can't return.' He smiled grimly. 'I don't think you'll like it there.' The Laird's reaction to this, however, wasn't what Jacob had expected. He didn't protest, he simply looked at Jacob thoughtfully and the sly smile that slowly spread across his face made Jacob wonder what he was missing.

'Hold out yer hands,' Noah said. 'Ye will be bound, taken to the edge of the valley and there cast into the outer world. yer crow can go with ye. Jacob, will you secure the Laird? Joshua, the Crow.'

Two lengths of rope appeared on the table and Jacob took one of them. To his surprise, the Laird didn't offer any resistance. With a sly smile still on his face, he compliantly held out his hands while Jacob put down his claymore and tied his hands together. The smile had made him nervous, so he tied the rope tighter than was good for blood circulation. Even so, the Laird didn't complain. Joshua had more trouble with the Crow, who cried and whimpered and even tried, half-heartedly, to run before being brought down by the flat of Joshua's sword.

As Joshua was dragging the Crow to his feet, the Laird, still smiling. He whispered in Jacob's ear, 'Poor Myriam. She'll never see you again, nor you her. All those long nights alone, seeing each other only in half remembered dreams. It's not enough, is it? Not nearly enough.' He laughed, softly and savagely. Jacob said nothing but pushed him roughly down the hall and towards the door.

When they got to the stairs, Joshua went first, followed by the Laird and the Crow. Jacob came behind them with Noah bringing up the rear. Neither prisoner offered any resistance, and again their good behaviour made Jacob wonder what he was missing. In truth, there was not much that either could have done to resist, but a meekly obedient Laird just seemed wrong.

At the bottom of the stairway, they found that the entrance chamber had been sluiced out with water and the metal balls stacked in a corner. The four strongmen were waiting for them. They took over guarding the prisoners and Noah led the small group across the courtyard, with Jacob and Joshua coming behind. Noah was soon joined by Father Augustus as they made their way down to the village.

When they got to the village, people came out of their houses to trail along behind as they walked down the street. The word had quickly spread that the Laird and his crow were to be banished and it seemed that the whole village wanted to be there to see the Laird's demise. The five former Riders joined Joshua, grim faced and angry, and Jacob fell further back into the crowd. He was looking around, trying to find Myriam but she seemed to be the only person in the village not in the procession. Even when they went past the lane that led to the cottage, she didn't appear.

At the entrance to the valley, the crowd paused near the oak tree while Noah and Father Augustus; Joshua and the other former riders; and the two prisoners continued down the ravine. Jacob stopped to collect his pack from where he'd left it. He put it on, taking a long time to adjust the straps. Still she didn't come. Jacob didn't know whether he was pleased or saddened by this. Much as he longed to see her, to hold her one more time, that would have made doing what had to be done even more difficult. Perhaps it was better this way after all. He turned and followed the others down the ravine.

The sun was now high in the sky and it shone brightly into the narrow valley. The mosses were a brilliant green and, in places, covered with small, white flowers. None of this did Jacob notice. The village might soon be leaving but he had absolutely no desire to leave the village. He had long known the high price that duty demanded but now, walking away from Myriam, all worlds seemed dark to him: dark, empty and cold.

CHAPTER TWENTY-SIX

Resolution

The prisoners and their escort stood in a small group at the entrance into Jacob's world. The Laird was smiling broadly and Joshua was finding it difficult to contain his growing anger. When he started to laugh as he saw Jacob walking down the ravine alone, Joshua grabbed him violently by the front of his coat, almost lifting him off the ground.

'What are ye smiling at, ye piece of filth?' he snarled.

The Laird ignored him and spoke directly to Noah. 'Don't you see, old man?' he said. 'I've won. Through all of this, I've won!' He was answered by a stony silence and he laughed again. 'What have I lost? The castle? The place was a prison to me and I treated it like a sewer. The village and its people? I despised them. What have you lost? Everything. Your son, the one grabbing me like some ignorant ape, has lost nearly twenty years of his life and is forever separated from the girl he loved. The one man your daughter has ever loved is now walking away from her and I will be the cause of him going into exile. Both your children will live long, lonely and miserable lives.' Again Joshua snarled. This time he physically lifted the Laird off the ground, and threw him against the wall of the ravine.

Noah was calmer. 'This isn't about ye or me, about winning or losing. It's about the villagers, who can now live their lives free of fear and intimidation-'

'Fool!' the Laird said, as he struggled to his feet. 'What do I care about the villagers? This was never about them. This was always about you and me. I was the legal son and my mother the rightful wife but who did my father care for? It was always about you and me.'

Jacob joined the group. 'He would be less annoying if he was gagged,' he suggested casually.

One of the former Riders smiled nastily and produced a rag. 'You still lose,' the Laird shouted. 'I don't care what happens to me but you care about your children. Only those who care can ever lose. Only th…' 'His voice was cut off as the rag was roughly tied across his face. Noah looked at him in grim anger and Joshua looked as if he was barely restraining a desire to beat the Laird to a pulp.

Jacob was almost unnaturally calm. 'You're wrong you know,' he said. 'You can 'not care' all you like and still lose everything. In fact, if you truly don't care, you already have. It's only those who care who can ever win.' He took a deep breath. 'Come on. Let's get this over with.'

He walked forward and once again looked out onto his own time and place, onto the wild valley and the neat walking track maintained by the national park's rangers. If he took another step he would leave, forever, Myriam, the cottage, and the village. Behind him, the Riders were rough handling the Laird and the Crow, preparing to throw them out of the ravine. Jacob took a deep breath and stepped forward.

'No, wait!' a voice he knew well cried out behind him. He turned to see Myriam running down the ravine, dressed in the same blue cloak she had been wearing when he first met her. 'Wait!' she cried. 'Wait!'

Jacob looked at her, her pale skin flushed by the run, her wild, red hair flying behind her, and he simply ran to meet her, brushing past the group at the entrance. He gathered her and held her, feeling the warm softness of her body. He breathed deeply, taking in the sweet smell of her hair and the sweat on her skin. He felt her arms grip him and their bodies simply relaxed into each other, holding each other close.

'It has to be done, Myriam,' he said. 'I have to leave. I have to make sure that he's taken far away from the valley. Far enough away, so that he can never return.'

'I know,' she answered softly, 'and I thought to stay away. I thought I couldn't stand to say goodbye. Then, I just knew that I had to be here. I had to see you one last time.'

He kissed a tear away from her face, looked into blue eyes, now filled with tears, and knew then that he couldn't leave her: his time was with her, his place was where she was. Behind him, the Riders threw the Laird and the Crow, stumbling and cursing, out into the modern world.

Immediately, the world seemed to shift and change. The sky spun, the sun went dark, and the wind cascaded through the ravine like a wild river. Jacob didn't care, didn't even notice. He held Myriam and, for the moment, was aware only of her.

The Laird and the Crow found themselves in a Tasmanian valley. When they turned around, the rocky ravine had gone and there was now only a steep slope leading to a clump of wind twisted Huon pines. The Laird spat the gag from his mouth.

'Don't just stand there, you idiot,' he said to the Crow, holding up his still bound hands. 'Find a sharp rock.'

* * *

Two months later, Jacob was sitting outside the church with Father Augustus, sipping some of the good priest's wine. Around them, the tall brown hills of the Scottish

Highlands were not that dissimilar to the Tasmanian highlands he had left behind. Father Augustus was explaining what had happened on that day when Jacob had left his time and place.

'It seems,' he said, 'that the curse the Laird placed on the village wasn't permanent. It wasn't even for the life of the Laird, as I had thought. It appears that the curse was attached to the person of the Laird himself. As soon as he set foot outside the valley land, the curse was broken and the village returned to its proper place and time.' He waved his arms at the hills around him. 'These are our proper hills. We are back where we belong.'

Jacob smiled and took another sip of wine. 'Time has passed though,' he suggested.

'Yes,' the priest agreed. 'Time is as it would have been if the village had never been cursed.'

'What do you think happened to the Laird and his crow?' Jacob asked. 'Does he just wander as a vagrant in my world?'

'Possibly, but I don't think so,' the priest replied. 'Of course, we can't be sure, but I think he took the curse with him and that he, himself, is now cursed in the way that the village once was: a vagrant not just in your world but across all time and space. Alone, because I think his Crow will abandon him at the first opportunity. If I'm right, then it's a terrible fate. Unless he can find a way to repent his sins, eventually, he will be lost in the between place.'

Jacob gave a dismissive shrug of his shoulders. 'I wish I could say I feel sorry for him but, honestly, I don't. In my book, justice is served. How have the surrounding villages taken the valley's sudden return?'

'Surprisingly well,' the priest said. 'I think they always considered this valley a little odd and when, from their point of view, it simply disappeared for twenty years, leaving only a barren hollow filled with brambles and thorns, they just thought the place cursed. They wouldn't talk about it or even look at it – bad luck to do so apparently. In the early years, young Agnes was always up here waiting for Joshua to return, they say, and look what happened to her – her husband died. Fifteen years and four kids later, mind you, but, apparently, that proves the point.'

Jacob gave a wry smile, 'From what I hear, he was a bit of a loser and his death was far more unlucky for William Campbell than it ever was for Agnes.'

'Yes, maybe,' the priest said, 'although I fear you have been listening to a biased source. Anyway, I explained to my brother priests that the Laird had sold his soul to the devil, which is true enough, and used the dark arts to banish us from time and place. I told them that it was only after twenty years of prayer and penance that we were able to break the curse and return home. That also is true enough.

The upshot is that they'll accept us back, although we'll be treated with a great deal of caution and I don't believe this incident will ever be spoken of again. Bad luck, just look what happened to Agnes.' The priest took a long draught of his wine and smiled contentedly.

Jacob laughed. 'But Agnes is getting married to Joshua next week, and he'll make her a finer husband than that William fella ever could.'

'Yes,' the priest murmured happily. 'Things do seem to work out, don't they? And how are you getting on in the cottage? Not too lonely I hope.'

Jacob shook his head. 'Too busy. Who knew that animal husbandry and farming were such hard work?'

'Only those who have tried them, I imagine,' the priest said mildly. 'And the dreams, the anxiety? What of those?'

Jacob shrugged. 'Deep breathing and meditation helps with the anxiety, stops it turning into panic, at least most of the time. I think that maybe I will always have the dreams.' He smiled ruefully. 'Of course now, if they get too bad, there's this beautiful dreamkin of mine who enters in and holds my hand. Then the dreams aren't so bad. Myriam also gets down in the waking world whenever she can get away from all the preparations. That's also great.'

The old priest nodded. 'And how are things going up at the castle?'

Jacob gave a slight shrug. 'Well, they're all working hard to try and put the place back into some sort of proper order. It's not easy. There are years of neglect. Still, Noah is determined that his father's house should be restored.'

Father Augustus nodded. 'Speaking of which,' he said, 'I think that Noah's chances of being declared the rightful Laird are very good. Excellent, in fact. You might tell him that when you see him later. I've shown the copies of both the parish marriage register and the baptismal registrar to the local magistrate and I've just gotten word back. The marriage and baptismal dates were clear and, since the old prince is long dead and there's no interference from any existing claimant, it should be a straightforward decision and declaration. Actually, I don't think anyone else will want this 'cursed' village. I expect Noah to be declared the lawful Laird and landowner within the month. That means, of course, that Joshua will be his heir and, unless he and Agnes have more children, your eldest son will be the Laird after him.'

Jacob laughed. 'You're rushing just a little, Father. We're not even married yet.'

The priest shrugged. 'The time will come soon enough. Tell me, man of the distant future, what advice will you give your sons?'

Jacob looked thoughtful for a moment. 'Unfortunately, my knowledge of Scottish history is a bit sketchy,' he said. 'I think I will just say to stay out of politics as much as possible and to have nothing whatever to do with a place called Culloden.' The priest looked at him, puzzled, but he continued. 'Also, to find a pretty girl, get married, and have lots of happy children.'

'Amen to that,' the priest said raising his glass. 'Amen to that indeed.'

Epilogue

It seemed like the whole village followed them, all the way down from the church to the cottage: Jacob in the hiking clothes he had arrived in, cleaned and pressed, and Myriam in her most beautiful dress and crowned with a wreath of wild flowers. The crowd even followed them into the cottage garden and cheered when Jacob picked up Myriam as if she were a child and carried her across the threshold. There at last, when the door was closed, they had some privacy.

'Put me down,' she said. He complied but still held her close, her body pressed against his.

'Tonight, we dream together,' he said softly.

She stood on her toes and whispered in his ear, 'Husband, tonight there will be neither the need nor the time for dreams.' Then she kissed him hungrily and urgently.

* * *

Two men stood in the cottage garden as the villagers all turned and went home. They were dressed in long robes; one in bright colours and the other in simple white.

The one in the coloured robes said angrily: 'So, this is your victory? Let me tell you it's not going to last. I'll not give up. Don't ever think I'll give up. Do you imagine they'll live happily ever after? They won't. Hard times will come and I'll be there. I promise you, the time will come when each will think the other the most annoying person on earth, when this warm infatuation will seem like something that happened to someone else. True love is a myth and 'happy ever after' doesn't ever happen.'

His companion smiled and bent down to smell a rose. 'I may have mentioned this before, but I really don't think you understand love – or happiness,' he said. 'Yes, their feelings will come and go. But love isn't based on anything as fleeting as feelings. It's a decision they've made. They're committed to each other and in that is the love that will see them through all the troubles they'll face and bring them that happiness which we wish for them. A happiness you'll not be able to take from them. You'll not get them to share in your misery. You will be there? Then, I promise you, so will I.'

'What difference will that make?' the first man yelled. 'Regardless of what you say or do, they'll eventually join me in knowing the only truth there is: that life is full of pain and ends in death. They'll come to know their weakness and curse all they once loved. Happy ever after? What nonsense! That's nothing but a foolish dream; a fairy tale fit only for children.'

'No, my sad friend,' the other man said. 'All of this is very real. This delusion you have, of equal parts power and despair, that's the fantasy. It's love and hope that are real, just as it's the broken who are strong and those who consider themselves whole who give way and are lost. My hope is always in broken things and my hope is sure.'

The first man stood in angry silence, looking long and hard at his companion. Then he said, 'Bah! If you're not even going to try and be rational, I refuse to listen to you.' He turned and vanished into the darkness.

The other man turned and smiled as the last candle in the cottage was extinguished. It was a clear night and the sky was filled with stars. He walked slowly up the chestnut lined path, to find a hill and wait for the light of morning.

If anything in this book has raised issues for you, or if

you know a veteran in need of healing and support with

regard to PTSD or related issues, please contact the

Veterans Care Association: www.veteranscare.com.au

If it is non-veteran related then please contact

Beyond Blue: www.beyondblue.org.au